The Devil's Mountain

The Devil's Mountain

Mountain

H. G. de Lisser

MINT EDITIONS

The Devil's Mountain was first published between 1922–1923.

This edition published by Mint Editions 2023.

ISBN 9798888970096 | E-ISBN 9798888970249

Published by Mint Editions®

 MINT
EDITIONS
minteditionbooks.com

Publishing Director: Katie Connolly
Design: Ponderosa Pine Design
Production and Project Management: Micaela Clark
Typesetting: Westchester Publishing Services

Contents

I

"A Detestable Person"

Lawrence Beaman was one of the first to see the members of the moving picture company when they arrived. The motor cars rolled swiftly up to the porch of the hotel and discharged their occupants; then through the lobby came trooping the actresses and actors, who were immediately joined, with friendly welcoming greeting, by many of the guests.

Lawrence moved forward with the others; he approached a tall girl, hot and dusty, just now, but of striking appearance. She flashed a bright smile at him and gaily put out her hand.

"We have just come in," she laughed, "and I am a sight! I am covered in dust. Have you been here long?"

"About half an hour. How did you get through today?"

"Pretty well; the director was less cross than usual, and we took some good scenes."

"You must be very tired, my dear," broke in a decisive voice behind her, and, next moment, a decisive-looking lady was at her side. This lady bowed coldly to Lawrence, who returned her stiff saultation with a precise inclination of the head. Then she gave her attention to the girl.

"Come right upstairs now, Marian, and refresh yourself before we have tea. I will come into your room and help you change, or perhaps you had better first come into mine. Shall I order tea to be brought upstairs for both of us?"

"Oh, it's awfully good of you to suggest that, Lady Rosedale," replied Marian, "but I'd rather come down to the lawn for tea, if you don't mind."

"Well, it may be nicer," Lady Rosedale agreed; and linking her arm round the girl's waist, she took possession of her and carried her away.

Lady Rosedale, in spite of her fifty years, was a very vigorous woman. Her hair had silvered early, but her face was still fresh-looking; her eyes were masterful, her mouth determined. Just a shade below average height, she was inclined to be stout. But she carried herself erect; she walked briskly, spoke briskly; she made her presence felt and seemed to find delight in doing so.

Lady Rosedale was the widow of an English baronet and had been wintering in Jamaica, at the Myrtle Bank Hotel, for about a month when the moving picture company arrived. She was a woman of sudden fancies and quick impulses; her title, her social position and her reputed wealth rendered it easy for her to take under her patronage any girl in the hotel, or in the island for the matter of that; and she did not hesitate after meeting Marian to declare that she had fallen in love with her at first sight. Certainly she always treated Marian with mother, if somewhat fussy, kindness: she seemed devoted to her. But she did not like Lawrence Beaman, Lawrence had had more than one intimation of that fact of late, and the lady's manner this afternoon had conveyed something more than a hint of it.

He turned and strolled about the lawn, between tea tables set out with tea and cake and surrounded by women and men in afternoon attire, the dresses of the girls rivalling the rainbow in variegated hues. The clatter of cups and of voices made a not unpleasant sound, suggestive of human comradeship, and the lighter, pleasanter things of life; the stylish frocks of the younger woman, the care-free air of the men, the rippling laughter, the setting of green sward and slender palms under a canopy of soft blue appealed to him subtly. For with the eye of his fancy he saw Marian everywhere in this beautiful tropical setting; at home in it. She endowed the scene with meaning for him, established a bond of delightful sympathy between it and him. He was waiting for her now to reappear. He was determined to spend a few minutes in her company this afternoon despite the objections of all the Lady Rosedales in the world.

He was quiet and self-contained, a man of few friends or even acquaintances. Well-built and of middle height, with light brown hair and steady, clear, blue eyes, he gave one the impression of self-confident strength and even of obstinacy. The brown moustache which covered his upper lip did not conceal the firm set of the mouth; the chin was almost square, the nose straight; the forehead suggested keen practical intelligence. Lawrence was of English descent, but Jamaican by birth. He was associated with an English shipping company; held locally, in connection with it, an important position, and was much trusted by his chiefs at the London head office because of his tried and tested devotion to duty. Some of those who worked with him had more than once laughing remarked that Lawrence had no romance in his composition but was merely a business machine, with work and yet more work as his passion in life. He was thirty-three, and they doubted if he had ever once had a love affair; they were positive that passion and he would always be strangers. Thus their judgement, based upon years of association and upon what they believed to be an intimate knowledge of the man. Yet this afternoon he was waiting for a moving picture actress, and counting the moments until she would reappear.

He had met her three weeks before, a few days after her arrival in Jamaica. The company had come to the island to take a series of tropical pictures: during the day they worked outside of the city, but in the afternoons and evening they were free. Most of them lived in the hotel, though some, chiefly men, preferred private lodgings in the upper part of Kingston. In a little while they had made numerous acquaintances; they were sociable in their habits; and, as strangers and artists, they were greatly in demand for all sorts of private social functions. Someone had casually introduced him to a group of them one afternoon: Lawrence had looked into Marian's eyes and heard her laugh; he had talked with her for a little while; he had lingered longer on the lawn on that occasion than was his wont. Then the habits of reserve, the habits of years, were shaken to their foundations. The next day he returned, and the next; and in the evenings now he was a visitor at the hotel, a rare thing with him in former days.

Sometimes he sat with her alone: these were his times of good fortune. Oftener he had to share her society with others. Not many persons seemed to notice that she was his particular attraction; but there were some who did. Her brother, for example, and Lady Rosedale. Mr. Phipps also, but Mr. Phipps was generally regarded as a curious, prying sort of person, who apparently made it his business to notice everybody and everything.

It was nearly five o' clock in the afternoon. The early February sun was westering, the sky was azure, dotted here and there with patches of fleecy cloud floating slowly, changing their shapes as they drifted, and sometimes dissolving into the golden, all-pervading ether. The strong wind that had blown steadily during the day had died down, but the air was delightfully cool. There was no sharpness in the sun. The branches of the coconut palms caught and reflected its rays, the metallic surfaces of their fronds shining as they slightly swayed in a gentle breeze. Merely being able to breathe was happiness, and the laughter that rand out at frequent intervals on the lawn told of enjoyment and of delight in life.

Presently she reappeared. She had changed her dress, and all traces of dust and fatigue had gone from her face. Her tall figure, bent slightly forward as she moved, was sinuously graceful; you noticed at once that she had dark, brilliant, slightly slanting eyes, a mass of dark and glossy hair, which even the hat she wore could not completely hide, and a nose, sensitive, delicate, and Grecian. Her face was oval, her complexion ivory, touched by the sun; her lips, pink, and parted now in a little smile, revealed two rows of even, well-formed teeth, and her smile lent to her face a singularly winning if mischievous expression. There was a suggestion of something foreign about her. She looked what she was in reality—a daughter of the South.

Piloted by Lady Rosedale, Marian moved towards one of the small tea tables that had just been vacated by another couple; and, seeing that she was with Lady Rosedale, many of the young men about, both guests in the hotel and residents of the city, hesitated as to whether they should venture to join her. It was a tribute to Lady Rosedale's personality that few persons ever dared to join her or her party unless distinctly encouraged to do so. Lady Rosedale never froze them with the stony British stare: she simply did not notice them at all. She could be a very tolerable impersonation of the iceberg when she liked, and she very often liked if she happened to disapprove of the person or persons seeking her society.

But Lawrence Beaman was a man of resolution. He followed Marian and her friend, and when they sat down, and Lady Rosedale had summoned the waiter to order tea, he approached the table and addressed Marian.

"There is only one dance that I know," he began at once; "the new dances I have never learnt. But once I could waltz, and I hope you will reserve a waltz or two for me this evening. Will you?"

"How long ago was it that you last waltzed?" asked Marian mischievously. "You speak as if it were ages."

"Nobody waltzes nowadays," broke in Lady Rosedale; "the waltz is no longer popular. I don't say that I approve of the change, but young people do and their tastes ought to be considered. I believe it is now considered positively tedious to waltz."

"I am sure I would not deliberately ask Miss Braeme to do anything painful," replied Lawrence with a slight smile, understanding perfectly well that Lady Rosedale was suggesting that Marian should not dance with him. "By long ago, Miss Braeme, I mean eight or ten years."

"Then probably you have forgotten by now," said Lady Rosedale. "You must be awfully rusty at least."

"Is that what you think?" he asked, addressing himself directly to Marian.

"You deserve to be," she replied evasively. "Fancy living in a country where there is dancing all the time, and not joining in a dance even once!"

There was a moment of silence. Lawrence realised that by his own admission he had shown plainly that it was Marian and Marian only with whom he desired to dance. Lady Rosedale had voiced the thought that was in all their minds.

"But for you, my dear," she remarked, "Mr. Beaman would not think of evening being here tonight. But as you will be dancing he is quite willing to indulge in a pastime in which he indulged but rarely, I imagine, even when he was much younger than he now is."

"He pays me a great compliment," Marian answered gaily; then: "I believe there are sixteen dances tonight, Mr. Beaman. I will put down two waltzes for you if you like. They are the only two on the programme."

Both of them saw the look of disapproval on Lady Rosedale's face; but Lawrence had previously noticed that while Marian seemed always solicitous to please her friend, she had continued to be nice to him despite that friend's obvious objections. He was about to bow himself away, having now no further excuse for loitering near them (much as he desired to do so), when, to his surprise, Lady Rosedale herself requested, or rather ordered him, to remain where he was.

"Don't go, Mr. Beaman," she said sharply but quietly; "don't go now, for heaven's sake!" Her ensuing words gave her reason for this unusual request. "There's that detestable American person coming, and I don't want him to join us, which he will certainly do if we two are alone."

The detestable person, of American nationality, was Mr. Phipps. Lawrence knew him well; he knew also that Mr. Phipps was one of those people who would never be abashed by Lady Rosedale or anyone else in the world. The next moment Mr. Phipp's voice was heard proclaiming a greeting: it occurred to Lawrence that there was evidently to be no escape for Lady Rosedale.

"Ah, Lady Rosedale, and our little movie star! Just the two folks that I would have picked out to meet this afternoon, and here they are! To tell you the truth, I was looking for you. Seek and ye shall find, saith the Scriptures, and I sought and have found."

"So it seems," remarked Lady Rosedale distantly.

"Beaman, too. Say, but you know I am in luck!"

"Why, Mr. Phipps?" asked Marian.

"Because, my little movie star, I am a man of varied social tastes. I admire nobility of mind as expressed in uplifting conversation, and though I am American I have an inborn respect for noble birth. Lady Rosedale fulfils these requirements. Beauty, too, I simply adore, and youthful innocence and grace and that's sure you. And I like manly strength and dogged devotion and all the rest of the sort of thing that you get in a fifth chapter of the latest novel when the strong, silent man comes upon the scene and begins to be strong and silent. Friend Beaman here fills that part beautifully, especially the silent part. And how are you, this afternoon, Lady Rosedale?"

"As well as I was at noon, when I saw you last," replied Lady Rosedale, bringing her arctic manner into play, though with a despairing sense of its being sufficiently adequate to freeze Mr. Phipps.

"Well, that's a blessing!" exclaimed Mr. Phipps fervently, "I am always anxious about your health, Lady Rosedale, for you are not yet acclimatised, and there is no telling what may not happen to one between lunch and tea in the tropics. I have known men die between those two meals."

While speaking, his quick eyes had been roaming about the grounds in search of something. "Wait a moment!" he cried, "I'll be right back in a moment." He darted away, towards a chair from which someone had risen the instance before, and probably intended to resume almost immediately. But Mr. Phipps seized the chair, and, with a rapid, "thank you," to its original possessor, he sped back towards Lady Rosedale's table. Placing the chair near the table, he sat down as though he had been expressingly invited to form one of the party, and took out his cigarette case. Lady Rosedale ostentatiously poured out tea without offering to order a cup for him.

"Tea," said Mr. Phipps, "is an English institution implanted out here by the English, along with the penitentiary and the protestant religion. All these are useful things, the penitentiary being especially good for the natives. As an American, I have never taken to tea. Will you have a cigarette, Beaman?"

Lawrence smilingly refused.

"The ladies don't mind my smoking," Mr. Phipps explained. "I regard them as old friends now, though we haven't known one another for long. It is community of spirit and not length of acquaintanceship that makes friends, isn't it, Lady Rosedale? The moment I saw you in this hotel, giving us object lessons in true majesty of deportment and nobility of mind, I said to myself, 'I can see we two are going to be friends.' As to my little movie star, why, we were all in love with her from the star. Why don't you sit down, Beaman? What's the big idea in your standing?"

Lawrence hesitated. He had been invited by Lady Rosedale to remain, but the purpose of that invitation had not been achieved; still, he had been invited, but no seat was available. Again Mr. Phipps's keen eyes swept the grounds, and he pointed out to Lawrence a vacant chair some distance away. "Better run and get that one," he advised, "or it will be snapped up by some selfish person. There is not much consideration for others to be expected in this world."

Lawrence walked leisurely away to fetch the chair, meanwhile Lady Rosedale angrily resigned herself to another quarter of an hour's torture (so she inwardly termed it) in the company of two persons who she detested.

Mr.Phipps appeared to be enjoying his cigarette. He was a spare, middle-sized man, about fifty-and-five years of age, with scanty hair, small mobile features and agile manner. A heavy pair of moustaches, once brown, now almost completely grey, covered his lip; but a careful observer would have noticed that that lip was a very long one, coming firmly down on the under-lip, and that the chin beneath, though small, was well formed and strong, with a slight suggestion of aggressiveness. Mr. Phipps's keen grey eyes seemed hardly ever in response; he was constantly glancing at everything and everybody. He was well-dressed, a sort of elderly dandy. Light flannel trousers, a dark blue jacket beautifully cut, an upstanding collar set off with a spotted blue butterfly tie, a jaunty straw hat and highly polished brown shoes completed his attire this afternoon. His hands were small and well-kept; his whole appearance indicated a man who thought very highly of himself and treated himself very well indeed. He apparently assumed that his company was in request by everyone, and his conversation most entertaining. Mr. Phipps, it was said by his acquaintances, loved the sound of his own voice.

"A nice young man that," he observed, when Lawrence had got out of hearing distance, "A reliable, intelligent young fellow. I feel that I share your opinion of him, Lady Rosedale."

"I am not aware that I have ever expressed any opinion of Mr. Boman," replied Lady Rosedale, purposely mispronouncing Lawrence's name to show her general lack of interest in him.

"You have not in so many words," Mr. Phipps agreed heartily; "but I often see him about you, and you would not have anyone about you that you didn't like. That's what struck me the first time I saw you, Lady Rosedale. You can keep people off. You have the distinguished manner. 'Even the lowly farm can teach us there is something in descent,' as one of your poets said—I forget who it was. It is the privilege of birth that it makes itself felt, and the way I saw you freeze off some folk the other night was a corker. That's a nice boy, as I was saying, and I'm glad you like him."

This personal conversation was interrupted by the return of Lawrence with the chair. Marian, who was well aware of Lady Rosedale's true feelings with regard to both Mr. Phipps and Lawrence, had been listening to the former with much amusement. She now turned to Lawrence, offering him a slice of cake.

"There's no tea left," she said, "but you will join us in cake, won't you?"

Lady Rosedale darted a warning looking at her, which she affected not to see. Lawrence, feeling awkward, accepted the cake. Mr. Phipps, with characteristic impetuosity, immediately begged for a bit of cake.

"It isn't the cake I really want," he explained, "but the pleasure of receiving it from such lovely hands. That's what you ought to have said, Beaman. You young fellows are slow at saying the right thing, but it was different in my day. When the three of you are as old as I am—and that will be many, many years to come—you will treasure in your memory all the nice things said to you and about you."

Lady Rosedale was not visibly mollified by this suggestion that she was still young. She desired no compliments from Mr. Phipps. She finished her tea and rose.

"Miss Braeme will have to get ready for dinner and the ball," she remarked, "so we had better go upstairs now. Are you ready, Marian?"

"Quite," said Marian brightly. "Shall we see you tonight?" she asked Mr. Phipps.

"Always on the job, my dear," answered the gentleman, agilely rising with Lawrence. "It is on festive occasions that I am at my best. I do my finest work then."

"Work?" cried Marian; "do you ever work?"

"Someday you may find that I do," he protested. "I toil and spin while others enjoy themselves. Beaman, let's go and have a drink."

Mr. Phipps led a protesting Lawrence in the direction of the bar, while Lady Rosedale took Marian upstairs to her own room.

II

LADY ROSEDALE'S ADVICE

Lady Rosedale's room, one of the largest in the main building of the hotel, was on the first floor, looked directly out upon the gently slopping metal roof of the verandah below, and commanded a view of the gardens that fronted the Myrtle Bank Hotel. The entrance to the hotel faced northwards; less than thirty yards from the northern verandah was the street. Glimpses of flaming red from the low-growing poinsettias in the garden, the flash of a fountain playing in the sun, the welcome green of tender grass, and the purples and yellows of broad-leaved crotons attracted and charmed the eye as one's gaze travelled onward to the ornamental iron fence which seemed to shut off the hotel from the outer dusty city with a touch of finality. This was the view which greeted Lady Rosedale's eyes when she looked out her window, but it is to be feared she did not greatly appreciate it.

On entering her room Lady Rosedale latched the light slatted half-door at the top, but left the heavy wooden door ajar, so that there should be plenty of air. She seated herself in a straight-backed chair, insisting that Marian should take a rocker. "You must bathe in my bathroom this evening, dear," she began at once, "and you must use my bath whenever you like; that's one reason why I got you to change to the room next to me. And now, my dear, I want to talk to you seriously; I am sure you won't mind, for I am old enough to be your mother, and you know I am your friend. Don't you think that young man, Mr. Beaman, is just a little too pushing where you are concerned?"

"What do you mean, Lady Rosedale?" asked Marian, looking with a twinkle in her eyes at her friend. She had taken off her hat, and her hair, tumble, but wonderfully thick and glossy, lent to her face a singularly childlike appearance, which, however, was contradicted by the laughter in her eyes.

"I mean that he is trying to make love to you," said Lady Rosedale directly. "I have noticed it now for the last couple of weeks. Before you came, that young man, whenever he happened to come to this hotel on an afternoon, would moon about by himself, hardly talking to anyone, and certainly never to a woman, so far as I could see. Now he is about the place everyday, and if he is not with you, he manages to be as near you as possible. He tries to make opportunities for speaking to you. He wants to dance with you tonight, and I can't guess what he will not be doing next. Proposing, I suppose!"

Marian laughed. "Surely you take him too seriously, Lady Rosedale! He is very pleasant—and very quiet. But he hardly ever pays me a compliment, and I don't think he would know how to propose!"

"Don't you think that," returned Lady Rosedale seriously. "Every man knows how to propose, whatever he may say. I think, too, he is being encouraged by that detestable Mr. Phipps, who simple cannot be insulted. Except for being positively rude, I have done all I can to show Mr. Phipps that I do not desire his company, but it is of no use whatever. And now I am sure, he is egging on that young man to make love to you."

"It is very foolish of him, if he is," replied Marian thoughtfully. "I do not care that way for Mr. Beaman; I like him as an acquaintance, that is all. It ought to be plain to him."

"My dear," said Lady Rosedale, "you believe today that you only like him as an acquaintance, but, if he goes on following you about with his eyes, as if you were the only girl in the world, you may begin to feel tomorrow that he is more than an acquaintance, more than a friend. It is a dangerous game he is playing—for you. Who is he? And what is his position?"

"And who am I, Lady Rosedale, and what is my position?" asked Marian laughing. "A movie actress of the fifth or sixth class. That isn't much, is it?"

"But you may be of the first class tomorrow," protested Lady Rosedale. "I have heard," she continued, "that the movie people make fortunes when they become popular."

"I am afraid I am not one of those," said Mariah a little sadly, shaking her head. "They give me roles of a very ordinary description to play. The directors say I have no sufficient personality for success on the screen."

"You have all the personality that a moving picture play can possibly want," asserted Lady Rosedale, who was scandalised at any moving picture director having an opinion differing from hers. "I am afraid that moving picture directors are not an estimable body of persons; but if you are patient your time must come. If you throw yourself away on a young man with but a few hundred pounds a year, and who does not seem to be even in such society as this place affords—which is not saying much—you will regret it. I am sorry you promised to dance with him tonight Mariah. I was trying to catch your eye when he was asking you to, but I couldn't. Take an older woman's advice, my dear, and be cold and distant to him. I wouldn't say this if he were merely nice and courteous to you, but he is in love with you, and that is a very serious matter. Would your brother approve of him?"

A shadow passed over Marian's face at this question. "He would not," she answered simply, "but there will be nothing to disapprove of, I can assure you." She paused for a moment, then continued slowly. "I like Mr. Beaman, as a friend. He has always treated me, not as an actress to be flattered and made love to, but as a lady, as a—a—"

"Divinity," suggested Lady Rosedale. "Yes, I have seen it. I don't say the young man is not nice in his own way, though he appears to me to be rather wooden; and I am glad that you don't care for men who think that because you are a picture actress they can be familiar. If anyone here does it," she went on, with haughty asperity, "I wish you would let me know who it is. I should certainly seek and opportunity of speaking to him: once would be all that would be necessary. You cannot, however, give up your career because Mr. Beaman seems to you to be more gentlemanly than someother men. He is not the man for you, my dear; with your looks and disposition and youth, you could marry anyone. I said as much to your brother yesterday."

"And what did he say?" asked Marian.

"He said he would look after your future and would take care that you made no mistake. Which is the proper sentiment for a brother to express, no doubt, though how he is to act up to his resolution I do not know. Your future is in your own hands, my dear, not in the hands of any brother, however affectionate or careful he may be. You don't mind my speaking to you as I have done, do you?"

"No, dear Lady Rosedale," cried Marian, "but I wonder why you take all this interest in me. I am a stranger to you; you know nothing about me."

"I know you are a good little girl," the elder woman was on the point of saying impulsively, but checked herself and replied instead, "I like to see things going as they ought."

Marian laughed. She knew that Lady Rosedale did indeed love to play the part of a dictatorial Providence; Mr. Phipps had more than once said so in quite a disrespectful manner behind Lady Rosedale's back, and Mariah had already come to perceive that Mr. Phipps formed remarkably accurate estimates of the characters of the people with whom he came in contact. Perhaps it was because Lady Rosedale had some inkling of this that she never felt quite at ease in the society of Mr. Phipps.

"And now," she said, rising with a self-satisfied air, "we had better call the maid to see about the bath. And, by the way, I want you to wear my pearls tonight, Marian, they will suit you beautifully. I have set my mind upon seeing you wear them, so I'll take no refusal."

Marian was about to say something, but Lady Rosedale would not listen.

"Not a word!" she cried, "I have made up my mind about the pearls."

Marian said nothing, knowing well that Lady Rosedale would listen to no protest.

III

Mr. Phipps's Advice

The Myrtle Bank Hotel was ablaze with light. The long walk leading from the south verandah to the seawall and the pier was an avenue of colour formed by the many-tinted electric bulbs; the rustic summer houses on the lawn glowed in the cardinal hues; to the east the annex flared; along the seawall ran a row of little glittering electric lamps.

Above, serene ineffably, shone myriads of stars in a deep blue sky, and westward faintly gleamed a crescent moon. The night air was cool and crisp, bracing; and as one watched the wonderful constellations that blazed overhead, one might see at intervals the meteors as they rushed through space, trails of fire, things of evanescent beauty. In a few moments they had flashed in all their glory into human ken, and then faded entirely out of the tropic sky.

The dining room of the hotel was crowded to its utmost capacity. Flower-bedecked tables set close to one another were surrounded by diners, the men in regulation evening dress, the women in low-cut gowns of soft silk and glossy sating, with jewels flashing from fingers and bosom, with fire glinting from their eyes and laughter pealing from their lips. Black waiters clad in white hurried about bearing dishes, bottles of hissing, sparkling wine, and boxes of fragrant Jamaica cigars. The guests were at different stages of the dinner's progress. Some, coming late, had just begun, others were sipping coffee or liqueurs, and smoking cigarettes, the girls delicately blowing the smoke into the air, the men puffing with more deliberate enjoyment.

On a stand on the lawn a military band, each musician a native soldier, crashed out a popular air. But the music was scarcely heard because of the hum and clamour of hundreds of voices, each striving to make itself distinct.

Lady Rosedale had a table for four. Marian sat opposite to her; her other two guests were the director of the moving picture company, and his leading lady, a Miss Hellingworth, who was being "featured" in a play in which Marian had some part. Lady Rosedale considered the director a vulgar, odious person, but she had asked him to dinner for the purpose of influencing him in Marian's favour; for much the same reason had the star actress been invited. These appeared highly sensible of the compliment which Lady Rosedale paid them, and delighted, for in the recent past they had suffered something from her marvellous faculty of keeping people at a resentful if not respectful distance.

Not far from this group, at a table for two, sat Mr. Phipps and Lawrence Beaman. Now and then Lawrence would steal a look at Marian, and Mr. Phipp's eyes invariably followed his glance.

"She is not looking happy tonight, Phipps," said Lawrence guardedly, after one of these swift glances. "I can see that even from here."

"Do you attribute her unhappiness to an insufficiency of champagne?" enquired Mr. Phipps. "Lady Rosedale may be somewhat parsimonious when it comes to the drinks. She may believe in a dry country when she has to stand treat. I think I have noticed that peculiarity of hers."

"I don't think Miss Braeme is particularly fond of drink," returned Lawrence with perceptible coldness; "she may be ill."

"Miss Braeme, like the modern girl, and especially the girl who acts for the movies, is not likely to be a strenuous advocate of a dry Jamaica, my boy," said Mr. Phipps tritely. "I have not observed that she regards a cocktail with marked disfavour, or refuses to look upon the wine when it is white."

"Can't you be serious for once?" asked the younger man impatiently. "I feel sure she is being bored. Look at that little ass of a director who is just hanging upon every word spoken by Lady Rosedale. What sort of a company is that for a sensible girl?"

"Meaning that she would have been happier had she dined with you? Did you ask her?"

"How did you know that I wanted to ask her?" demanded Lawrence.

"I didn't know; I merely guessed. Well, why didn't you ask her?"

"Hadn't the opportunity."

"Lacked the nerve, you mean: you could have written her a note. Nothing incriminating, you know: a few words of chaste politeness signifying a meal and a bottle of iced fizz. You thought of it, and then funked it. Isn't that so?"

Lawrence admitted by his silence that it was. Mr. Phipps glanced quickly around him. No one was likely to hear what he might say. "What's the big idea?" he questioned. "Are you serious about the little movie star?"

"I have a high regard for her," replied Lawrence with a reserve of a manner that was not lost upon Mr. Phipps. "That is all. Even Lady

Rosedale, as you have observed, has take to Miss Braeme. If it were anyone one, I should think that Lady Rosedale had an ulterior object."

"You don't credit the old lady, then, with any kindly human feeling, Beaman?"

"Do you?"

"Well, I don't know. She sure don't love me, and that isn't likely to prepossess me to a favourable view of her moral qualities. As for you—"

"She detests me," admitted Lawrence.

"Bull's eye!" agreed Mr. Phipps. "She is true to form in dealing with you, son; she suspects you have an eye on her little favourite, and she thinks it is awfully cheeky of you. She's got that girl's future all mapped out in her mind. She wants to do great things for Miss Marian at a minimum of personal expense and with great self-satisfaction, and you threaten to butt in and spoil the plan as duly outlined by her ladyship. I guess she is top-notch in selfishness all right; but I think she rally had a soft spot for Marian."

"She is thinking more of herself than of Marian," said Lawrence angrily. "Ever since that girl came here Lady Rosedale has hardly let her have a minute to herself. You would think Miss Braeme was her property."

"Has Miss Braeme shown any objection? Said anything to you to indicate that the old damne is a kind of old man of the sea on her shoulders?" asked Mr. Phipps.

"No; I can't say that she has," admitted Lawrence.

"Then I reckon she can bear the burden of Lady Rosedale's interest in her life. One can stand much from a title, as you are now finding out. Look at your friend the director. He's so proud to be seen in her ladyship's company that he'll die of excessive delight if he don't look sharp. Perhaps it's the way too with your movie star—and yet—"

"Yes?"

"I'm not so sure that it is. She hasn't dropped you, as I am dead certain the old lady has asked her to do. But don't be too sure that she won't cut you some day, Lawrence. There's something in the Jamaica atmosphere that leads people to treat their bosom friends like dirt if they only for a moment in the company of someone bigger than themselves. It is habit of you people here, and a man is liable to acquire it after three weeks' residence in the country."

"She's dancing with me tonight," Lawrence reminded him.

"Make the most of the giddy mazes of the waltz," urged Mr. Phipps. "If you want the girl to like you, push ahead and get in your spade work at once. You are reserved and shy. Drop it. In a girl's eyes a shy man's a fool, a sissy. But, say, look at how she is dressed, son; simply stunning, ain't it? The man who marries her will have to have some pieces of the golden calf, and I don't know that you are quoted as a millionaire yet. Thought about all that?"

"I have thought nothing of the sort," said Lawrence. "Who am I that I could think of—you know what I mean. I have some money saved, yes; and a salary. But you are right; she would want a man much better circumstanced than I am. I am a fool."

"With your opinion of yourself it would be impolite for me to disagree," said Mr. Phipps; "but a fool will act according to his folly, Lawrence, and you are going to do that. Sure!"

Lawrence smiled; then made haste to finish his dessert. The rom was now thinning rapidly, and he saw Lady Rosedale and her party preparing to rise. The military band on the lawn had ceased to play; the dance, he knew, would shortly begin. "Are you ready?" he asked his companion after a little while, when Marian and the others had disappeared from view into the crowd outside. Mr. Phipps signified that he was, and together they strolled on to the verandah and towards the open doors of the ballroom.

The lobby and the verandah were crowded with people, the younger ones eagerly booking dances, the older ones looking about for comfortable seats. The ballroom itself, when Lawrence and his friend reached it, was already filled to its utmost capacity. A native string band, the musicians swaying to the sound of their own music, was playing a popular ragtime and under parti-coloured lights and a roof profusely decorated with flags the dancers moved round and round the room, a kaleidoscope of brilliant colours and of flushed and merry faces.

Now and then Lawrence could see Marian as she came abreast of the door by which he stood and swiftly passed him, her partner a tall good-looking officer of the British West India Regiment. Lawrence's waltz with her was third on the programme, and he knew that to every dance there would be an encore or two. He had therefore sometime to wait, and, as he could not possibly hope for a word with Marian before his dance, he turned to move away. As he did so he came face to face with Marian's brother, Stephen Braeme. From the expression on the latter's face, Lawrence realised that Stephen had been watching him for some moments as his eyes had followed Marian's movements.

Stephen Braeme was one of the actors of the moving picture company who lived outside of the hotel, in private lodgings, but at the Myrtle Bank he was a frequent visitor, and there he had been introduced to Lawrence. At first he had been cordial; a little later on his manner had distinctly changed. Stephen was much taller than his sister and decidedly darker; he looked about thirty years of age. Their mother (it had got about, as these things somethings will) had been a lady of a good family in Peru, their father an Englishman who had met and married her there. Of aquiline features, his black eye quick and glittering, his hair coal black, and with full, clean-shaven lips, Stephen Braeme was unquestionably a very handsome man; a book companion too and of sociable disposition, though patently vain. Lawrence knew that the reason of Stephen's dislike of him was the attention which, however unobtrusively, he paid to Stephen's sister. Stung to resentment by Stephen's change of manner, and realising that he exercised an immense influence over Marian, Lawrence had come to detest him heartily. Yet when they met, as othey often did of necessity, there was a fair show of politeness in their greeting. At the very least Stephen Braeme was never quite so distant in attitude as was Lady Rosedale, and Lawrence appreciated the pride he so obviously took in his sister.

The two men bowed to one another, Lawrence endeavouring to inform his salutation with a degree of friendliness which he did not feel. Mr. Phipps grasped Stephen warmly by the hand and was greeted with equal enthusiasm. He immediately invited Stephen to come and have a drink; the latter appeared on the brink of accepting this invitation, but altered his mind, and murmured something about having to find his partner for the next dance. Lawrence guessed that this excuse was given because Stephen did not wish to be in a party of which he, Lawrence, would necessarily be one; Stephen desired to keep aloof from him. This reflection stung him to anger, and Mr. Phipps remarked instantly the frown on Lawrence's brow.

"A handsome fellow that," observed Mr. Phipps as they moved away; "but he thinks an almighty lot of himself—that's the Spanish blood. He think an almighty lot of his sister too," added Mr. Phipps slyly.

"There is reason for that," said Lawrence, "but he sometimes acts as if he owed her. Is that a Spanish custom?"

"My dear boy, you would never have got to know her had she not been here as an actress, and he had desired that she should not know you! There is no such thing as the emancipation of woman in Spanish-

American countries; there are still the watchful father and brother, the vigilant duenna, the barred windows, the whole blessed family on the spot when a man wants to say a nice word to the girl of his admiration. That tall fellow regards himself as father and brother in one, so far as authority goes anyhow, and you have got to reckon with that until you can get him round. What with him and Lady Rosedale, son, you are in for a bad time!"

To this Lawrence made no reply: he was thinking much the same thing himself. His pride was hurt; but he was willing to make a sacrifice of pride if only he could bring these two to a better frame of mind towards him. And yet, he asked himself as he had done more than once before, what exactly did he have in view?

Mr. Phipps had pointed out to him that he might be too poor for a girl who dressed as Marian did, who was probably so accustomed to hectic excitement that it had become a necessity of her existence. Hitherto he had had no good reason to be discontented with his position, or discouraged by his prospects: now it seemed to him that that position was utterly miserable, those prospects appalling. He supposed that both Stephen Braeme and Lady Rosedale knew all about them: in a small city personal information could be gathered from the garrulous in a week. Those two would probably use all their influence with Marian against him, they had shown him plainly that they did not regard him as desirable, while he—he did not dare go further than sit with her for an hour or ask her for a dance.

"Beaman," said Mr. Phipps firmly, breaking in upon Lawrence's reflections after a silent walk that had lasted for several minutes, "you are coming with me to have a drink. You could not possibly take that stunning young woman into the ballroom feelings as you are, and with a face such as you are wearing. Whisky had been universally pronounced good for snake bites in the United States, ever since prohibition was put over the people in that free and enlightened country. You have been bitten, my boy—I won't say by a snake, but you have been bitten. Come and have a drink."

IV

"It Is Impossible"

They went into the bar, and Lawrence, usually an abstemious man, had one whisky and soda, after which Mr. Phipps declared that he looked better. "It is about time that I should go back now," he said to Mr. Phipps, as soon as he had finished his drink; "you must excuse me, I'll see you later." He hurried out of the bar to look for Marian, and he found her, as he had expected, standing by Lady Rosedale's chair.

The waltz was beginning. He led her in, and together they began to dance. But in a crowded room Lawrence soon realised that the was but an indifferent dancer; do what he would, he could not prevent himself from bumping up against other waltzer, and, though these took it all in good part, he flushed hot with annoyance at his own clumsiness.

"I am afraid that I am making you appear ridiculous," he whispered to Marian with a blank look of chagrin, after a vain struggle to keep out of other people's way.

"Let us go outside," she replied quickly. "We can sit the rest of it out together. It's close in here; and I don't feel that I want to dance tonight."

"You wouldn't want to, with me," he agreed grimly, as they made their way outside and walked slowly toward the sea-front. "I am ashamed that I have spoilt part of your evening."

"No; you are quite wrong," she assured him earnestly. "I really don't want to dance."

She spoke with an earnestness that surprised him, and he experienced a strange thrill of elation. She was not, then, a girl who would care for a man's company only if he could keep her always amused. These little revelations of character that she made from time to time were always a delight to him. It seemed to him that he was always discovering something new and wonderful about her, something finer and more loveable than he had suspected before. He wondered, too, if she did not care to dance because she preferred to be alone with him: a thought which, if he instantly dismissed it as vain and presumptuous, imparted to him, nevertheless, an exquisite glow of pleasure.

"Marian!"

They were nearly at the end of the lawn when a voice behind called out to her. The speaker was not far behind.

"My brother," she murmured quickly, and stopped dead. "He—he probably wants to say something to me, and I have—I must go and hear what he has to say. Wait; I will come back in a moment."

Stephen himself, after calling to her, had paused, making no attempt to come up to them.

She hurried towards him and joined him: Lawrence could see them both dimly where they stood. He guessed that Stephen was remonstrating with her for being with him, and his lips closed ominously. Whatever Stephen said to her, however, did not prevent her from keeping her word; for she came back, and quickly, as she had promised, without any reference to the brief interruption. They resumed their walk towards the seal; where he found a vacant garden bench. The seawall itself was deserted. They seated themselves in silence. He was angrily moody; she seemed somewhat depressed and sad.

"Your brother does not like me," he said at last.

"No," she replied with a frankness which he hardly expected. He resolved to be equally plain.

"Why?"

She made no reply at once. He glanced at her face, discernible in the light shed by the lamps that stretch overhead along the seawall's length. It was drawn, nervous: she was visibly agitated.

"I can't say," she answered, after a little while; "but he is like that at times. He takes likes and dislikes to people for no reason whatsoever. It is foolish of him."

"Shall I tell you why?" he asked, and it appeared as if she did not hear him. "I will tell you," he continued, with a ring of determination in his voice.

"It is because he knows I love you. He has seen it, and he thinks I am not good enough for you. I am not, dear; but I love you though I never meant to tell you so tonight, or at any other time."

He had spoken without premeditation, uttering words that had been in his heart for days, breaking through all his habits of reticence and reserve. And now that he had told her he loved her, he found further speech, and gave full vent to it.

"I love you, dearest, love you as I never could have thought it possible for me to love a woman. I have been very lonely all my life, but I never felt it before. I did not wish it otherwise; but you came, and I saw you, you who are so beautiful, so wonderful, and now I could wish only to live for you, to be everything to you. I should not say it, for how can I ask you to marry me? I, who am nothing, compared with you—a mere sort of clerk, I suppose, at best. And yet I am glad I have told you what an hour ago I should have thought it foolish to mention, for you know now that to me you are everything, everything. . ."

The lap, lap of the waves against the seawall, the gentle rustle of coconut palms in the avenue behind them, the hum of the tropical night insects among the trees, the sound of the music, softened as it came to them throbbing through the air, the murmur of human voices from the lawn, all these they heard with a strange distinctness when he ceased and waited for her reply. They were listening to nothing, intent only upon themselves. Yet all these mingled sounds impinged upon their consciousness with peculiar insistence as they stared at the dark sea in front of them, with the light lighted ships at anchor upon its bosom.

"I know it," she replied at last, "but I wish you hadn't said it. It's no use," she went on, as if talking to herself; "it is impossible. You don't know how impossible it is."

"I do, only too well," he answered bitterly. "I have known it all along. It is hopeless, but who would blame me for daring to hope? And yet I did not even dare to hope!"

"What is the good of hoping?" she asked. "I am going away in a few weeks, and then it will be all the same to you. Some day you will wonder why you cared for a moving picture actress you knew nothing about—and you will feel ashamed."

He exclaimed passionately against the suggestion; suddenly he seized the hand lying nearest to him and would have carried it to his lips had she not quickly pulled it away.

"If you do that now you will do it again," she said softly, "and then you—surely you must know what yielding to temptation mean? We yield once and say it is only for that once; and after that we yield again, and again, and then—! You mustn't. And I mustn't let you. It would not be fair to you."

"I am a Bohemian," she continued, "a wanderer; here today and gone tomorrow, and I do not love you. Besides, I am afraid. . ."

"Oh what?" he demanded.

"Of everything, I was always a coward. I am afraid now, horribly."

He glanced at her, and her face bore witness to her words. His gorge rose. "Afraid of your brother?" he cried. "If that is all, there is nothing to be afraid of. I would tell him now."

"No," she protested; "No. You must not. You promise me that you will not?"

Involuntarily she had placed her hand upon his, as if to beseech him by touch as well as by word. "If you wish it," he said, gladly obedient to her faintest desire.

A slight pressure of her hand on his suggested that she realised why he so readily consented to do what she wished.

"And this is the end?" he asked her, after another pause.

"Of our friendship? Why should it be? I like you; you have been very nice to me. I like you to be near me; I know I could trust you at anytime. Why should it be the end?"

"I would be your friend and your lover forever," he answered, "Your lover I shall be always. If you let me continue to be your friend—"

"Yes;" she interrupted softly. "I want you to be."

And again a silence fell between them, and they heard the soft lapping of the waves at their feet.

To Lawrence everything seemed a blank; he was conscious of a peculiar feeling of numbness in his mind, numbness and intense stillness. He has said he had not dared even to hope; he knew now that he had been deceiving himself, that he had hoped much with all the strength of his being. And now he felt this absolute refusal of him with every nerve of his body. She did not love him; she had said so frankly as if to put that matter at rest forever. But if he should persist in offering her his devotion, might she not feel differently towards him, come to care for him? But did his position warrant that? Would she be satisfied with what he had to offer? These questions thronged through his mind half unconsciously. He could find no answer to them.

"I have missed one of the dances," said Marian, rising at last, "and my partner must be looking all about for me. We ought to go back now, don't you think? They'll wonder what has become of us."

Thus brought back to practical realities, Lawrence led her from the seawall and towards the ballroom. At one of the entrances of this room they were met by the young man who had engaged Marian for the sixth dance; the fifth was now in progress: she had, involuntarily, cut that. The young man suggested that they should sit together until his dance came round; and at this moment Mr. Phipps made his appearance.

"Not a dance for the old man!" he exclaimed, shaking his head in affected sorrow. "No one wants him, and yet I can foot it deftly with the youngest of them. Never seen me dance, have you?"

While speaking he had been keenly scanning Marian with admiration in his eyes. She was dressed in rich yellow satin: the skirt covered with beautiful lace. On her bosom and neck glowed with soft lustre, a wonderful necklace of pearls which he had seen on Lady Rosedale more than once. Some flowers were fastened at her waist by a diamond brooch; but these were wilting already and hanging lose.

"If you are not careful," went on Mr. Phipps without waitinf for any answer to his last question, "you will lose that fine brooch of yours, young lady. The catch seems weak, or something."

Marian glanced at the brooch. "I must get it tightened," she said a little absently; "but it's all right, the catch will hold." She took out the faded flowers and threw them away.

"Careless, careless," reproved Mr. Phipps, "you deserve to lose it to teach you a good lesson for the future. Sometimes we want what we say we don't, and sometimes we lose what we think we have certain, and then waste time in regrets." He spoke with the most innocent of expressions, but Marian and Lawrence shot a sharp look at him. They were extremely sensitive just now to any remark that might appear to have a hidden meaning.

"Let us all sit down while we may, and before the chairs are monopolised," counselled Mr. Phipps. He shepherded them to a small table with chairs set around it, and placed between two low, broad-leaved palms: here they could the see the ballroom distinctly. He suggested drinks. It was a habit of his, and he bade a waiter take the order before his invitation could be refused. For himself he chose a low rocking chair next to Marian and luxuriated in its comfort. He seemed to realise that no conversation was to be got out of Lawrence or Marian just then, so turned his attention to the strange young man and animatedly chatted about nothing in particular with him until the refreshments were brought. These consumed, the sixth dance began and Mariah and her partner rose to go; so did Lawrence, who, informing Mr. Phipps that he would see him later on, moved away also. When Marian and her partner had nearly reached the verandah, Mr. Phipps rose briskly, paused and seemed to change his mind, then returned to his seat. He elevated his feet on a chair and smiled as if amused by everything around him. He was still sitting in the same spot and in the same posture when Lawrence came back about an hour afterwards to rejoin him.

"I am a very active man," observed Mr. Phipps, "but when I see a host of young people moving to music for hours, I just want to sit still and watch them do the exertion. Then I understand the meaning of real rest, and appreciate the charms of an idle life. Had your second waltz yet?"

"I could not dance the first, so I don't know if I shall attempt the second. It is low down on the programme, anyhow," said Lawrence.

"You ought to cultivate poetry, like I do," advised Mr. Phipps. "'If you try and don't succeed, try, try, again': I guess it was an American who invented that line. Long ago I asked the same girl to marry me no less than five times. How's that?"

"Yes?" said Lawrence, abstractedly, and with obvious lack of interest.

"Yes, sir. And she refused me everytime. She was a real good kind of girl, now that I come to think of it. She refused me to the last, and now I could not sufficiently express my gratitude to her. I showed her what perseverance meant, and, by Jove! She proved that she had a wrinkle or two on that same moral quality. She out-persevered me; but I'd have been ashamed if I had given up at the first No. I would have gone on suggestin' the altar and the happy hearth if she hadn't accepted someone else; but she did. Man wasn't a patch on me, but there's no accounting for tastes. I have been happy ever since her marriage: she was tall and slender just like our movie stat here. She is now tall and stout."

Lawrence made no comment.

"I did not take No for an answer thill there was no sense in asking the question anymore," Mr. Phipps insisted.

But Lawrence was evidently not to be led into making any disclosures. He knew Mr. Phipps's methods of indirect enquiry, but was not disposed to be communicative just then. He allowed the hint to pass.

Mr. Phipps did not try again, but, instead, took out his cigarette case, and, finding but one cigarette in it, hailed a passing bellboy.

"Run up to my room, Ethiopa," he commanded, "and you will find a tin of cigarettes on my table or on the dressing table, or the bed—if you use your eyes you will see it. Hurry back with it." The boy grinned and went quickly to do as he was ordered. Mr. Phipps was known to be generous in the matter of tips.

Mr. Phipps lay back in his rocking chair. "The charm of the tropics," he soliloquised, "is its cheap labour. Cheap and inefficient, but wonderfully willing at the prospect of modest remuneration. These bellboys now; they never say that a thing can't be done, or confess that they do not know how to do it. They make a real effort to help you. Only last week there was a busy American down here, and he wanted to telephone someone. Asked a bellboy to bring him a telephone directory, and that boy said, yes, he would, and went away at the double-quick. Stayed a little longer than seemed necessary, but came back at last with a lemon squash. It wasn't quite what was wanted, but the helpful intention was there. Ah, here's my boy! Well, where are the cigarettes?"

"Please, sir," said the boy, "there is no cigarettes on the bed or the dressing table, sir."

"And it didn't strike you to look elsewhere, is that it? Too much of a demand upon your imaginative powers, eh? Well, I am not going to smoke any other cigarettes except my own, so I guess I'll just foot it upstairs and get them. Beastly shame to have to do it."

"Don't trouble," said Lawrence, seeing that Mr. Phipps did not wish to stir. "I'll run up and get them for you."

"Will you, son? That's kind of you, sure. You'll find me right here when you come back."

Lawrence was away for quite ten minutes before he came back. "No wonder the boy couldn't find then," he observed, handing an unopened tin of cigarettes to Mr. Phipps; "you had none out. I had to hunt for them, and found two or three tins at last in the bottom drawer of your dressing table." Mr. Phipps said nothing, but opened the tin, extracted some cigarettes, with which he filled his case, and proceeded to smoke. He made no effort to draw Lawrence into conversation; the look on Lawrence's face was not inviting. Only one question did he ask: "About what time is your second waltz?"

"Somewhere between twelve and one o' clock," said Lawrence, and Mr. Phipps knew that he would remain till the dance was over, or till Marian went upstairs.

At midnight Mr. Phipps got up to retire. "These festivities will go on until three o'clock," he observed, "and you are likely to be here until then. You want to see the last of everything, Lawrence, meaning thereby one certain young person. But I see no reason why I should stay down here any longer, so I'll go and hit the hay. And take my advice: quit looking so darned grim and gloomy. Anyone seeing your face will know that something has happened to you. Well, goodnight."

"Goodnight," echoed Lawrence.

V

The Jewel Robbery

The bellboy who first heard Lady Rosedale's bell flew incontinently up the stairs, showing a celerity not habitual with persons of his profession. But there was something so loud, so imperative, so persistent about the summons, that he felt impelled to swiftness; even as he sped up the servants' stairs he heard that summons shrilling below him and knew that whoever was ringing would tolerate no nonsense on his part.

He had no need to knock at Lady Rosedale's door. It was wide open, and that lady's voice was heard calling out to her neighbour, who was Marian Bareme, and telling her of a terrible misfortune. Guests on the opposite side of the corridor, some of them awakened suddenly, were hurrying into bathrobes and kimonos, preparatory to emerging upon the scene. Maids were speeding to the spot. Lady Rosedale was not loud or hysterical, but the word she had sent out to Marian had been caught by one other person, and (so significant and sinister it was) had been instantly repeated to another. It was "theft," a sort of magic talisman for unlocking all kinds of fears. By the time the bellboy reached Lady Rosedale's door he was joined by a little crowd of people, and the crowd grew momently.

The boy heard Lady Rosedale gasp, "My diamond necklace—gone!" and in his innocence he answered, "Yes, ma'am," as if it were the most natural thing in the world that a diamond necklaces should disappear overnight out of a lady's room.

"The manager; quick, bring the manager!" ordered Lady Rosedale, as Marian joined her. Marian's face was bloodless, her lips white. She it was to whom Lady Rosedale had first called out on discovering her loss; she had thrown on a loose robe as quickly as she could, and had hurried to join her friend. Her eyes looked frightened, as indeed did the eyes of everyone in the corridor. The diamond necklace they had all heard of; its reputed value was ten thousand pounds. It had been stolen? . . . surely, surely, there was some mistake. "Why not telephone for the police?" suggested one of the startled guests, and, without waiting for an answer, flew to the telephone nearby.

The manager made his appearance, having been given to understand by the bellboy that Lady Rosedale had been robbed of everything she possessed, and nearly murdered in addition. The boy had been dramatic in his relating of Lady Rosedale's condition; consequently the manager was considerably relieved at seeing her alive, and apparently perfectly well, even if somewhat agitated. He looked congratulations, Lady Rosedale, aware that he must have heard of her loss, regarded his look as a premeditated insult. She turned upon him with dignity.

"So this is how guests are treated in this hotel, is it, sir?"

"It is impossible, Lady Rosedale, quite impossible," protested the manager, who was a Frenchman with a plentiful supply of ingratiating gestures. "It has never happened before, and it cannot have happened now. Have you searched? Maybe a little oversight: mislaid, perhaps. I assure you we shall do everything to find it for you. With your permission, we shall look at once."

The dapper little man was ready to conduct the investigation himself. The very idea of policemen in the hotel filled him with consternation and dismay.

"Search!" exclaimed Lady Rosedale, who, in her flowing kimono, chocolate coloured, and embroidered with bright birds that flew in every direction, appeared now of almost striking height as she looked down upon the manager from the summit of her great indignation— "search! Do you think I would make a fuss about nothing? Will any amount of search account for my trunk being open? Yu can search if you like; that will be necessary, I dare say. But I inform you at once that I shall hold you and your hotel responsible for my loss."

The manager shrugged his shoulders deprecatingly. "The hotel is not responsible for any money and jewellery not deposited in the safe downstairs," he reminded Lady Rosedale, but succeeded in throwing to his words and attitude a suggestion of regret that such responsibility could not rightly be placed on the hotel. "But the necklace, it is safe, I am sure. Let us begin to look."

By this time most of the people on the first floor were in the corridor. Among these was Mr. Phipps, who was already completely dressed. Mr. Phipps pushed his way to Lady Rosedale's door, outside of which stood the other guests, then calmly entered the room. One or two others, emboldened by his example, followed suit, but drew back hastily as a withering glance from Lady Rosedale's eye fell upon them. It fell upon Mr. Phipps also. But he did not seem to see it.

"Your diamond necklace gone?" he enquired of Lady Rosedale. "Too bad, too bad! Sent for the police yet?"

"Yes," answered someone in the corridor. "They are coming along immediately."

"In the meantime," said the manager, "let us search; there is no knowing—"

He began energetically to peer about, looking at all the places where, if the necklace had been there, Lady Rosedale herself must certainly have long ago discovered it. Everybody who could see him followed his movements closely, Lady Rosedale with obvious disdain. At length the manager desisted, with the remark that a more thorough search could be made later on. There was nothing to do now but to await the arrival of the police.

"But are the police going to be a week in getting here?" demanded Lady Rosedale impatiently. It seemed not. Just then, indeed, two men appeared upon the scene, pushing their way into the room with a businesslike air. One was a slim man, not more than thirty, dark brown in complexion. The other was over forty; a black man, big and burly, with tiny, prying, suspicious eyes and heavy lips. These men had been sent posthaste from the Kingston detective office, which was not quite half a mile from the hotel, on the telephone message being received there that a robbery had taken place at the Myrtle Bank Hotel.

Lady Rosedale looked them over critically. Her look said as plainly as speech could have done that while these men might be useful in dealing with an ordinary theft, they did not seem capable of handling an important case such as hers. Her next words gave expression to her feeling.

"Is there no such thing as a white detective in Jamaica?" she asked.

"The detective inspector is a white man," Mr. Phipps informed her, "but he is not supposed to know anything about detective work. He is an administrative officer with very little experience in criminal investigations and an astonishing acquaintanceship with fishing, shooting and other manly sports. I would suggest that you contented yourself with the aid of the two men."

Lady Rosedale made a gesture of despair. The elder of the two detectives, with a slight movement of annoyance at the almost openly expressed disbelief in the skill of himself and his colleague, now took a definite hand in the business. "If the lady will tell us what she lost and how she found it out," he suggested, "we can get to work. But standing here and doing nothing is not going to help us."

Even to Lady Rosedale this appeared an eminently sensible way of stating the situation. She collected her thoughts, and proceeded at once to give her statement.

She had retired at about one o'clock in the morning. On entering her room she had observed nothing peculiar. During the rest of the night she had slept soundly; she had, consequently, heard nothing, if there was anything to hear. This morning she had got up at her usual hour; while dressing she noticed that the hasp of her largest trunk was hanging down. She felt at once that something was wrong. On searching the trunk and her jewel case she missed her diamond necklace, by far the most valuable trinket she possessed. Immediately she had given the alarm.

The older detective looked narrowly about him; then eyed the manager suspiciously for a moment. The manager stared back haughtily at him. The detective began a cross-examination.

"You say, ma'am, that your trunk was locked last night. Are you sure?"

"Perfectly," answered Lady Rosedale. "I will tell you all about it. I don't travel with much jewellery as a rule: a couple of necklaces, a few rings, a couple of brooches, and a pendant or so. I leave the rest with my bankers in England; but I never leave my diamond necklace behind. I have always liked it have it with me: I see how unwise I was. When I came to this hotel I saw no reason why I should put away my jewel box in the hotel's safe; I had never any reason for doing so at any other hotel, and I had always heard that the Jamaica thief confined his attention to trifling articles, things of really no value, such as a banana or coconut."

"As a general proposition, that is quite true," interrupted Mr. Phipps. "The native mind has not yet attained to the heights of scientific burglary. But it will improve."

"Have the goodness not to interrupt, sir," growled the big detective, with an almost malevolent look at Mr. Phipps: he did not like the latter's reference to the native mind. Lady Rosedale, who had also favoured Mr. Phipps with an indignant stare, continued.

"I took out the jewel case last night. I want to—to," she hesitated, glanced at Marian, then hurried on. "I wanted Miss Braeme to wear a pearl necklace of mine. I opened the case, and after we had taken out the necklace and a small pendant for myself, we closed the case and put it back in the trunk. The trunk was then locked, and shortly after we left the room."

"You locked the trunk yourself, ma'am?"

"No; I asked Miss Braeme to do that for me. But I saw her lock it: I saw it with my own eyes. She handed the key back to me."

"And you had the key with you when you were downstairs?"

"No. It is one of a bunch, you see, and I don't care to carry a thing like that about with me. But I have a safe hiding place for it in my room; besides, this morning I found the keys exactly where I had left them. My trunk must have been opened with a false key; it could not have been opened in any other way."

The younger detective went over to the trunk and examined the lock. He took the key, placed it in the key-hole and turned it again and again. "The lock has not been broken," he remarked, "and no false key for this lock was ever made in this country. There's nobody here who could make it."

"Evidence again of the undeveloped state of the native mind," murmured Mr. Phipps, but this time no one took any notice of him.

The man raised the trunk-lid, disclosing a deep tray with several compartments, in some of which, as he opened them, he perceived a number of articles. One fairly large compartment contained the jewel case.

"I always keep it there," explained Lady Rosdeale, and lifted it out.

The case, a flat, beautifully inlaid box of polished ebony, was placed on the dressing table; in the presence of the people in the room Lady Rosedale now opened it. As she had said, she did not travel with many articles of jewellery, but some that she took about with her were still lying in the box: the diamond necklace was all that had disappeared. She opened several compartments; then, lastly, the little drawer at the bottom where the necklace had been kept.

"Why," questioned the elder detective, "did the thief take only one thing and leave the rest? It looks very funny."

"It is positively hilarious," agreed Mr. Phipps. "You suggest, I see, that the thief had a sense of humour, and left something behind him to show that he could resist temptation. That is certainly not a common characteristic of burglars."

"Has this gentleman anything to do with you, ma'am?" asked the detective, turning to Lady Rosedale.

"Certainly not," she replied haughtily.

"Then," began the detective, but though better of it, and closed his lips. But he gave a warning glance to his subordinate, who seemed to understand what was passing in his mind.

"Did you see the diamond necklace"—he called it "diamond necklace"— "in the box last night?" he resumed.

"No; we did not open the drawer in which it was," Lady Rosedale answered.

"And the case was opened or locked when you took it out this morning?" continued the detective.

"I—think it was locked," said Lady Rosedale, puckering up her brows to remember. "I know I put the key into the lock and turned it. I don't quite remember you see; I was excited when I found my trunk open, and knew I had left it locked last night, so I am afraid that in my hurry to find out if I had lost anything I did not very closely observe what I did. But almost any key could open a box like this," she added.

"But if a thief had opened it, he would not have taken the trouble to locked it again," pointed out Mr. Phipps. "Indeed, I don't see why, when he opened Lady Rosedale's trunk, he should have taken the trouble to close it after him. That looks like a precious waste of valuable time."

"If the thief was anybody in this house," returned the detective darkly, "he would close the trunk if he had time. He wouldn't want his robbery to be found out too quick; for that wouldn't suit him."

Mr. Phipps, with a slight nod of the head, admitted that there was something in this way of looking at the matter. Then an idea seemed to strike him.

"Anybody else lost anything?" he enquired suddenly, "or is it Lady Rosedale alone who has been the victim of a burglarious attention?"

No sooner had the question crossed his lips than there was a general scurrying of the people in the corridor to their rooms. Ina few moments some were back at Lady Rosedale's door, their momentary apprehensions relieved. Others soon followed these, and yet others, and when it had been ascertained that none had lost anything they all prepared to enjoy with disinterested thoroughness a sensation that would have been considered delectable even in a European or American city. Mr. Phipps had not stirred, nor had Marian, while the other guests were busy with their search.

"What about you?" he enquired, turning to her jestingly, when everyone had declared that he or she had lost nothing. "As for me, not even a tin of my cigarettes has been touched. Good fortune dogs my heels."

"Yes, dear, you had better go and look," advised Lady Rosedale, and Marian left the room.

In a minute or two she was back, her face and demeanour eloquent of calamity, "Everything is gone"; she exclaimed. "The pearls, my rings, my brooch—everything!"

VI

Mr. Phipps Goes Out

If Lady Rosedale had been excited before, she was struck with absolute consternation now. The first blow she had sustained with a fine appearance of righteous indignation tempered with dignity; under the second she staggered. She stared at Marian in blank astonishment, unable to utter a word. There were murmurs of surprise and commiseration from the spectators, an exclamation of horror from the manager. The elder of the two detectives was again about to begin a sharp interrogatory when Mr. Phipps intervened.

"What did you say had been stolen?" he asked, looked narrowly at Marian.

"Everything I wore last night," she answered. "Lady Rosedale's pearls and my own things. I put them in the upper drawer of my dressing table after taking them off before going to bed. I thought that they would be perfectly safe there. I keep all my jewellery there, and nothing has ever been stolen before."

"Are you sure you were wearing the pearls when you came up to the room last night, or rather, this morning?" enquired Mr. Phipps. "You might have dropped them, you know."

"Miss Braeme was wearing the pearls when I left her downstairs at a little past twelve o'clock last night," interrupted Lady Rosedale, sharply, annoyed that Mr. Phipps should be interfering in a matter which did not directly concern him. "She must have come to bed very shortly after that."

"I came upstairs with Miss Hellingworth," Marian resumed. "About the last thing she said to me when I bade her goodnight was how beautiful the pearl necklace was. That was at my door."

"I only asked for the purpose of not leaving any possible explanation unexplored," explained Mr. Phipps. "You were about to say something," he continued, turning to the chief detective.

"I was about to say, sir," replied that individual, "that if you were going to ask questions, I had better stop."

"Please proceed," implored Mr. Phipps; "the sagacity of your enquiries simply fills us all with admiration. I can already see the necklaces being discovered in an hour or two, thank to the local Sherlock Holmes."

"Did you lock your drawer after you had put the necklace and other things in it, miss?" the detective asked Marian, merely giving a glance at Mr. Phipps which seemed to threaten future trouble.

"I did," said Marian in a low voice, "and I think the lock has been forced. You had better come and see for yourself."

Led by the detectives, the party now went into the adjoining chamber occupied by Marian, which was smaller than Lady Rosedale's. Here both the detectives examined carefully the lock of the first drawer of the dressing table, a standardised piece of American furniture with three drawers whose locks were all opened by the same key. It was easy to see that the lock of the first drawer had been picked, not by any means a difficult matter to accomplish. Satisfied on this score, the two detectives withdrew into a corner of the room and whispered together. Lady Rosedale, Mr. Phipps and Marian watched them keenly, Mr. Phipps being intent on studying the expression on their faces.

The conference lasted but a few minutes; when it was over the elder detective turned to Lady Rosedale.

"Did you lock your room door last night, ma'am?"

"Yes," she replied, "I always do."

"And you, miss?"

"Yes," said Marian.

"So that the thief must have entered through the window," observed the irrepressible Mr. Phipps; "and he must have done so after two o' clock in the morning. But would he have not been seen by the night watchman? There is a watchman always about, isn't there?" he enquired.

"There is," the manager hastened to affirm, "and he is a most zealous and competent man. I am sure he would have seen any thief clambering through a window."

"He would have seen the thief if there was enough light and if he was where he could see him when he was climbing in," remarked the younger detective, somewhat incoherently; "but there is nothing about this window to show that anyone came in through here."

"No," admitted Mr. Phipps, who was already at the window conducting a personal examination. "There are no finger prints observable, and the curtain shows no sign of having been disturbed." He threw open the window and peered outside. "No footprints visible on the verandah's metal roof," he added, "this roof being rather remarkable for affording what naval strategists would call 'a low visibility': in fact, it is too hard and clean for the traces of footprints to be left on it. It would seem that the thief did not enter this way; and yet he must have. A wide-awake and active man would have avoided disturbing anything or making any noise, wouldn't he?"

"This thief, whoever it is," said the elder detective dogmatically, "is somebody who knows this place well. It is nobody from the outside." He gave the slightest of signs to his colleague, who, with well-affected indifference, sauntered out of the room. "It would be easy for anyone who is active to get on to the verandah roof," the speaker continued; "but it would take him sometime to get into one room and open a trunk and then climb out again and get into another room and open a drawer. Could you send for the night watchman, sir?" he asked, addressing the manager.

"Certainly," said the manager and he hurried out of the room. Without a word, Mr. Phipps followed him; seeing which, the detective, hastily asking Lady Rosedale and Marian to remain where they were until he returned, quickly left the room also.

Lady Rosedale had seated herself on one of the chairs, her eyes fixed on Marian's face with an expression in which were blended amazement and dismay. The discovery that her pearls were indubitable gone had apparently touched her heart and bewildered her mind. It could not be said that she was utterly crushed, for it would have taken mountains of calamity to crush Lady Rosedale's spirit. She gave one the impression of being always able to rise superior to circumstances. Yet she was grieved, profoundly disturbed; it also seemed as if something unexpressed and perhaps inexpressible were perplexing her greatly. Marian noticed her troubled appearance, and now that the temporary absence of the detectives and the withdrawal of Mr. Phipps and the manager gave her the opportunity of a word or two with lady Rosedale, she looked at that lady pathetically and with obvious regret.

"I am so sorry this has happened," she said in broken tones, "you know I did not want to wear the pearls last night."

"If you had only been a little more careful, my dear Marian," retuned Lady Rosedale with the first touch of bitterness she had ever imported into her voice in speaking to Marian, "if you had only been more careful it might not have happened. A drawer is hardly the place where one should place a valuable necklace for safe keeping."

"Your trunk did not seem to have been safer," retorted the girl, trembling, but with some spirit. "Yet you know I locked it securely; I saw you try the hasp after I had handed you the keys."

"That is quite true," replied Lady Rosedale with dignity; "I always make sure that things are properly done. And if only one of my necklaces had been stolen I should not now feel so distressed. But both! Just think of it." She added after a pause, more kindly, "But I am not blaming you, dear; you must not believe that."

Before Marian could say anything further the elder detective and manager reappeared, the latter explaining to Lady Rosedale that he had sent for the night watchman, who would shortly be there. As for the detective, he showed quite plainly that he was waiting for someone or for some development, for he made no further effort at finding out anything by search or question, but merely pretended to be making notes in a little pocketbook. Everyone noticed the absence of Mr. Phipps, but no one commented on it.

Presently a heavy tread, accompanied by a jingling sound, was heard in the corridor, and then it the doorway appeared a tall, handsome young English-man, spurred like a cavalry officer, and dressed in the white jacket and dark-blue trousers of an Inspector of the Jamaica Police. On seeing the ladies, his hand flew to the salute, and he greeted Marian by name, as one who knew her. He turned to Lady Rosedale, who had risen from her chair at his appearance.

"I am exceedingly sorry to hear about your loss," he said to her courteously, in a pleasant but business-like tone of voice. "Brown,"—he indicated the detective—"Brown telephoned for me to come down, as the case seemed a peculiar and delicate one, and I hastened down in the hope of being of some service. I trust we shall be able to recover your diamond necklace very shortly, Lady Rosedale."

"My pearl necklace also," said Lady Rosedale. "That—"

"If you please, Inspector, I would like to say a work to you by yourself," interrupted Detective Sergeant Brown.

"Certainly, Brown," agreed the Inspector, and retired with his subordinate into the corridor, which had by this been deserted by many of the guests, who had gone to breakfast. Some persons still hung about, however, eager to learn at first hand the latest developments of this interesting situation. These keenly followed Inspector Harmsworth and his subordinate with their eyes, though their ears could catch nothing of what passed between the two, who spoke to one another in whispers.

When Inspector Harmsworth returned, after about five minutes' whispered conversation with the detective, he was looking exceedingly grave and embarrassed. He muttered a word or two in the manager's

H. G. DE LISSER

ear, and the manager, in his turn, went into the corridor and hinted to the people who still lingered there that the dining room would shortly be closed. He also managed to suggest delicately that the Detective Inspector would like to conduct his investigations in private. This hint had the desired effect, and when the last of the curious and excited spectators had disappeared, Inspector Harmsworth closed the door of Marian's room, and, seating himself at the writing table by the window, rapidly filled in some official forms.

"I hold a commission as a Justice of the Peace," he explained to the manager as he wrote; "it is useful in emergencies. I am afraid we shall have to search one or two of your rooms."

"But which?" cried the manager; "surely you can't interfere with everybody's private apartment!"

"There is no such intention," said Inspector Harmsworth soothingly; "Indeed, I am sure no one will make any difficulty about a search quietly conducted by experienced officers. I am sorry, but, in the circumstances—"

His eyes rested on Marian apologetically, and at once, he saw, with relief, and yet with something like shame, that she understood the look. Before she could make any remark, Lady Rosedale replied;

"Both I and Miss Braeme will be glad to have our rooms thoroughly overhauled, Inspector," she said, "you can begin with mine. What other rooms do you intend to search?"

Inspector Harmsworth pretended not to hear the question. More embarrassed than ever, he resumed his remarks.

"You should yourself go over every article of—er—clothing, Lady Rosedale, so as to be absolutely certain that nothing has been mislaid in them. Miss Braeme will no doubt assist you."

"And Lady Rosedale can assist me," said Marian quickly. "We had better begin with my room. After we have searched, your people could go over the rooms for themselves if you like. Mightn't that help?"

"It would, immensely," agreed the Inspector, greatly relieved: "and you had better get one of the hotel's maids to help you; you'll need someone to move the things in the room."

He hated the job he had in hand; he had never done anything like it before. But the girl's quickness of wit had saved him from making any deliberate suggestion that a search of persons as well as of property was desirable if suspicion was not to continue to rest on Marian. The police could not venture to search anyone unless he or she was arrested, and there was no good grounds as yet for the arrest of anybody. But Brown had stated plainly to him his suspicions of Marian, and in the latter's own interests it was best that it should be settled once and for all that she had none of the missing jewellery hidden in the room or concealed on her person—that is, assuming that Sergeant Brown was wrong. Marian would now, he hope, insist upon Lady Rosedale "assisting" her in a minute investigation, and, to save Marian's face, Lady Rosedale would also submit to a similar search. The police would not be called upon after that to go through either lady's person or things.

For himself, the Inspector thought Detective Brown's suspicion of Marian absurd; but the man had had much experience in the detection of robberies, and duty was duty. It was Harmsworth's duty, as head of the local detective department, to discover the thief and recover the jewels. The value of these, the position of Lady Rosedale, the peculiar circumstances of the double theft, rendered this case the most important of which he had ever had the handling. There was going to be a great fuss and to-do about it; that he could already see: what he could not see was his way to success if the jewels had really disappeared. The whole business seemed to him an infernal nuisance, and one, moreover, with which a gentleman should have nothing to do. But there it was: he was Detective Inspector, and Brown had sent for him because Brown had felt that he could not personally deal with a white lady as a suspect, however much he might suspect her: that was a job for an Inspector at least. She was not, however, the only person against whom Detective Brown entertained suspicions; he had also whispered the name of Mr. Phipps. In one of the search warrants just signed appeared the name of Mr. Phipps, whom Inspector Harmsworth knew very well indeed. Often he had enjoyed Mr. Phipps' hospitality. Now to be called upon to countenance and then to order a search of his rooms was positively awful. Police work, when it touched the better classes, was decidedly not work for a man with decent feeling, though Inspector Harmsworth, as he silently sympathised with himself. He was sorry he had not applied for protracted leave of absence a week or two before.

"We shall remain outside until you are ready for us," he said, rising from the table as he finished writing, and addressing Lady Rosedale. He would not venture to look at Marian. "Please take your own time," he added, anxious to be as nice as possible, and bowed himself out of the room.

Once outside, he breathed a sigh of relief, and turned to the stolid black man at his side. "Now, Brown," said he, "shall we go to Mr. Phipps' room? The manager here will help us."

The manager's face indicated quite plainly that there was nothing that he could possibly desire less to do; but he contended himself with shrugging his shoulders.

"And where is Mr. Phipps?" asked Inspector Harmsworth.

"When I sent Sampson to telephone to you, Inspector, Mr. Phipps walked out of the lady's room, where he had no right to be from the first. I knew he was trying to get away, so I went after Sampson and told him to follow Mr. Phipps wherever he went. Sampson hasn't come back yet, nor Mr. Phipps either."

"There's a Mr. Phipps now," said the Inspector as he caught sight of the well-dressed, jaunty figure of that gentleman stepping lightly along the corridor towards him. "He must have just come in."

"Ah, Harmsworth," cried Mr. Phipps heartily, "on the job, I see. I guess from the start that this sable Sherlock Holmes would send a lightning summons to you. Holmes will make a great reputation yet if only he lives long enough, avoids drink, and conquers the tropical tendency to inertia: I especially want to advise him against drink. Your other man has been following me all over Kingston in a cab. I say, old chap, I am awfully sorry to put the Jamaica Detective Department to such expense. Seems that I am suspected of harbouring diamonds and pearls on my person against the Aliens Immigration Act or something. Is that so?"

"The matter is rather serious, Mr. Phipps," replied the Inspector. "We have to do all that we can to recover Lady Rosedale's jewels, so you must excuse me if I—"

"Say, you aren't going to arrest me, are you?" asked Mr. Phipps.

"Oh, no. There's nothing whatever against you: don't imagine that for a moment. But as a matter of form, you understand, we, that is to say—"

"Just what, son? Say the word!"

"We shall have to go through your rooms. It is in your interest really. You see that, don't you?"

"No, *sir*, I don't. What you mean to tell me is that this bright and shining son of Ham has got out a search warrant against me and that it is now to be executed. Well, I have no kick coming, and it wouldn't matter a brace o' sour apples to King George's Government if I had. So get along, and make your search, and if you can haul up any diamonds and pearls among my belongings we'll just divide the graft between us. Come along."

Mr. Phipps, smiling as though at an excellent joke, led the way to his room. Detective Brown lingered in the corridor, while Harmsworth followed Mr. Phipps. Brown then ran downstairs, with a celerity of which he would not commonly have been suspected, and there, as he had expected, he found his assistant, Sampson, waiting for him.

"Where did Mr. Phipps go?" he demanded brusquely.

"To Jones and Bedlaw," answered Sampson, mentioning a leading firm of city solicitors.

"What did he want to go to lawyers for at this early hour? He went nowhere else?"

"No, he came right back, and I came behind him."

"Alright, Sampson, wait down here till I want you; but it he comes down before me, follow him. But try and don't let him see you." And with that Detective Brown hurried back up the stairs and into Mr. Phipp's room.

The search warrant was produced, and the search took place, the Inspector watching it with a shame-faced expression. Brown looked everywhere, leisurely, knowing that the ladies would take sometime at their own task; but his heart was not in the job. The fact is, he did not expect to find anything. Mr. Phipps had left the hotel, and if Mr. Phipps was the man who had stolen the jewels he surely would not have left them behind him. They would not be on him now, either: Brown was convinced of that. Sampson had followed him in a cab; but had Sampson been as watchful as possible? Mr. Phipps' cabman, too: who was he? Sampson should be able to recognise him; possibly he was a creature in the pay of Mr. Phipps. That cabman must have his room searched this very day, if the Detective Inspector would consent; but a man like Mr. Phipps wouldn't leave anything valuable in a cabman's room for ten minutes. If the cabman could be questioned properly— Brown was a staunch Presbyterian, but at the moment he thought with great approval of the means of investigation which, as he had read, had in former days been employed by the Spanish Inquisition.

"There is nothing here, sir," said he at length to Inspector Harmsworth, "nothing at all."

"And did you think anything would be there, O wisest of detectives?" asked Mr. Phipps. "In the meantime, what happens to my reputation if the story of this search gets about?"

"But it must not!" cried the hotel's manager: "it must be kept a secret."

"It will be," promised Inspector Harmsworth; "I am sorry the search had to be made." He looked reproachfully at Brown.

"You can say, sir," suggested that worthy, "that Mr. Phipps was trying to help us, and we had a talk together in his room—for people have seen us come in here, and will wonder why."

"That is an excellent suggestion," agreed Mr. Phipps. "I perceive that there are depths of intelligence in Sherlock Holmes which I have not yet plumbed. I have heard of rough diamonds, and of Lady Rosedale's diamonds, and now I have met a black diamond. The age of discovery is not yet closed."

A knock at the door sounded, and a maid's voice was heard informing Inspector Harmsworth that Lady Rosedale was asking for him: he, the manager and the detective went out to meet here. Mr. Phipps accompanied them.

Lady Rosedale and Marian were standing in the corridor waiting for them. "There is not a jewel to be found in either of our rooms," said Lady Rosedale at once. "I am certain of that. We have both search thoroughly. Have you made any search yourself, Inspector?"

"We have, but discovered nothing, Lady Rosedale," Harmsworth replied. "And now Brown will take down your full statement and that of Miss Braeme, and then we'll go and see the Inspector General. But first we must talk to the night watchman and one or two other persons in this hotel. We are only at the beginning of our enquiry," he continued hopefully, "and before long I trust you will have your necklaces back again. You are not going today to take pictures, Miss Braeme?"

"No; nor tomorrow. I don't come into the scenes the director is taking today," explained Marian.

"I am glad of that, after all the annoyance and excitement of this morning," courteously observed the Inspector. "Goodmorning. Goodmorning. Lady Rosedale. Brown will take down what you both have to say."

"May I hazard a guess, Harmsworth?" said Mr. Phipps, as they moved away together.

"What is it?"

"That the necklaces will never be found."

"That will be rather serious for me and for Lady Rosedale," said Harmsworth grimly.

"It might be much more serious for the thief," returned Mr. Phipps, "and, as a man of humane feeling, I am bound to think of him also. I sympathise with you; but, frankly, for Lady Rosedale I have not the slightest sympathy. She does not deserve it."

VII

THE POLICE CONFER

Some hours after the robbery at the Myrtle Bank Hotel the Inspector General of the Jamaica Police was seated in his office, a spacious room situated on the ground floor of a large block of yellowish ferro-concrete buildings in the lower or business section of the city of Kingston. Two wire-screened windows, facing westwards and opened at the top, admitted light and air, while shutting off the interior of the room effectually from all curious or impertinent glances thrown towards it by those who passed without.

The Inspector General was a short, thick-set man, with perky features and of martial appearance. He had been a Major in the King's Army, and was now head of the semi-military police organisation of Jamaica by virtue of having served in India in an entirely differently capacity from that of a policeman. Ordinarily, in spite of its self-sufficient expression, his face gave one an impression of determination and shrewdness; and indeed those who knew him best were satisfied that Major Fellspar was anything but a fool. Just now, however, he was looking neither shrewd nor self-confident, but irritable, worried, perplexed. For now he was faced with the biggest problem of his life— the recovery of Lady Rosedale's jewels.

He sat at his desk, and his Deputy, a tall placid person of noncommittal features, was seated at his right hand near the desk. Inspector Harmsworth occupied a chair a few feet away from the Deputy, while against the western wall of the office, in an attitude of alert attention, stood the two detectives who had conducted the investigation at the Myrtle Bank Hotel that morning.

Inspector Harmsworth had been specially summoned, with Detectives Brown and Sampson, to a conference with the Chief and his Deputy. At present the role of the Deputy seemed to be to show sympathy with his puzzled and sorely-tried superior officer.

The latter had read through carefully the statements made to Sergeant Brown by Lady Rosedale, Miss Braeme, Mr. Phipps, the hotel's watchman, the night maid on the first floor of the Myrtle Bank, and one or two of the bellboys. Brown had been thorough in his efforts to educe information which he thought likely to be at all valuable. The names of persons who were known to have been in the vicinity of Lady Rosedale's room during the night before, and their movements, in so far as these could be ascertained, were duly recorded in the papers on the Inspector General's desk. A bellboy—the same whom Mr. Phipps had sent for his cigarettes—had mentioned that Mr. Beaman had also searched Mr. Phipps' room for cigarettes, and had remained upstairs for several minutes. The night watchman had stated that he had seen no one on the roof of the verandah, or making any attempt to reach it from the ground. The Inspector General, after reading through this man's statement twice, turned to the Deputy with a gesture of irritation.

"It would seem from what this night watchman has said," he fumed, "that he is a model of vigilance and did nothing all last night except keep his eyes fixed on that part of his hotel where Lady Rosedale's room is situated. I gather that, for some entirely inexplicable reason, he had that room under surveillance for several hours. Now how can we be expected to believe any such preposterous thing?"

"Quite so, sir," murmured the Deputy; "his statement isn't worth much to us."

"There is this man, Beaman," continued the Chief: "what was he doing so long in Phipps' room?"

"I understand that he was worried last night; gloomy and abstracted," explained Harmsworth. "He wouldn't be very quick and lively in the circumstances."

"But what was he gloomy about? That's something for you to find out."

"Very well, sir."

"Then there is this actress: you tell me that Brown suspected her from the start?"

"I did, Chief," put in Detective Brown himself respectfully; "for thought it is true that she did lock the lady's trunk after she put back the jewel box, she might have taken out the necklace while the box was on the table, when Lady Rosedale wasn't looking, and slipped it into her pocket."

"A lady's evening dress does not contain pockets," remarked Inspector Harmsworth. "Ladies' dresses are not made with pockets nowadays."

"You seem to know a great deal about ladies' dresses, Mr. Harmsworth," said the Inspector General grimly. "Could she not have slipped it into her bodice?"

"But Lady Rosedale is positive, as you will see from her statement, sir, that she did not take her eyes off the jewel case while it was on the dressing table. In fact, she opened it and handled it herself up to the moment she asked Miss Braeme to put it away in the trunk. There can be no doubt of that."

"So that takes suspicion off Miss Braeme," said the Inspector General: "and of course the pearls and her own jewellery were stolen out of her room."

"But what about Mr. Phipps?" asked the Deputy.

"I am coming to that," said Major Fellspar. "Phipps admits that he retired to his room last night almost before anyone else did. His room is situated near to Lady Rosedale's and Miss Braeme's. It would be easy enough for him to slip out of his room on to the verandah, and enter room nearby, wouldn't it? He could do so at different hours of the night if he is a man of nerve. But how would he know where Lady Rosedale kept her diamonds?"

"The young lady might have told him, Chief," remarked Detective Brown bluntly.

"Brown still suspects the actress," the Inspector General went on; "and he may be quite right. But how can we establish complicity between the two?"

"That is the question, sir," said the Deputy.

"It is, and it is only one of the questions we have got to answer. The Governor has already heard of this robbery, and has telephoned me to say I must leave no stone unturned to get back the necklaces. He doesn't understand the difficulties in the way. This Police Force was never intended to deal with such problems!"

"I think Phipps above suspicion myself," observed Inspector Harmsworth. "And as Miss Braeme has been in the island for less than a month, she could hardly be a confederate of Phipps."

"But what do we really know about him?" asked the Chief. "Who is he? His name by the way"—he took up a paper from his desk—"is Archibald K. Phipps. What does the K stand for?"

"Nobody seemed to know; but, from the look on his face, the Deputy apparently considered the question one of vast importance, the answer to which would materially assist the Police in a solution of the problem before it."

"What does the K mean?" again demanded the Inspector General, looking round the room for information. His eyes happened to rest upon the face of Detective Sampson. The latter, thinking that he was directly addressed, and wishing to be helpful, hurriedly suggested that the K might mean "Cupid."

"You ass!" stormed the head of the Police, "Cupid is not spelt with a K! How am I ever to find these necklaces if I have a staff that cannot even spell? What do you know about this man, Phipps, Mr. Harmsworth?"

"He is an American, sir, who has been about two years in the colony. He owns or rents a small property in St. Ann, about fifty or sixty miles from here, and is believed to be pretty well off. He has been back to the States three or four times since he settled in Jamaica."

"Is he really well off?"

"Nobody seems to know exactly. But he is a very pleasant sort of man. Quite sporting."

"He seems a suspicious sort of person to me," sniffed the Inspector General; "besides it is decidedly queer that he should have hurried away to his lawyers while Brown was investigating the robbery. What did he go to Jones and Bedlaw for?"

"That of course we don't know," murmured Inspector Harmsworth.

"No; and it is a pity that we don't. But we can't ask a man's lawyers anything about him, and a firm like Jones and Bedlaw can't even be remotely suspected of receiving stolen goods—that is quite out of the question."

"True," agreed Inspector Harmsworth. "I don't quite see myself that there is anything to connect this robbery with Mr. Phipps," he added.

"We may know more about that later on. His movements have been very peculiar. Still, it seems to me that Brown has been clinging far too much to his belief that the robbery was committed by someone in the hotel; why should it have been done by one of our ordinary burglars? Why should we insist upon leaving well-known burglars out of account?"

"We are not doing that, sir," Inspector Harmsworth hastened to assure him. "We propose to search the rooms of those we have any reason to imagine might have been connected with this theft. I have already made arrangements for that. I think it quite likely myself that someone of them may have committed this robbery."

"But, begging your pardon, Inspector, no thief from outside could know about where Lady Rosedale kept her necklace, or that Miss Braeme next to her had a necklace for him to steal at the same time," insisted Detective Brown.

"As to the necklaces," replied Inspector Harmsworth, "any burglar might have heard of them from a bellboy. From the same source he could have obtained an impression of Lady Rosedale's locks. I don't think it all impossible for false keys to be made by clever crooks here. Why should it be?"

Brown was about to retort to the effect that a Jamaica burglar who only searched for an expensive necklace on breaking into a jewel case would be a type quite new to his experience, but the look on the Inspector General's face did not encourage him to an argument with Inspector Harmsworth.

"Have you questioned all the bellboys?" asked the Inspector General.

"Yes, sir," said Harmsworth; "but what they said was quite straightforward, and their movements last night can easily be accounted for. They are all fellows of good character: we have nothing against them in our records."

"We are all good character until we are found out," muttered the Chief sententiously. "But if these boys have no police records, we cannot of course arrest any of them on suspicion. That's a great pity. Perhaps you could find out something about one of them by enquiring of previous employers?"

This question having been addressed to Brown, he answered that he would do his best, his manner suggesting that he had no doubt whatever that, by enquiring closely enough, he could discover much to the detriment of anybody's character.

"If one of our ordinary thieves has stolen Lady Rosedale's jewels," continued the Inspector General, "their recovery will be an easy matter. You will find them under his bed, or under the flooring of his room: they never seem to hide their booty anywhere else. But if someone of a different type has got hold of them, then only an accident, so far as I can see, will put us on their track. We have almost nothing to go upon. Lady Rosedale completely exonerates Miss Braeme, and, anyhow, nothing is found in Miss Braeme's room. Baeman's movements after he went to Phipps' room, and after he left the hotel, have yet to be thoroughly investigated, but I don't see that that will help us at all. We come back to Mr. Phipps; but what is there damaging against him? Nothing. He is laughing at us; that is plain from what you told me this morning. If he is an American crook, he knows that we are not organised here for dealing with a man like him. I don't know what the devil we are organised for," he concluded angrily, "since I can never get the Government to give me the money I need for making this Force worth a curse."

Here the Deputy gurgled some words of sympathy and Detectives Brown and Sampson assumed expression indicative of their deep disapproval of Government parsimony. But they did not dare to gurgle. That would have been indiscipline and rank impertinence.

"I shall have to take an active part in this enquiry, Harmsworth," the Inspector General resumed; "the Governor has asked me to do so. Well, have the room of every habitual criminal searched thoroughly; you can put all the detectives on the job, save those we have at the Myrtle Bank Hotel. How many have you go there now?"

"One, sir—Dixon. He was left there to watch the movements of persons connected with this case."

"Very good. I think I shall call on Lady Rosedale this afternoon. It will encourage her to know that I myself am looking after her case."

He rose from his chair, signifying that the conference was at an end. As he did so, the telephone tinkled.

The Deputy, who was nearest to the telephone, put the receiver to his ear.

"Yes; this is the Inspector General's office; yes, Inspector Harmsworth is here. Dixon wants you, Harmsworth," said the Deputy handing Inspector the receiver; "he is speaking from Myrtle Bank."

The Inspector General paused in the act of putting on his helmet, his interest fully aroused. Harmsworth listened attentively to the voice at the other end of the phone, then called out to Detective Dixon to "hold the line."

"Dixon says," he informed Major Fellspar, "that Mr. Phipps left the Myrtle Bank in his big motor car a few minutes ago, going at full speed. Phipps seems to have sent over to the garage for it, and Dixon believes he is not returning tonight. He wants to know what he is to do."

A look of triumph fitted over the heavy face of Detective Brown, who evidently saw this latest move of Mr. Phipps' ample justification of all suspicions entertained against him. Major Fellspar smote the desk with his open hand.

"Gone, eh!" he exclaimed; "gone to his country home as quickly and as unexpectedly as possible. What do you make of that, Harmsworth?"

"He is always coming and going, sir."

"I don't like the look of it all the same," returned the Inspector General. He came to a swift decision. "We must keep a sharp eye on that man. He'll repay watching."

"Could we get a car and follow him?" suggested the Deputy.

"We could, but it would be half an hour at least before you could start, and he is probably expecting that we'll make some such effort. We'd hardly be able to overtake him if his car is a good one—and I suppose it is."

"A Hudson super-six," said Harmsworth.

"That makes any pursuit we could offer quite out of the question; and if we did overtake him, what could we do? It would not be wise to arrest him without good reason to believe that he had the necklaces with him. He may be a crook; I believe he is myself; but you can never be certain about Americans. He may be a second cousin or something of some Senator we never heard of, and we don't want any talk about American citizens being brutally mistreated by the Jamaican Police. Let him go! Let him believe that we entertain no further suspicion of him; that may make him careless. Tomorrow I will tell you what steps we must take with regard to him if we don't find the necklaces in the meantime."

He nodded and walked out of he office, the others following, after Inspector Harmsworth had informed the detective at Myrtle Bank to proceed at once to the Police Station to await further instructions.

Major Fellspar emerged upon the public gardens in front of the building in which his office was, but had no glance to waste upon the grass plots and graceful palms that relieved the harshness of the ferro-concrete buildings on every side. He strolled towards the sidewalk shaded with low, thick-leaved trees, and hailed a cab. The street was filled with men and woman of variegated complexions hurrying home after the day's toil and talking loudly of the things that interested them; the black, uniformed policeman at the corner drew himself up to attention and saluted, but neither people nor policeman did Major Fellspar notice. It was a glorious afternoon, an exuberance of happy spirits seemed to characterise everyone that passed that afternoon along the principal business thoroughfare of Kingston. But Major Fellspar did not feel exuberant and was interested in nothing at that moment save necklaces and their recovery. The Governor's telephone message to him had been far more peremptory than he had mentioned to his subordinates. The Governor had said that the necklaces *must* be found.

"I am a soldier and not a damned detective," reflected the Inspector General, but that was not an answer he could return to His Excellency. His feelings towards Lady Rosedale, as he entered the cab and ordered the driver to take him to the Myrtle Bank Hotel, bordered on personal hate.

VIII

LADY ROSEDALE'S SUSPICIONS

Major Fellspar do the bar, and Lawsistent with his dignity thar he should be personally identified with this search for stolen jewels. That was work for his Detective Department, which should report progress every now and then to him, and possibly ask him for directions and advice. It would have been so had the articles stolen been of ordinary value, and the loser of them of ordinary position; in such a case the Governor would have taken not the slightest notice of the matter. But Lady Rosedale on her arrival had called at King's House, and the Governor and his wife had returned her call. She was a woman whose name had appeared in the English society papers and about whom the London *Morning Post* had more than once published a paragraph. She was therefore, if but in a minor manner, something of a personage in England, which meant that in a British West Indian colony she was a very important personage indeed. Dignity had to be somewhat set aside even by an Inspector General in dealing with such a lady: this Major Fellspar distinctly realised. But this reflection did not tend to make him feel kindly disposed towards Lady Rosedale. He wished that she had never come to the island, and, but for the fact that the reputation of the Police was at stake, would have been glad to believe that her necklaces would never be found, a punishment which he thought she merited for her crime of losing them.

A short drive through dingy streets of low, wood-and-brick houses with their short flights of steps built out upon narrow, unpaved sidewalks, and of little shops presided over by placid Chinamen attending to numbers of dark-hued people making purchases for the evening's dinner, brought Major Fellspar to the Myrtle Bank Hotel. Received with marked deference by the porter, he handed his card to a bellboy with the order that it should be taken up to Lady Rosedale. The lobby was filled with people, many of whom eyed him curiously, his uniform indicating his connection with the Police, and his authoritative appearance suggesting that he was someone very high up in the Force. The Inspector General seemed quite unconscious of the glances and conjectures which his presence had evoked, but nevertheless was keenly aware of them. He was aware that he was, at the moment, a centre of attraction and attention; this appealed to his vanity and at once he began to feel that, after all, there might be compensations for the work he had been called upon against his will to undertake. The amiability of his manner, as he walked to the foot of the staircase to meet ady Rosedale, was therefore not altogether assumed. He felt more genial now than he had done but a brief five minutes before.

He knew Lady Rosedale slightly; had met her at a reception given by the Governor some three weeks before. They greeted each other with much cordiality.

"It's so good of you to come round yourself," she smiled. "I feel almost certain now that the thief will be discovered. Shall we have tea on the verandah or on the lawn: you take tea, don't you?"

"I shall be delighted to have a cup," he answered. "Here? Excellent." He seated himself at a spot indicated by Lady Rosedale, on the lawn just beyond the edge of the right wing of the southern verandah, from which a view of the lobby, the lawn and the rest of the verandah was easily obtained.

"I have had a day of it," began Lady Rosedale, after she had given the order for tea. With a quick sweeping glance she had taken in the scene round and about her. There were at least two hundred people on the lawn besides those sauntering about the lobby and on the verandah. And momently the number grew. No person there but knew now who she was and of the great misfortune that had recently befallen her. They must know, moreover, that this military-looking man was one of the big men of the colony, and the word would soon go forth that he was no less than the Inspector General of the Police himself, a man at the mention of whose name (so she thought) every criminal in the colony trembled. As a matter of fact, most of the criminals had never heard of him, and would not have been greatly disturbed if they had. Their main concern was with the common interfering policeman and the prying plain-clothes detective. But Lady Rosedale would never have imagined that, and certainly, to those persons in whose opinion she was interested, the Inspector General stood as the embodiment of the might, majesty and unceasing vigilance of British Law. The whole hotel was now taking note of the circumstance that, beginning with the advent of two native detectives to investigate her loss, the day was closing with the coming of the Inspector General himself to talk the matter over with her. But when she said she had had a day of it, she meant merely to imply that she had passed through a most trying ordeal. The keen satisfaction she had extracted out of that ordeal was not to be suspected by anyone.

"I have had a most trying day of it," she said. "After your detectives left, some reporters came and asked to see me. I thought of refusing to see them, but that might have been churlish: after all, newspaper must print news. Those of the city are usually without any."

"Yes; and I wish they would confine themselves to news," said Major Fellspar, with a nasty feeling that, if the necklaces were not speedily recovered, the newspapers might begin to say unpleasant things about the local Police and its head.

"That is what I said to the young men today, when they asked me for a photograph. I hate seeing my picture in the papers; I have always avoided it when I can. But they were quite pressing and I did not know how to refuse them. I suppose one must do in Rome as Romans do. Do you take sugar, Major Fellspar?"

"One cube, please. I would not advise you to do in Jamaica as the Jamaicans do, though."

"What is that?"

"Oh, everything," he replied rather vaguely, but with his mind still on the possibility of bitter and unnecessarily personal criticism if the necklaces should not be found. "So you gave them your photograph? That was very kind of you, I am sure. Did they get one from Miss Braeme?"

"Mariah? No; she would not hear of it. And I did not press her to give them one. As a matter of fact she would not see the reporters: she has not left her room all day, she is so disturbed and distressed by all that has happened."

Lady Rosedale did not mention that why she had not aided the reporters and pressed Marian to have her photograph reproduced in the newspapers, was because she had seen no necessity why, the really valuable jewels being hers, anyone else should appear before the newspaper footlights as a sufferer. Marian would be mentioned in the reports, of course; but she herself would dominate the stage of publicity. Considering the magnitude of her loss, there was nothing unfair about that. It was indeed eminently just.

"So Miss Braeme would not allow her picture to appear," commented the Inspector General. "But she is an actress, and can have no real objection to publicity. She gets it everyday."

"She said she'd rather not; and, anyhow, she had no photograph with her and would have had to take a new one. The one of myself that I gave the reporters as taken two years ago, but of course I could not think of being photographed specially for a newspaper in connection with a robbery. I don't know that I ought to have given them my photograph at all."

"One has to do these things now and then," remarked the Inspector General sympathetically, "but I can quite understand the ordeal through which you have gone. The loss first, and the confusion and the interviews after—terrible. But we'll get the jewellery and the thief; both yours and Miss Braeme's. You can depend upon us for that." Thus he spoke, with a fervent hope that some special Providence would come to the aid of the Police. Less than this he did not dare to say to Lady Rosedale.

"Whom do you suspect?" she asked him.

"In a case of this kind," he answered confidentially, "the Police have cast their net wide. We have our eye on several persons. You may rest assured that the Police of England and America have been informed of this robbery, and your description of the jewels has been telegraphed to them. Everybody leaving this island during the next few weeks will have their luggage carefully examined on the other side. There is no possibility of their being smuggled through any foreign custom house."

"And you suspect several persons?"

"I do. And, as I have said, I have my eye on them."

"There he is again!"

Lady Rosedale spoke with petulance, and, following her glance, the Inspector General found himself looking at a quiet, strong-featured young man who had just come out of the lobby and was busily scanning the lawn in evident search of someone.

"Who is that?" he asked.

"A Mr. Beaman. He makes it a practice to come here everyday now."

"He is the man who went upstairs to Mr. Phipps's room last night and remained there for sometime, isn't he?" enquired Major Fellspar, looking narrowly at Lawrence, who was totally unconscious that he was an object of scrutiny and discussion.

"Did he?" asked Lady Rosedale. "I hadn't heard of it. Besides—"

She paused as an idea seemed to dawn and develop in her mind. "How did you hear that, and why?" she demanded.

Major Fellspar was sorry he had said anything about Lawrence; but there was no evading an answer to Lady Rosedale's question.

"It is our business to make an enquiry into the movements of everyone who was in your part of the house last night," he replied. "It doesn't mean anything more than a necessary precaution."

"Do you believe that a poor man who is deeply in love would commit a burglary?" suddenly asked Lady Rosedale.

"Being in love would have nothing to do with the theft, so far as I can see," replied Major Fellspar, thinking that she was making a humorous sally. "Love and theft have no necessary connection, have they? A poor man, if a thief, would steal whether he were in love or not. Unless he was taken with sudden ambitions about reforming and becoming honest; but those wouldn't last, I am afraid. Once a thief, always a thief."

"But," insisted Lady Rosedale, "if a man was poor and desperately in love, and wanted money badly; if he could not get the girl he loved while he remained poor; do you think he would rob?"

"He might," admitted Major Fellspar, "that has happened again and again."

He fixed his eyes keenly on Lady Rosedale's face. "What are you thinking about?" he asked, now fully aware that her remarks were not intended as light conversation and meaningless.

"Well," said Lady Rosedale slowly, "it is only an idea that has just occurred to me, and I don't say or think myself that there is anything in it. Still, I suppose I should not conceal anything from you, should I? That would not be quite fair to you?"

"It would not," agreed the Inspector General.

"That young man,"—her voice was hardly above a whisper—"comes here to see Miss Braeme: he is deeply in love with her. Her brother knows it and is furious at the very thought: quite rightly, for I feel the same way myself. I am trying to do what I can for Marian, of whom I am very fond, and I agree with her brother that it would be madness for her even to think of a young man who has only his salary, which may not be very much, and who has to live all his life in a country like this."

"The salary may be ample," replied Major Fellspar, a little stiffly, "and I have been in many worse countries."

"But this man is not an official," Lady Rosedale hastened to explain, conscious that the Inspector General was offended. "He has no position. It is really presumption in him to have fallen head over ears in love with a bright and promising girl like Marian: don't you think so?"

"I am not acquainted with Miss Braeme," returned Major Fellspar, "but you should be able to judge admirably."

"He was here last night, and you say he was near my room for sometime. Well, I would not dream of accusing him of anything, but I know he was looking desperate last night: perfectly miserable. I hope he did not yield to any sudden temptation. . . What do you think?"

"I can hardly believe that he would have robbed Miss Braeme if, as you say, he is desperately in love with her. That doesn't seem reasonable, does it?"

"But the pearl necklace was mine, and not Marian's, and perhaps he knew it. He saw her wearing it; why should she not have told him whose it was? There was nothing to hide."

"Oh, that puts a different complexion on this business!" exclaimed Major Fellspar. "You think he may have robbed you first and Miss Braeme afterwards, knowing that both necklaces were yours. And of course he would take the rest of the things he found in her drawer. The wonder is that he—or rather, the thief—didn't take everything you had in your jewel case."

"I should imagine that he took quite enough," said Lady Rosendale. "He did not rob everything from Marian either. Only the things in her top drawer."

"He would have had to be contemplating the robbery for sometime," reflected Major Fellspar aloud; "no sudden impulse would have enabled him to get an impression of your locks. There was nothing sudden about this business, I am afraid."

"I don't suppose there was, and mark you, I am suggesting nothing against this unfortunate young man. But I should like my jewellery back, and he was poor a week ago as he was last night. Would anyone have required more than a week to plan a burglary like this, do you think?"

"Not necessarily. I will keep in mind what you have said, and of course you will mention it to no one else: you understand, don't you? I say! He seems to be coming up to us."

This was true. Lawrence, satisfied that Marian was not within sight, had determined to ask Lady Rosedale about her. The latter's aversion for him did not affect him greatly now; it was Marian's own declaration of hopelessness of his love for her that at present dominated his thoughts.

He went up to Lady Rosedale, indifferent to her attitude of aloofness, and as he had already heard of her loss, begged to offer his sympathy. Lady Rosedale made no attempt to introduce him to Major Fellspar, who, while Lawrence stoof there, studied him quietly. He remembered having seen the young man before, but had not observed him particularly then. As for Lady Rosedale, she thanked Lawrence for his sympathy and said she hoped and believed the Police would be successful.

"And Miss Braeme was also robbed?" said Lawrence. "I was extremely sorry to her of it. Is she down?"

"She had not left her room since morning," replied Lady Rosendale.

"Do you know if she is coming down?"

"I believe she said she might; she wasn't sure."

There was nothing to say after this. Lawrence decided to wait and see if Marian would appear. He bowed and walked away.

"What do you think of him?" enquired Lady Rosedale of the Inspector General, after Lawrence moved off.

"First impressions may be absolutely deceptive," said that gentleman, "but he looks to me about the last man I should suspect of breaking into your room. He has the face of the sort of men who make reliable officers. I know the type."

"Well, that is something in his favour," admitted Lady Rosedale; "but I don't think he is a very popular young man; he has very low friends. The only person wo speaks highly of him is an American called Phipps. Do you know Mr. Phipps?"

"I seem to have been hearing of almost nothing but Phipps today," said the Inspector General. "Everybody mentions him."

"Lady Rosedale—Miss Braeme—Mr. Carfew—Mr. Smith—Miss Hellingworth—" a bellboy with a bunch of telegrams in his hand was lustily "paging" several people without, as it seemed, pausing once to take breath. He was hurrying by, when Major Fellspar called out to him: "Here's Lady Rosedale." To that lady he handed a telegram and sped away on his voyage of further discovery. With an "excuse me," Lady Rosedale opened the telegram and swiftly perused its contents. "From Mr. Phipps," she said.

IX

THE INVITATION

"Ah, here is Marian."

Major Fellspar, though burning with anxiety to know what Mr. Phipps had telegraphed to Lady Rosedale about, followed with his eyes the movement of her head and saw coming quickly towards them a tall, graceful girl, with a rich brunette complexion and large dark eyes. "Pretty creature," he commented, and the next moment was introduced.

"How are you feeling now, my dear?" enquired Lady Rosedale kindly, after Marian had accepted the seat which Major Fellspar had hastened to secure for her. "Any better?"

"Much better, thank you," said Marian, and Major Fellspar admired the low musical tones of her voice. "The headache's gone, but of course the anxiety is not."

That it had not was evident from the strained expression of her eyes and lips. She felt the catastrophe more keenly than Lady Rosedale, concluded the Inspector General, and it came to his mind that one of his detectives had suspected her of the theft. "Just like a damned detective," he reflected wrathfully, for he had taken at once to Marian, and it was always as an officer of the King's Army and not as a policeman that he thought of himself.

"Be anxious about nothing," he assured her; "you must leave the Police may not be quick, Miss Braeme, but there are wonderfully sure. I have known them discover a thief six month after he had made a haul."

"That thief must have been very stupid then," was Lady Rosedale's comment. "Six months! I do not propose to remain here for half that time."

"Nor will it be necessary," said the Inspector General, with well-assumed conviction.

"Telegram for you, miss!"

The bellboy with the telegrams had returned; he handed Marian one of the messages which he had been charged to deliver.

"From Mr.Phipps," said Major Fellspar smiling. "I'll bet anything on that."

Marian opened the envelope. "You are right," she smiled in reply, and read aloud:

"After the fatigue of last night, I propose excursion to my country home Sunday. Gone to arrange it. Returning tomorrow. Do you good. Will take no refusal. Others invited. Cards to take you."

"He invites me also," cried Lady Rosedale; "only he says I can bring a party. Considering that I know the man but slightly, this is strange."

"He seems to have invited a lot of other people here, judging by the batch of telegrams that boy was carrying round," said Major Fellspar. "But why telegrams, and where did he send them from?" The question was casually put, but Major Fellspar very much wanted to have an answer.

Marian glanced at the paper in her hand. "They were handed in at the central telegraph office in Kingston an hour ago," she said; "the place is not much more than a quarter of a mile from here. He could have written us notes in this hotel."

"He went or sent from here to the central telegraph office and wasted money in despatching these messages," said Lady Rosedale. "But that's just the sort of thing you would expect him to do," she added. "The man is perfectly eccentric."

"He certainly does thing in a way of his own," agreed Major Fellspar, who was now wishing very much to meet this strange and eccentric Mr. Phipps who threw away money on telegrams without any apparent reason. Half-a-dozen other persons had these messages in their hands and were comparing them. The picnic that Mr. Phipps was arranging was evidently to be on a considerable scale.

Some of these people now came up to Marian with kindly enquiries. They had not seen her the whole day; they wanted to hear from herself all about her sensations; she was, in their minds, the central figure of a very interesting drama.

She soon found herself in the midst of them, and drawn away from Lady Rosedale and Major Fellspare. These, looking on, saw Lawrence Beaman join the group. The Inspector General felt that he had been with Lady Rosedale long enough; it was time for him to take his leave. He rose to go.

"This Mr. Phipps," he remarked casually, preparatory to saying goodbye, "has shown a good deal of interest in your loss, I believe?"

"Far more than acquaintanceship would seem to warrant," replied Lady Rosedale. "And what is more, he looked thoroughly unsympathetic. I shall not accept his invitation."

"Well goodbye for the present," said Major Fellspar; "I hope to see you shortly again, and with good news."

"Come in whenever you like," said Lady Rosedale; "it will be a comfort to know that you are doing something to help me;" and the Inspector General walked away.

As he passed through the lobby, he met a number of men and women who were just coming in. He formed the corrected conclusion that these were the members of the moving picture company that had been taking pictures that day. These strolled out into the lawn, and all of them, the director included, rushed up to Lady Rosedale to express their sympathy, though to some she had never spoke before. With her the director and his star actress remained after the general expression of condolence, the rest of the company trooping off towards Marian.

Marian was obviously the heroine of the hour. Everybody was eager to know if, during the night, she had not heard some stealthy, mysterious step, or stirred in her sleep with a premonition of imminent danger. "That's how it ought to have happened," protested the company's chief actor. "You should have awakened just in time to see a man disappearing through the window, and you should have dimly recognised him by saying something similar about his form. But say, Marian, it's all very well for Lady Thing-am-bob over there to lose her pretty thing, but what about yours? That is a real shame. The crook might have left you something."

"He didn't take absolutely everything I possessed," smiled Marian; "I have a ring or so left."

"Yes; but that diamond broach of yours was a beauty, and that's gone. Say, boys, what about giving Marian a broach as a birthday present to make up for the one she has lost."

"But my birthday isn't for some months yet," cried Marian.

"It's going to come quicker this year than ever before," asserted the star actor, a merry handsome fellow. "It's going to be this month. I am down for fifty dollars. Who's next?"

The idea was caught up by other members of the company, and the news of what was afoot flew swiftly among the guests. The holiday spirit implies a generous mood. Everybody wanted to subscribe something; insisted upon it. A subscription list was opened at once, and in their eagerness to collect a large sum of money, Marian's colleagues forgot about her completely and went about their undertaking, leaving her alone with Lawrence. He had refrained from putting his name down as a contributor to the present suggested; he felt instinctively that she would not like him to be one of the donors; he did not believe that she even favoured the suggestion. But he was glad that it caused her to be alone with him, and she seemed glad of this also. "Let us go on the pier," she said quickly, "before they come back: there may be nobody there."

"I heard all about this robbery today," said Lawrence gently, when they found seats. "You must have had a dreadful time."

"More dreadful than you think," she answered, and now her face was no longer smiling. There was no longer any reason why she should act as though she were not deeply affected. "The detectives suspect me. They believed that I had stolen the necklaces."

"What!"

"It is true; but Lady Rosedale was very nice about it. The suspicion exists, though, and I feel that I am going to hear more about it yet."

She was very distressed. For the first time since he had known her, he saw her eyes fill with tears and a wave of wrath swept through him. It was monstrous that she should be worried like this, and that anyone— anyone—should dare to suspect her of theft.

"This comes," he said bitterly, "of that old woman's interference with you. I am sure you did not want to wear her pearls."

"I did not, but she insisted; it can't be helped now. But I wish I had never come to this country. I have hardly been happy since I came—at least, well, I don't know—"

"You have been unhappy; why?"

"I can't tell you, though you are the best friend I have here, you and Mr. Phipps. He sent a note up to my room today to tell me not to worry about anything. He was present when the detectives were making their enquiries, you see, and he followed their meaning."

"There is nothing for you to worry about," said Lawrence vehemently. He looked at her, a somewhat pathetic figure now in the waning light. He long to take her in his arms and tell her that if she would trust to him no evil should come near her. He felt capable of protecting her against anyone or anything, if only she would give him the right to do so. As it was, he felt strangely impotent, realising as he did that, as matters stood, he could do nothing to take her troubles upon himself.

The hold and crimson glory that had flamed on the western horizon had suddenly passed into deep purple, and here and there in the sky above a silver star peeped forth. The sea murmured, darkling, and a vague melancholy seemed to creep slowly over sea and sky, in tune with the sad spirits of the girl who rested her head wearily against the railing of the pier.

"You are overwrought," he said gently. "You have been working hard in an unaccustomed climate. You were dancing last night until a late hour, and from morning you have been worried almost to death. That is why you feel so cast-down and distressed. The feeling will pass; what can it matter what a stupid policeman thought or suggested? He would not dare to put his impertinent suspicions into words. Don't think anymore about it. Phipps sent you an invitation to go to the country on Sunday, did he not?"

"Yes; I intended to tell you of it."

"He telephoned me from the hotel today to say that he was going to arrange for the trip and the picnic at his place in St. Ann. I believe he has done it all on your account; he wants to get you away from here, even for a day. You will go?"

"I don't know. My brother—I don't know if he has been invited."

"Others have been. You can go without your brother, though probably he too has been invited. You ought to go; promise me that you will?"

"You are going? You know the place, I suppose?"

"Very well indeed." He smiled slightly. "It belongs to me, as a matter of fact. I leased it to Mr. Phipps a few months after he came to this country. I was born in that house, and I love it I should like you to see it. Will you go?"

"I think I will: I should like to see your old home."

She rose, and wiped her eyes with a little lace handkerchief she carried. "I suppose I must go upstairs now and change for dinner," she said; "you are coming down there tonight?"

"I am remaining right on; I'll stay here and dine," he replied. "You won't mind my telling you now that I want to be near you always, especially if you are in anyway worried and distressed. Remember you can always depend upon me in any emergency. I want you to feel that I am ever ready to do anything I can or you. That is the least that can be said by—by a friend."

She looked at him gratefully. The brief talk had done her good, had relieved something of the oppression at her heart. There was almost a happy look on her face as they left the pier together.

X

A Passage At Arms

They strolled up the gravel walk towards the hotel, now blazing with light at every window and through the graceful arches which supported the verandah's roof. As they entered the lobby Marian was gaily greeted by a tall fair girl who was sitting just by the staircase with Stephen Braeme. Both rose to meet them.

"Marian, I hardly saw anything of you last night!" exclaimed the girl, impulsively kissing her. "I was mostly with your brother, and you were with everybody. How popular you are!"

"So are you, Nora," smiled Marian. "If you didn't dance with a lot of men last night, that was because you didn't want to. How many did you refuse?"

"Oh, a host. But this brother of yours and I get on famously, so I gave him most of my dances. My dear—" she turned abruptly to another subject—"I have been hearing all about the burglary from Mr. Braeme. I think I should have died of fright if I had got awake and seen a man robbing my room! It's a blessing that you slept through it all. I'll tell you what I have come down here for tonight: I want to take you and your brother off to dinner; you must come."

Lawrence felt himself out of the picture. He knew Nora Hamilton, a bright attractive girl, fairly well, and he admired her freshness, her gay spirits, her impulsiveness. Her white and pink complexion, hazel eyes, her soft bronze hair and finely moulded features, delighted the eye; and, as Marian had said, she was immensely popular. You thought of her at once as "a nice girl": the expression described her perfectly. Like Lawrence, she was Jamaican by birth, her parents being Scotch settlers in the colony. She herself had been educated in England, and had been back in Jamaica now for something over a year.

Lawrence was a mere acquaintance of hers. He had not gone much into society when younger, the hard conditions of his life, as well as his naturally reserved and proud spirit, forbidding, and society had come to the conclusion that he was out of it. He had never been out of it, so now there was a sort of subconscious determination on the part of some of its members that he should never be. He himself never made any effort to extend the narrow circle of his friends; on the other hand it was quite clear to him that very few people of the class to which Nora belong showed any desire to make a friend, a circumstance which had never troubled him, since it fitted in so well with his own inclinations. Nora would not willingly have hurt his feelings: she would have done anything to avoid doing so. Yet it never occurred to her include him in the invitation she was extending in his hearing to Marian and Stephen. Both of these had often noticed before that Lawrence was by a sort of general agreement excluded from social functions by people who pressed their invitations on the members of the moving picture company, and Lawrence knew that they had noticed it. This, he was also aware, could scarcely help to induce Stephen Braeme to adopt towards him a particularly friendly attitude. Stephen chose fashionable company by preference, though in his relations with everybody he was certainly not a snob.

"It is awfully nice of you to want me, but I am afraid I cannot come tonight, Nora," said Marian. "I shan't be up late tonight; I have had a pretty troublesome day of it."

"Then come and spend the day on Sunday."

"I am going down to St. Ann to spend Sunday with Mr. Phipps."

"Phipps!" broke in Stephen; "has he invited you too? He seems to have asked a lot of people here."

"Aren't you invited?" enquired Marian.

"No," said Stephen, "I cannot understand it; he must have purposely forgotten me. Have you been invited?" he questioned Lawrence.

"Yes," answered Lawrence dryly.

"I might have guessed it! I hope you are going to refuse the invitation, Marian. Even if Mr. Phipps has no liking for me—though I thought we were friendly—it would at least have been polite of him, remembering I am your brother, to have included me in his party. I say it is downright rude of him!"

Stephen looked intensely annoyed, his eyes rested on Lawrence as though he believed that Lawrence had had something to do with his being ignored by Mr. Phipps. He clearly wished Marian to refuse the invitation.

"I have made up my mind to go," she said quietly, but with a ring of determination in her voice. "I don't suppose my going will make any difference to you."

"What do you mean by that?" he demanded.

"Just what I have said. I cannot imagine that your not being with me at Mr. Phipps's house will in anyway disturb you."

"I wouldn't have gone if I had been invited," he retorted hotly, though with evident insincerity. "It is not his invitation that I desire, but polite treatment."

"I did not believe you really wanted to go," she replied.

"No; and I do not want you to go either."

Nora looked from the one to the other with a smile at first, then realised that both were in deadly earnest.

"Oh, come," she cried, "you two are surely not going to quarrel! I am not a stranger, but a row always makes me feel uncomfortable. Never mind Mr. Phipps, Mr. Braeme; he is a little peculiar, but such an old dear. He doesn't mean anything by not asking you; but he is just the man to think that a brother is a nuisance when a sister is around. Brothers think sisters *de trop* at times also," she concluded archly: "I have known such. Besides, he hasn't invited me either, and I am not vexed."

"Mr. Phipps can be counted on to make special facilities to assist those in whom he happens to be interested," said Stephen, still in angry tones. "He has done so now."

"Why, what do you mean?" asked Nora curiously; then noticed that Stephen's eyes were fixed with a contemptuous expression on Lawrence Beaman. A swift look of comprehension swept over her face. It flashed upon her that perhaps the reason why Marian had refused her dinner invitation was because Lawrence had not been included. She hesitated. Lawrence Beaman—well, but Lawrence Beaman was not in society, not in her set, how could she invite him without her mother's permission? She thought it best to bring the conversation to an end.

"I should love to have gone with you Sunday, Marian, if I had been invited," she said gaily; "you are sure to enjoy yourself." She turned to Stephen: "Are you coming now? You won't need to go home to dress; it's nothing formal."

With narrowed eyes Marian watched her brother and her friend leave the lobby and go out upon the porch, whence they were whirled away in Nora's big motor car. She made a quick little gesture with her head, as if dismissing Stephen from her mind; then, with a nod to Lawrence (as if, in her present mood, she would not trust herself to speak) she began slowly to mount the stairs. "I will wait for you down here," he called out to her, and again she nodded.

He sat down by the foot of the staircase to think. Watching Stephen and Nora closely while the little scene of a few minutes before was being enacted, he had become acutely conscious of something which he had vaguely felt rather than realised previously. Stephen was evidently attracted by this bright, fresh-looking girl, and it had been borne in upon Lawrence, with the full force of conviction, that Nora liked, and perhaps more than liked, the handsome actor. How much did she like him, he wondered. Somehow he did not feel that it was all quite right; he became aware of a certain prejudice in his mind against the Peruvian because he was a Peruvian and a moving picture actor. Lawrence had always liked Nora; he tried now to envisage her as his sister, and he asked himself the question: were Nora his sister of a truth, how would he view this attraction between her and Stephen? Would he be pleased with this growing intimacy between them? The question was answered almost before it was put; yet Lawrence recognised that these reflections were, in a way, an act of treason to Marian. For she too was Peruvian, she was an actress, and perhaps she had perceived in him that strain of racial pride which had just stirred to active consciousness within him, and of which he had not himself been aware before. He felt ashamed.

He tried to get to the root of this feeling of his. Was it, after all, only his personal dislike of Stephen, a dislike engendered by the latter's frank and unconcealed antagonism to him, that caused him to regard Stephen as an inferior? For the word inferior exactly summed up and expressed the content of his mind and attitude towards Stephen Braeme. And yet, reflected Lawrence with a touch of scorn, the man was made welcome by people who professed to be select, who set themselves up as arbiters in the little social world of a little country. Nora had gone off with him to her home, and all Nora's friends would be glad to see him and would make much of him. He was a stranger, he was "romantic," he had a sort of meretricious brilliancy about him that passed among superficial observers for the real thing; they were ready to regard him as a great actor on the strength of his own suggestion: they took him at his own valuation, and that was high. They would gladly agree with him that it was impertinence and presumption on the part of a man like Lawrence Beaman to love his sister; some would be ready to take a hand in punishing such a presumption with all the weapons of social boycott and expressed disdain they could command.

Nora Hamilton, whose natural fineness of disposition could never be wholly spoilt by any extraneous influences of snobbery and littleness, had defended Mr. Phipps when Stephen had spoken disparagingly of him; but most of the people in her set would be surprised that Phipps should have invited Lawrence Beaman to this picnic on Sunday, and have ignored Stephen Braeme. Indeed, they would be greatly astonished that he (Lawrence) should have been invited to the picnic at all. At the point of his reflections Lawrence realised that jealousy of Stephen had suddenly taken possession of him, and that, by the mere act of being jealous of another man, he was acknowledging an inferiority to that man. Lawrence was fair-minded: he perceived that, the personal relations between them being what they were, he could never be just to Stephen.

But this intellectual admission in no way affected his feeling that Stephen and Nora were worlds apart and should so remain. "They are as different as Scotland and Peru," he muttered to himself.

He rose for Marian was coming down the stairs with Lady Rosedale. Two hours before, that lady had greeted him, if not with cordiality, at least with politeness passable enough if somewhat frigid. Now, he noticed as she reached the lobby, her manner had definitely and perceptibly changed for the worse. Marian's attitude also suggested to him that something had occurred upstairs. There was constraint in the manner and appearance of both.

Lady Rosedale, as a matter of fact, had since his departure been thinking of the chance remarks of the Inspector General as to Lawrence's movements on the night before, and of her own question whether a man, poor and in love, would become a burglar for the purpose of obtaining at one stroke a large amount of money. And the more she had pondered over these things, the more inclined she had become to believe that Lawrence was in some intimate way connected with her loss. Not that she had clearly formulated in her mind the bald proposition that Lawrence was a thief; but, without any regard to logic, she had concluded that he would need to explain a very great deal if he were wholly to free himself of suspicion. This belief of hers she had just imparted to Marian, who had vehemently repudiated the very suggestion of Lawrence's being suspected of dishonesty. For the first time since their friendship, there had nearly been a quarrel between Marian and Lady Rosedale. But the latter had not pressed her point; she had contented herself with an admonitory shake of the head and a word of general warning. "I don't like your defence of him, my dear; it is altogether too warm. You tell me that you like him only as a friend, and when I merely hint that perhaps the young man, overcome by temptation, may have done something which he ought not have to have done, you flare up in passionate anger. Well, let us say nothing more about it. But it is always an advantage to be warned about other people's characters. It often saves us from many a serious mistake."

She was not, however, even to please the girl she liked and desired to befriend, prepared to treat Lawrence as though nothing had happened. To her mind, something very serious indeed had happened, and he had to be regarded as a possible suspect until his innocence was fully established. Marian had agreed to dine, as usual, at her table; on descending to the lobby, therefore, Lady Rosedale walked straight towards the dining room, not giving Lawrence a moment's opportunity to utter a word. Moral reprobation was expressed in her brisk, masterful walk and attitude of aloofness. A bellboy who witnessed her progress to the dining room, whispered to a colleague that "the duchess was great this evening."

Bellboys are sometimes keen observers of character in spite of their apparent devotion only to the matter of tips. Some of them at the hotel had already come to name Lady Rosedale "the duchess," standing all the while in great awe of her and being painfully alive to the circumstance that while she always acknowledged services with a dignified "thank you," she was often backward in the production of the sixpenny pieces and other coins so dear to the bellboy's heart. They also knew from brief but infallible experience that when she donned her grandest manner the idea of remunerating the humble and meek never entered her mind. On such occasions they stood in greater awe of her than ever. But they did not appreciate her.

Lawrence guessed that, so far as she was able, Lady Rosedale would keep Marian from him that evening. The event justified his belief. After dinner he lingered in their vicinity, but the elder lady seem solicitous to guard Marian against his approach. Nor did Marian manifest any desire to be with him; she was patently more depressed than she had been in the afternoon, ill in mind and almost ill in body. What she had heard from Lady Rosedale as to the latter's suspicions of Lawrence had disturbed her gravely; she knew that Lady Rosedale, though not exactly garrulous, was not, on the other hand, a model of reticence. What she whispered to one person she might vaguely communicate to another, and rumours detrimental to the character of a man or woman are rapid of circulation in communities where interest in personal matters take precedence of interest in almost all things else. She dared not hint to Lawrence what was in Lady Rosedale's mind; she could only hope to disabuse Lady Rosedale of her extraordinary suspicion. Lady Rosedale, though she might not dare, without adequate proof, to put her suspicion into words when speaking to strangers, might indirectly suggest almost anything, and that, Marian thought, might be harmful to Lawrence.

Half an hour after dinner she intimated that she intended to retire. She bade goodnight to Lady Rosedale quickly, before the latter could offer to accompany her upstairs. Then she crossed over to that part of the lawn where Lawrence was sitting, by himself, and bade him goodnight also. "I want to rest," she explained, "and am going to bed. Perhaps I shall feel better tomorrow. I am not working tomorrow and on Sunday the trip to St. Ann may do me good."

"I'll probably see you tomorrow here," said Lawrence, and bade her goodnight. He observed that her eyes wore a troubled expression, and her distress affected him deeply. What, he wondered, after she had left him, would be the final outcome of all this coil of worry. The robbery and her connection with it—slight and accidental as it seemed to him— he regarded as of no importance; her future relation to him—for hope he would and must in spite of all that she had said—was what he dwelt upon. Lady Rosedale's antagonism was of itself but little; she was a stranger to Marian. But Stephen's hostility counted. With growing dislike on both sides, with his feeling of contempt for Stephen, which went so deep that he even objected to Nora Hamilton associating with Stephen as an equal, and with Stephen's unrelenting dislike of him, it would not be easy to persuade Marian to give herself to him, especially as he had no brilliant prospects to offer. The odds were against him. And, in a matter of this kind, he was disposed greatly to exaggerate these odds.

Yet one thing he had observed with secret satisfaction: Marian was becoming less disposed than ever to bow tamely to her brother's dictation. There was more than a suggestion of revolt in her manner; the brief passage-at-arms in the lobby that evening had signalled an open breach between them. That breach might widen—and if it did? Thus did he balance hopes and fears, possibilities on this side and on that, resolving to make the most of any favourable opportunity that might come his way, and even to create such opportunity. For even while he told himself that he had nothing to offer a girl like Marian, he pictured her as with him always; his doubts and fears were on the surface of his mind: unshakeable conviction of ultimate success lay deep within it. He knew he had achieved a certain measure of material prosperity; he had no doubt that more would come to him. He was ready to try his fortune elsewhere if Marian should desire that. The world was all before him, and, with her to plan and work for, what might he not achieve?

Thus he dreamt, the man who was believed to be without a spark of romance, and unimaginative.

Thus dreaming he went home.

XI

Major Fellspar Meets Mr. Phipps

The next day, Saturday, Major Fellspar on entering his office was presented with a telephone message from no less a person than the Governor of the Colony, asking him to go up to the King's House, the Governor's residence, at eleven o'clock the same day. It was then nine o'clock, and as soon as the Inspector General had interviewed Inspector Harmsworth and despatched one or two items of work he proceeded to obey the Governor's command.

He knew what he was summoned to discuss: it would be the robbery and nothing else. The Governor was something of a martinet, insisting on the utmost efficiency from his subordinates: it would not be to the credit of his Government that so great a robbery should not speedily be traced to its perpetrator and the stolen things restored. Major Fellaspar had all along feared that the Governor himself would take a hand in this business—it was just what might be expected—but he had hoped that he would be given a couple more days for investigation before hearing from His Excellency. Harmsworth had been diligently searching the dwellings of burglars under police supervision in the city, and enquiring into the whereabouts and movements of those who were not within easy reach. Nothing possibly connecting any of them with the robbery at the Myrtle Bank Hotel had been discovered. The enquiry was not yet over, however; later on that day, there might be more encouraging information. Major Fellsapr thought out the most promising presentation of the case that the facts permitted, and proceeded to the King's House in the hope that the Governor would agree that the Police was doing everything in the matter that could reasonably be expected of it in the circumstances. He was admitted immediately after being announced. The Governor was waiting for him.

"Found the thief who stole Lady Rosedale's necklaces?" demanded His Excellency curtly, after replying to the Inspector General's salutation.

"Not yet, sir," said the latter, "but"—(hopefully)—"I think it won't be long before we do."

"Why do you think so?"

"We are searching all the burglars' room in Kingston: we are having all the persons about whom there is any suspicion watched."

"Who are they?"

It occurred to the Major Fellspar that he really did not know. For, with the possible exception of Mr. Phipps, he had dismissed from his mind both Marian and Lawrence Beaman as in anyway connected with the crime. But the Governor was probing him with his eyes, and as he had spoken of the "persons" he could not well confine himself to mentioning but one name. "There are two men whose movements have seemed to me highly suspicious," he answered thoughtfully. "One is Mr. Archibald K. Phipps; the other is a young man by the name of Lawrence Beaman; and our men think that the actress, Miss Braeme, may be the guilty party."

"It is likely that three persons were concerned in this theft—they are not intimately connected, are they?"

"Not particularly, sir; and no, I do not think that they have been working together."

"Then are you suggesting to me, Major Fellspar, that three different persons, each without the knowledge and connivance of the others, have stolen Lady Rosedale's jewellery?"

"No, sir; you misunderstand me: what I meant was—"

"I am sure I understood you very well, sir. I understood and understand you to say that you have not the slightest idea as to who is the thief, that you are groping in the dark, and that there is not the remotest likelihood of your police being able to lay hands on either thief or jewels!"

"I am doing my best Your Excellency," replied the Inspector General stiffly. He had a great respect for the old martinet, and not a little fear. But there were limits to his official acceptance of rebukes.

"Your best, so far, Major Fellspar, has resulted in absolutely nothing. This man Phipps, for instance, who is he?"

"An American, sir."

"So is the American Consul; so is every other American in the country. Your explanation is not enlightening. Has it not occurred to you that Phipps may be an assumed name? That is how it sounds to me."

"It may be," agreed Major Fellspar.

"And this woman, Braeme: is her name Braeme? Who is she? You do not know, of course; but have you taken any steps yet to find out?"

"Not yet," admitted the Inspector General, "but it was only yesterday that the robbery was reported."

"In twenty-four hours a good deal may be done if you set about it the proper way. That is what you are not likely to do."

"I am sorry you think so, sir," said Major Fellspar, with what he flattered himself was a most impressive attitude of offended dignity.

"I am sorry I have to think so," replied the Governor grimly, in no wise impressed by the Inspector General's dignity. "I have a great deal of work to do, and should not be expected to look after yours."

Major Fellspar tried to control his temper; he felt that this attack was unwarrantable.

"I have always wanted to introduce the fingerprint system of detection here," he reminded the Governor, "but the Government has never authorised it. It might have been helpful in this case."

"It might," retorted the old man dryly. "It might have helped you, for instance, to set in motion enquiries into the past of Mr. Phipps, and Miss Braeme, and all the rest of those you have miscellaneously suspected of this theft. Major Fellspar, I desire you to get for me, by Monday at the latest, a photograph of this Mr. Phipps and of the members of the moving picture company here. I intend sending them to the British Counsul in New York, and asking him to obtain for me the aid of the New York Police in ascertaining if anything is known about these persons. Is Mr. Phipps from New York?"

"So I understand, sir; and the moving picture came here from New York."

"The Police Department of that city will doubtless know something about them, if there is anything to be known," the Governor continued. "I will ask there assistance in the name of my Government, and the British Consul General in New York will also ask it in the name of the British Government; the New York authorities will doubtless do all they can. But you must get the photographs."

Poor Major Fellspar wondered how in the name of reason he was going to do that by Monday, but he merely replied that he would do his best.

"Not later than Monday afternoon," said the Governor, and bowed in intimation that the interview was over.

The Inspector General withdrew in bad humour, and, to obtain some sort of emotional relief, sped down to his office to put the fear of God into the hearts of his subordinates. It was while engaged in this laudable undertaking that a brilliant idea occurred to him. He rang up Lady Rosedale immediately and asked if he could go and see her that day. The answer came back promptly: would he come and have lunch with Lady Rosedale? It was a little past one o'clock: lunch would be going on now at the Myrtle Bank Hotel. Major Fellspar telephoned to say that he would be at the hotel in ten minutes.

Arrived there, he was conducted to Lady Rosedale with whom he saw with Stephen Braeme, who, like his sister and someother members of the company, was not working that day. Stephen was introduced to him, and then the Major managed to suggest that he would like to speak to Lady Rosedale alone. Stephen was dismissed with a friendly word or two. "What is it?" asked Lady Rosedale; "or you can tell me at lunch if you like. We shall lunch alone."

"It's nothing very much," said the Inspector General, "but I think I am right in saying that Mr. Phipps invited you and your party to go down to his house christening tomorrow: isn't it so?"

"Yes, but it is not a house christening."

"That does not matter. Could I be one of your party?"

"Now this is strange," exclaimed Lady Rosedale; "you are the second person who has asked me to take him with me if I am going; though I did not intend to go."

"Who is the other one?" enquired the Inspector General, seeing that she expected the question.

"Stephen Braeme. It is just like Mr. Phipps to invite Marian and leave her brother out. I consider it very proper on Stephen's part to wish to be with his sister, especially as Mr. Beaman will be at the picnic. As you also wish to go, I shall accept the invitation of course; and if Mr. Phipps does not like my guests I shall not be to blame for that: he gave me carte balance to ask whom I pleased, did he not?"

"He did," agreed Major Fellspar, relieved that he had so easily gained his point.

"Why," asked Lady Rosedale, after they had sat down to lunch, "why, if I may ask, do you care to go to this picnic? I thought you didn't know Mr. Phipps."

"I don't, but I want to. You see, as I told you yesterday, it is absolutely necessary that we should keep in touch—merely as a matter of precaution—with everybody who is even remotely connected with this loss of yours. Mr. Phipps may be able to throw some light on it: one can never tell."

"He may be," agreed Lady Rosedale. "His trying to get Miss Braeme away from her brother, to throw her into the society of Mr. Beaman, seem to me a highly suspicious circumstance. I begin," she continued darkly, "to connect both those men with the loss of my jewels. Mr. Phipps said to me, only a few hours before the theft, that he did his best work at night. I suspected he had been drinking from the way he went on: invited himself to tea with me without being asked, you know, and talked a lot of nonsense. He is always drinking; and they say that drunken men and children speak the truth, though at the time I thought his remark was only one of his usual jokes, the point of which I can never see. What is the best work that a man like that can do at night?"

"I only wish I knew," said Major Fellspar frankly.

"I am glad that you have thought of going down to his house," continued Lady Rosedale. "Are you going to have it searched?"

"No; I haven't decided upon that. I merely want to learn something about him, and I can do that best by making his acquaintance. I can't say I like it," he blurted out.

"There is nothing to like about his acquaintanceship."

"It's not that I mean," confessed the Inspector General. "What I don't like is going to a man's house as a sort of friend—though, of course, I go as your friend, not his—and spying upon him all the time. It is not the sort of thing I should be called upon to do. But," he went on hastily, "we must leave no stone unturned to find your necklaces, and I need not accept any refreshment when I am under his roof. I will not."

"It will be awfully good of you to fast all day on my behalf," said Lady Rosedale gratefully, thinking as she did so that the Major would indeed show himself as a martyr to duty. For she judge, seeing the heart lunch he was making, and noting his well-fed appearance, that the Major never willingly missed a meal.

The prospect of a foodless day did, indeed, seem to depress Major Fellspar a little. With something like emotion he ordered a serving of Maryland chicken, having just demolished a lamb cutlet. "It is very important," he warned Lady Rosedale, "that nothing should be hinted as to my having asked to be taken down to the picnic. You will merely mention that you invited me. Better let him know that I was here when his telegram arrived; that will probably lead him to believe that you invited me on the spur of the moment."

"There's the man himself now," remarked Lady Rosedale. "He must have just returned from St. Ann."

It was indeed Mr. Phipps. He was hastening into the dining room, preceded by the head waiter, who was leading him to a vacant table opposite entrance. Mr. Phipps has to pass Lady Rosedale's table. Instead of walking on when he came up to her, he paused.

"Ah, Lady Rosedale, good afternoon," he cried cheerfully. "Heard anything yet about your things? I have been thinking a great deal about you since I saw you last."

Lady Rosedale, purposing to be at his house on the following day, could not but affect a certain degree of cordiality.

"No, nothing has been discovered yet," she smilingly informed him, "and it is very kind of you to have been thinking about me."

"The pleasure is entirely mine," Mr. Phipps assured her. "I feel distinctly better whenever I think of you. He glanced at Major Fellspar.

"Don't you know Major Fellspar?" asked Lady Rosedale: "Major Fellspar, Mr. Phipps."

"I am delighted to meet you," said Mr. Phipps heartily, as the Inspector General rose to shake hands. "If you have no objection, Lady Rosedale, I will have my lunch at your table. One eats ever so much more comfortably amongst friends."

"Very pleased indeed," Lady Rosedale murmured.

Mr. Phipps had seated himself in a vacant chair at the table even before Lady Rosedale had given him permission to lunch with her. He was beaming with pleasure. "You got my telegram yesterday, of course, and you are going with me to St. Ann tomorrow, aren't you?" he asked.

"You were so good as to invite me to bring one or two friends and I have ventured to ask Major Fellspar, who was with me when I received your invitation," said Lady Rosedale.

"I could have wished for nothing better," cried Mr. Phipps, "who else?"

"I have also asked Stephen Braeme, Marian's brother you know. You didn't ask him: I thought it was an oversight. I hope you don't mind?"

"Mind? Not a bit of it: only too delighted! I should have asked Braeme, but I had an idea that wouldn't care to come—stupid of me! I invited a few more folks this morning: wired 'em from St. Ann. The Emery-Smythes and the Hamiltons. Fine girl that, Nora Hamilton. Bright as a summer's day. And how's Miss Braeme?"

"Not as well as I should like," said Lady Rosedale. "She kept her room yesterday and only came down to dinner. She is having lunch upstairs now. The robbery has got on her nerves."

"Quite natural, Lady Rosedale. I must say that the way you bear your loss is a marvel to me. A diamond necklace, worth ten thousand pounds, a pearl necklace of much less value, but, still, one or two thousand pounds; I must say it requires the English noblewoman's sense of deportment and mental equilibrium to stand such a shock without any display of emotion. I will tell you, Major, I just admire the British *sang froid*. I have seen something of it in India, and am quite prepared to meet it anywhere else. It's marvellous."

"You have been in India?" questioned Major Fellspar, interested.

"Yes, *sir*: I have trodden on India's coral strand and wandered about her bazaars what the breezes were anything but spicy. *You* know. I always say that the English rule India by suppressing all symptoms of emotion, like Lady Rosedale does when she discovers she's been robbed, and as you do if the waiter brings you cold coffee in mistake, as I can see he has just done by the look on your face."

Major Fellspar laughed. "I am afraid that my emotions are rather forcibly expressed at times," he admitted. "Were you long in India?"

"Spent a year in that country way back in 1905. Wanderin' up and down, as the poet says, seeking whom I might devour. It is a country of wonderful extremes: great riches and great poverty: loin cloths and priceless jewellery. The ropes of pearls that some of those Indian Princes dress themselves in, Lady Rosedale, when they go to a big pow-wow, would make your mouth water. I have always had a weakness for pearls."

Lady Rosedale tried her hardest not to glance at the Inspector General to see if he had taken notice of this confession of Mr. Phipps'. She succeeded, and that she succeeded was proof that Mr. Phipps was right when he attributed to her great qualities of self-restraint. Major Fellspar, who had some knowledge of men and of the world, was absolutely convinced that Mr. Phipps was speaking thus of set purpose. He had felt on the previous day, from what Inspector Harmsworth told him, that Phipps had been laughing at the Jamaica Police Force. He experienced that unpleasant sensation again.

"There's a fine description of the robbery in this morning's paper," Mr. Phipps rambled on. "On my way to Kingston I stopped at a little country town and bought copies of today's issue: everything on the front page, with Lady Rosedale's picture adorning the display, like, shall I say, a bright star in a black sky—not a bad simile in a country where the darker brethren are in the vast majority, is it?"

H. G. DE LISSER

"Not at all," replied Major Fellspar, seeing that he was expected to answer, and wondering whether Mr. Phipps had had lunch before coming in. For he was hardly eating anything.

"The reporters have done themselves proud over this burglary," Mr. Phipps continued. "Language a little strained perhaps, but very effective for the purpose of conveying to the minds of the public the idea that Lady Rosedale might not have escaped with her life had it not been for her marvellous presence of mind in remaining asleep. Lady Rosedale's picture is quite nicely produced, too, all things considered. The foreign press correspondents here must have cabled a report of this robbery to their papers: heard anything about that, Lady Rosedale?"

"I believe that one of them did mention something of the sort to me yesterday," replied that lady.

"Sure they must have one so. There's nothing the English-speaking nations like better than a good robbery, unless it be a particularly barbarous murder. I always say, in noticing how closely crime is followed in England and the United States, that the popularity of the sensational newspaper in both countries is proof that the Anglo-Saxon peoples of the world are at heart the same, in spite of all outward differences of dress and accent. I believe, Major Fellspar, that together they are destined to rule the world as soon as they have learnt how to rule themselves."

"I have always been an advocate of Anglo-American unity," returned Major Fellspar politely.

"Same here," said Mr. Phipps. "And that is why, yesterday morning, the moment I heard that Lady Rosedale had been robbed of her jewels, I hastened to elucidate the mystery were exactly appreciated by your staff, but you are not responsible for that. There was one of your men loitering about here when I left for St. Ann, and he seemed to take a mighty keen interest in my movements. He was peeping at me when I scooted out in my car: I saw him through the corner of my eye right enough. Guess he thought I was bolting with the jewels in my pocket, but I only went to the telegraph office on my way to St. Ann, as that bright sleuth of sombre hue would have discovered if he had taken the trouble to follow me in a cab. Say, Major, you must have an awful lot of trouble with these fellows. Do they ever find out anything?"

Major Fellspar realised that he was in a cruel position. Here he was, at lunch with a man whose house he intended visiting the next day, and this man was not only telling him that his detectives had been watching him, but probably had not the smallest doubt that he, the Inspector

General, was going down to St. Ann because he suspected him. And this man was pretending to sympathise with him on the dullness of his subordinates, and treat him as though he had nothing whatever to do with the actions of his own dectetives! But for the Governor's sarcastic attitude and rebukes of a couple of hours ago, Major Fellspar would then and there have abandoned all thought of his visit to Mr. Phipps on the following day. As it was, he did not even dare murmur a sort of apology for hat members of his staff had done to Mr. Phipps. He took refuge in a glass of water. He had finished his lunch sometime now, and so had Lady Rosedale. The latter was merely pretending to toy with her coffee. He devoutly wished that Mr. Phipps would give a sign that he had launched and was ready to leave the table.

Perhaps Mr. Phipps guessed what was passing in Major Fellspar's mind. Anyhow, he abruptly announced that he would not have coffee and that he had made an excellent lunch, which was palpably untrue. The three of them left the dining room together, Mr. Phipps mentioning that he wanted to have a word or two with Marian if possible. He excused himself and went off to scribble a note to her. This he gave to a bellboy to take upstairs of Marian, then, catching sight of Stephen in the lobby, hurried over to him every appearance of friendliness.

XII

MARIAN AND MR. PHIPPS

"My dear boy, I am so glad that you are going down to my old ranch tomorrow," Mr. Phipps assured Stephen. "Should have invited you myself, but had a sort of hunch that you wouldn't want to come. Hunch all wrong, as it turns out, and nobody so glad as I. A liqueur now would not be out of place, would it?"

"No thank you, Mr. Phipps," said Stephen cordially; "I think I have already had about as much as is good for me just now. I prefer to indulge in the evening."

"Don't go!" cried Mr. Phipps, seeing Stephen make a movement as if to withdraw; "let's talk a couple of minutes. We see so little of one another. I want to explain that why I did not send you a wire like the rest because, of late, you don't seem to take me any: proud and aloof and all that sort of thing, you know: not like your charming sister. The fault must be mine, and now that you are going to pay me a little visit I feel that you are willing to let bygones be bygones: is that so?"

Stephen has a notion that Mr. Phipps was a trifle crazy. But he amiably remarked: "There are no bygones to let be bygones, unless perhaps I have been showing any foolish side. It's merely a manner of mine, Mr. Phipps; a silly manner, and I apologise for it. You have been so kind to all of us since we have been here that I did feel hurt at your leaving me out of your party, but I am afraid the fault has been mine."

"Say! Isn't that just fine of you!" exclaimed Mr. Phipps. "I begin to see that you have much of your sister's lovable disposition. And here she comes, looking a trifle worn out but still keeping her end up. How do you do, my little movie star?"

"Pretty well," Marian murmured with a not unsuccessful assumption of brightness, "and thank you ever so much for your invitation. We'll have a great day, I'm sure."

"We'll try and make it so," said Mr. Phipps. He was holding Stephen by the elbow, though the latter plainly desired to move away. "Your brother is coming with us," he informed Marian. "He's coming with Lady Rosedale, though it is I who should have invited him in the first place. Didn't think somehow that he would want to travel sixty miles to my old country home; but that's all my mistake. Plenty of other friends coming too; about thirty from here and twenty outside; the Emery-Smythes and the Hamiltons among them. Nora is coming, anyhow, and if Mamma and Papa Hamilton don't come, the loss will not be irreparable."

"Nora?" asked Marian with a side glance at her brother.

"Yes: great pal of yours, isn't she?"

"But she told me last night that she hadn't been invited."

"Battles have been lost and won between one day and the next," said Mr. Phipps. "I only invited her by wire this morning, when I found that we could accommodate at Triton—that's my place—more guests than I had asked yesterday."

"Did you know that Nora was going down to Mr. Phipps?" asked Marian, looking her brother full in the eyes.

"Yes," he replied shortly, "I heard of it today."

"From herself?"

"From herself. I had occasion to ring her up, and she mentioned it."

"I see!"

"What's the matter?" innocently enquired Mr. Phipps.

"Nothing," briefly replied Marian. "I got your note a few minutes ago; you want to see me?"

She had turned away from Stephen, completely ignoring his presence. He saw the gesture, but he hit back the words that sprang to his lips, and with a quick movement freed his arm from Mr. Phipps's grasp. He walked swiftly out of the lobby, Mr. Phipps staring after him as if surprised.

"That brother of yours is a man of impulses and sudden movements, my dear," he remarked. "He's angry with you: what about?"

"I don't in the least know or care," answered Marian; "you wished to see me?"

"Who does not always? I heard you were upstairs moping, and that's the worst thing you could do. So I sent up to say I wanted to see you, and here you are. You'll be better in the breeze, with friends, than shut up in your room thinking about a robbery that you couldn't prevent. You didn't steal the jewels, so why should you worry?" While talking Mr. Phipps had led her out to the northern verandah. There, in a quiet corner, they seated themselves in two comfortable straw rocking-chairs.

A sudden impulse seized. "But the detectives think I did still them," she murmured, and watched Mr. Phipps closely to see what he would make of this confidence.

"Of course they thought so," he admitted at once, showing no surprise. "The black man did and does, and I hear that he is considered quite a clever fellow in his limited way. But what of that?"

"And," continued Marian; then hesitated. She made up her mind to say what was in her mind. "You are a great friend of Mr. Beaman's, aren't you, Mr. Phipps?"

"That is how I regard myself," Mr. Phipps admitted.

"They seem to suspect him too," whispered Marian.

"Nothing at all surprising in that; they have got to suspect someone, and the more the merrier. That keep 'em guessing. Does Lawrence know this?"

"No; at least, I hardly think so. Of course it's all absurd; but don't you see that it may be rumoured about, and that that will do him harm?"

"And you don't want any sort of harm to happen to him, eh?"

She felt as if his eyes were peering into her heart, but in an instant they were turned away from her. He did not wait for any answer, but continued quickly.

"It may get about that he is suspected," he admitted; "such things have a way of achieving a might big circulation. It can't be helped, my little movie star: be thou as cold as ice and as hot as fire, thou shalt not escape calumny. That comes from one of your poets: I am thinking of your English connection, not of Peru. It's quite true: but Lawrence needn't trouble. He can prove all the alibis that circumstances may necessitate. Besides, their suspicion of him is nothing like their firm belief that I've got those necklaces somewhere. It's me that they are keeping their sparkling eyes upon; they have been doing so ever since Lady Rosedale raised the screech. The old girl herself has got it fixed in her mind that I'm a crook, and it's all she can do to keep herself from telling me so. Some day she may blurt out the idea; meantime she's got his high nibbs, the Inspector General himself, on my track. Don't let on to her that I know this, will you?"

"No," promised Marian, "but—"

"That's all right. Their beliefs don't worry me any. You see, it is simply impossible for them to have three different persons in mind and come to any reliable conclusion. And if they did come to a definite conclusion, they wouldn't know what to do with it. It isn't what they think, but what they can prove, that matters. So why should any of us worry?"

"It's easy for you to say that," answered Marian; "but not for me. You see, I wore the pearls, and they were taken from me."

"And Lady Rosedale hid her diamond, and they were taken from her," said Mr. Phipps with a twisted smile. "Why shouldn't we say that Lady Rosedale stole her own jewellery?"

Marian smiled in spite of herself. She felt relieved now that she had taken someone into her confidence; one that she could talk to freely about this matter because she felt she could trust him. She did not dare hint to Lawrence the suspicions entertained about him, but Mr. Phipps was his friend, and Mr. Phipps seemed impervious to care. And he too was suspected; so here were the three of them in much the same situation. She felt drawn nearer to Mr. Phipps.

"You like Nora Hamilton?" he asked her abruptly.

"Very much," she answered; "Nora is a nice girl, and friendly. She has been very kind to me."

"Your brother seems to be very fond of her. I was wondering—"

"What?"

"Whether he is in love with her; he is always with her when he has a chance, you know."

"He has no right to be!" retorted Marian warmly. "But it doesn't matter: Nora would not think of him."

"Why has he no right to be in love with her, and why would Nora not think of him?" asked Mr. Phipps banteringly, continuing the conversation.

"He isn't in love with her," replied Marian, severely. "Stephen is in love with no one but himself, and never will be. What I mean was that he has no right to make love to her, if he's doing so. He'd simply be deceiving Nora. He'll be gone from this country in another few weeks, and perhaps would never give her another thought. People here are very kind to us; but, after all, we are only a sort of strolling actors, you know; and we have no right to make love to people."

"I don't suppose that another member of your company would say as much," mused Mr. Phipps; "I don't believe they would even admit it to themselves—not the least of them. How long have you been connected with the moving picture business, Marian?"

It was the first time he had ever addressed her by her Christian name; but she showed no objection.

"About two years," she said.

"And your brother?"

"Off and on, for several years."

"And he would not think lightly of himself anyway," said Mr. Phipps emphatically.

"No; just the countrary."

"And Nora may think highly of him. He is young, handsome, dark. She is young, pretty, fair. There's the attraction of opposites to begin with. He is being made much of here, as much of as my friend Lawrence Beaman is made little of, for no good reason in the world except his cold manner. If your brother is making love to Nora, what is to prevent her from falling in love with him? There is nothing impossible in that, surely."

"It would be a calamity," said Marian bitterly.

"You and your brother are not on very good terms, if you will allow me to say so," commented Mr. Phipps. "I have seen that, and I mention it as I consider myself a friend of the family. I think you know your brother fairly well. I am a friend of Nora and her family too, and that's why I am talking to you like this. I don't myself quite see Stephen settling down into a model stay-in-one-place husband, and I don't see Nora travelling about with him making pictures: do you?"

"She should wish rather to die first!" exclaimed Marian.

"Perhaps she might wish to die very shortly after," said Mr. Phipps. "But I agree with you: Stephen is only passing the time with her: he is much too wrapped up in himself to love anyone—I am only agreeing with you, my little movie star, so don't cut up rough if I seem to disparage your brother. No doubt he is a man of great talent in his line; and he's a very nice fellow to meet. But Nora—well, Nora is still a girl, like you, and needs some looking after. Strange that her people don't see it; but in these days it is the children who look after the parents, not the parents the children. The time is coming when children will spank their parents regularly, and perhaps in public: don't you think so?"

But the question drew no smile from Marian. She was angrily grave. "He has no right to try to deceive Nora," she said vehemently, reverting to the subject which Mr. Phipps now appeared not anxious to pursue. "It is wrong of him. But that is just like him."

Mr. Phipps, however, thinking perhaps that he had said enough, rose abruptly.

Lady Rosedale had come out to the northern verandah, and was no surrounded by a number of people busily condoling with her. Since the robbery Lady Rosedale had decidedly unbent, and now graciously allowed strangers and others to tender her their respectful sympathy. "Misfortune has improved her," someone had said: she positively looked happy just now as she found herself the centre of attraction and knew that she and her necklaces were the hourly talk, not only of the hotel, but of the island.

"She sure is enjoying herself some," remarked Mr. Phipps glancing in her direction, "she's still on a pedestal, but another kind of pedestal this time. Will you join her Miss Marian? I've got to be going now to look after that picnic of mine: I am going to get some cars to take down those folks who have none. Remember, you travel in my care."

"I shall love to," said Marian, and Mr. Phipps jauntily took himself away.

XIII

"An Iron Strain in Him"

A February morning in Jamaica is a supreme delight. The sun rises at sometime after six o' clock, but long before its coming the skies are a shining blue from horizon to horizon; blue tinted with gold to east, and patterned with delicate streaks of frosted silver and pink.

The atmosphere exhilarates, there is a tang in the air that awakens pleasant memories and touches one's mind to romantic fancies. The new day means a new life; no feeling of enervation blunts the keen edge of enthusiasm; even the old are fired with something of the fervour that thrills through the soul of youth. One awakens to a delicious coolness, to brightness of spirits, to the splendour of glorious sunshine and magnificent sweep of sky, to the call of joy and gladness and a sense of the worth of living.

All the guests of Mr. Phipps, assembled early on Sunday morning by the porch of the Mrytle Bank Hotel, were affected by the spirit of the morning. Mr. Phipps had arranged everything beforehand, and now moved about busily, an efficient master of ceremonies. At his summons the first car rolled up to the porch, and into this went Lady Rosedale, with the righteous consciousness of doing something to promote Marian's welfare and progress in the moving picture life, had graciously invited to ride with her.

Lady Rosedale had done so, however, only after having asked Marian and Stephen to share the car with her and Major Fellspar. But Marian had excused herself by mentioning her promise to ride in Mr. Phipps's car, and Lady Rosedale had perforce to be content with this arrangement. She did not altogether approve of it, but admitted that if Mr. Phipps, their host for the day, had arranged that Marian should ride with him, there could be no reasonable objection. Stephen also had thanked her warmly for her invitation, but had mentioned that Mrs. and Miss Hamilton would take him over to St. Ann. So the moving picture director and Miss Hellingworth had been invited to travel with Lady Rosedale, to their own intense satisfaction, but somewhat to the uneasiness of Major Fellspar.

Truth to tell, Major Fellspar was not quite certain that it fully consorted with the dignity of His Majesty's Inspector General of Police (albeit only for the island of Jamaica)that the said Inspector General should be going to a picnic with one whom he secretly regarded as a vulgar if presumably talented moving picture man. Major Fellspar was not sure that he would relish being seen in such society. But Lady Rosedale's presence might be held sufficient to cover a multitude of minor social indiscretions, and the moving picture lady was undoubtedly pretty and extremely vivacious. Then the morning was so fine, the atmosphere so inspiriting, that Major Fellspar almost felt himself a boy again: he forgot his mission, he was conscious mainly of very agreeable sensations. He was attired, it may be mentioned, as a sort of tourist; that is to say, he had donned a flannel shirt, a gray tweed suit, and a soft felt hat; across his shoulders, by a leather strap, hung a camera which he sometimes took with him on excursions like the present. He did not expect to be called upon to operate this camera today, because of a circumstance which, he believed, would happily prevent his having personally to take snapshot pictures of Mr. Phipps and his guests, though, after leaving the Governor on the day before, he had decided that he would have to attempt something of the kind, however much against his will and his instincts it might be.

This fortunate circumstance was an application from Inspector Harmsworth, late on Saturday afternoon, for permission to spend the Sunday out of Kingston and in the parish of St. Ann. Strictly speaking, Inspector Harmsworth was entitled to the day: it was a Sunday when, ordinarily, he would not have to be on duty. But with the Rosedale jewellery theft still on his hands, the young man felt that every moment of his time should be at his department's disposal. On the other hand, the search under his direction of all the burglars' homes in Kingston had yielded absolutely no results, and his detectives had informed him that nothing of value was to be expected from any further investigation in similar quarters. It had therefore seemed to Harmsworth that no harm could be done by his going out of town for a day, especially as he was secretly convinced that he himself would never be able to do any good in this case, whether he remained in Kingston this Sunday or for the remainder of his life. Permission to leave the city, however, had first to be obtained from the Inspector General, and he had personally approached that authority, explaining to him frankly where it was that he desired to spend the following day.

He had half expected a stern rebuke. To his exceeding astonishment and joy, Major Fellspar had actually welcomed the suggestion. "And take a camera with you, Harmsworth—I know you have one—and get some pictures for me. Get the guests and the scenery, but especially the guests. I have promised to go myself, but I don't think I'll take any pictures."

Inspector Harmsworth thanked him with such warmth that Major Fellspar wondered if the young man was on the same job as himself and was glad because of this opportunity to demonstrate his interest in his work. Such zeal was eminently praiseworthy, thought the Inspector General, but also most unusual. Harmsworth was a gentleman, and the Major could not understand how any gentleman, and the Major could not understand how any gentleman could rejoice in a detective's task when he had to deal with persons among whom he moved on friendly terms. Whatever Inspector Harmsworth's motive, however, the Major felt that his desire to go to Mr. Phipps's picnic was the most fortunate circumstance in the world. It would save Major Fellspar from many qualms of conscience and much inconvenience.

So this morning, Inspector Harmsworth, clad in holiday attire of flannels, and with camera properly slung over the right shoulder, was among the party that had responded to Mr. Phipps's invitation. He attached himself to Mrs. Hamilton and Nora, who had come down to the hotel in their own car. With them was Stephen Braeme, and Stephen just now was not looking altogether amiable.

Stephen had expected to be the only stranger in the car, but he had just overheard Inspector Harmsworth ask Mrs. Hamilton if she could take him with her, and that lady, a pleasant-featured Scotch matron with homely figure and kindly eyes, had readily consented. Nora seemed delighted, said openly that she was glad Harmsworth was going to the picnic, and did not appear at all to regard his company as an intrusion. This had moved Stephen to some quite natural annoyance. He would gladly have dispensed with Inspector Harmsworth's presence for the day.

Mr. Phipps came bustling up. "You four together?" he asked, and ordered up Mrs. Hamilton's car. "In you go, Mrs. Hamilton," he cried cheerily, assisting her into the car. "Now, Miss Nora, you. You had better jump in, Harmsworth; Braeme will sit in front. He'll see the scenery better there; he'll want to: we are more used to it."

There was nothing to do but follow Mr. Phipps's instructions, though Stephen could not prevent himself from frowning at Mr. Phipps's officiousness. At the least he had counted upon sitting beside Nora, and now Mr. Phipps had completely upset his calculations. But the gentleman seemed sublimely unconscious of having caused anybody the slightest annoyance.

Car after car swept away, each one following the other at intervals of five minutes to avoid the dust. Soon there were only three persons left to go: Mr. Phipps announced that he would ride beside the chauffeur: Lawrence protested, with no warmth of conviction, that three could easily be accommodated on the back seat of the car. But Mr. Phipps ignored the suggestion, and Lawrence did not persist in it. Then, swiftly and easily, they glided out of the hotel and into the street, turning their faces towards the west.

The sun was rising now; the silent, sleeping city was flooded with light and looked strangely deserted to eyes that had usually seen it when its streets were peopled by the slow-moving, loud-voiced, dark-hued men and women in nondescript attire who formed the bulk of its population. A stray dog or two, searching diligently for the early bone with a persistent but futile optimism, were visible; beyond these there was no sign of life. Two minutes' running brought the car to the main thoroughfare of the city, Main Street as it would be called in an American town, King Street as it is styled in a colony of the British Crown; and then they turned northwards. Here were the best shops and stores in the island, two and three storey buildings of yellow-white reinforced concrete built on either side of a thoroughfare paved with hard brick and beautified by gardens in its centre, gardens of palms and green sward, and with trees which, in their season, bear a beautiful blossom of vivid gold. This street also was deserted, sleeping in the Sabbath calm; here too there was hardly a sign of life. To Lawrence it was all familiar; to Marian it wore an aspect of strangeness. She had known it raucous and busy and peopled by a motley crowd whose slow and heavy speech she could never quite understand. Now she saw it as though it were dead, while the sweet morning breeze swept through it.

Westward they turned again; suddenly they had passed out of the region of concrete buildings into an area crowded with low wooden structures, with shops and dwellings, some of the latter in the last stages of decrepitude. Fences bankrupt of paint remained in a semi-upright position apparently from sheer force of habit; doorsteps, irregular and broken, seemed negotiable only at the peril of those who used them. In this slum there was something like activity; some early risers

H. G. DE LISSER

were already about, exiguously clad in ancient garments, with vacant expression and uncombed hair. In another minute Kingston was behind: the broad road, with green pastures and thick woods on either side, stretched out before them: the mountains, grey and mist-wreathed, lifted their immense bulk to the right, while the low-growing shrubs and grass glittered with a million dewdrops.

Marian had never come this way before. She had worked with her company to the east and north of the city, and then she had always been in the midst of a chattering, laughing group of people intent upon the trifles and trivialities of their own little world. She was now seated beside a man who was instinctively able to sympathise with her silent admiration of the beauty of plain and hills which was beginning to unroll itself before her eyes. Hers was naturally a gay personality; she loved light and laughter, the sunshine, and all the bright pleasures and amenities of life. And she was young, and reacted readily to the stimulus of enjoyment. She knew she was speeding onwards to a day which would be brimful of brightness; she was looking forward to the hours to come with glad anticipation. The very calm of the morning, its coolness, its glory of sun and majesty of solemn mountains, filled her with a sense of separation from the worries and annoyances she had so recently endured. But she did not want to talk just then; but merely to sit still and look about her, happy in the presence beside her of one who had offered her everything that a man could give, and in whose love and sincerity she implicitly believed.

They swept by level fields green with the spears of the cane and the large drooping leaves of the banana; they passed by pastures where sleek brown cattle browsed; they rushed across a great iron bridge which spanned a sluggish river, green of hue, that wound its way between cultivated land towards the sea. Soon they were passing through another town which was just awakening to the day, and ancient town it seemed, with houses of an olden type; Lawrence told her that this was the former capital of the country, St. Jago de la Vega—St. James of the Plain—as the Spaniards had named it, and to this day called Spanish Town. Their way took them through its centre, and when she saw the square around which the old administration buildings had been built by the English, as they are built around the plaza of every Spanish city in every country where Spain has ruled, she experienced for a moment the nostalgia of the past.

"This is a touch of my old home," she cried; "there is something familiar here."

"Of Peru?" he asked.

"Yes; but I was thinking mainly of the little town I first knew before I left Peru; I was only a child then: it is very long ago."

"Long ago?" he smiled, glancing at her. "That is not to be taken literally of course." To his eyes she seemed little older than a child.

"Oh, I am older than you think," she retorted gaily. "How old do you think I am?"

"About nineteen," he said, and truthfully.

"I am twenty-five."

"You are jesting," he replied, and thought she was: she could hardly be more than twenty.

"Twenty-five," she repeated, nodding her head emphatically. "Quite a grown-up woman, you see. I spent five years in the States, and went back to Peru three years ago. I wish—"

"Yes?"

"Oh, nothing."

"Were you going to say," he asked insistently, "that you wished you had never gone back?"

"Did my voice suggest that?"

"I thought it did; why do you wish that?"

She evaded the question. "And yet," she said, as if merely continuing her own remarks, "only a minute ago a longing for the life of my childhood came over me, though I suppose if I were to go back to the little town that I have almost forgotten, near which my father lived, I should not be able to remain there for longer than a week. Still, in my heart, I love it."

"We love the places where we have been happy," he remarked, "and there is always a glamour about the memories of our childhood."

"I was happy," she said, "until my mother died. Then my father sent me away to the States. He would have preferred England, being English himself, but his only near relative, my aunt, was in America, and he had been so long away from his own home that he had no friends left there."

"Did you brother go to the States at the same time you did?" asked Lawrence.

"Stephen? Oh, no. You have never been to Peru, have you?"

"No; I have been to Colombia and Venezuela fairly often on business; never as far south as Peru. But if you were there I would come. I would go wherever you might be, I would—"

"Sh-h!" she warned, with a nervous glance at the two occupants of the front seat, though she and Lawrence had been speaking so quietly that they could not have been overheard.

"Is that to prevent my saying what I want to say?" he asked her, and she answered, "yes," but so brightly that his hand stole to hers and covered it, as it rested beside him. She gently disengaged it from his grasp, and with it made a gesture as if to point out to him some new aspect of loveliness without. But it was upon her and not upon the scenery that his eyes were fixed.

To their left a wide shallow river fretted itself into foam against the bowlers that strewed its bed; to their right, precipitous, towered to the sky the spur of mountains from out of whose side the road had long since been hewn. Beyond the river on the other hand the mountains also rose, from base to summit clothed in living green. Green with golden flashes was the water as it danced and foamed and glinted below, and wild cane grew upon its banks, and fish leaped into the air, sudden spurts of silver, to fall back into their native element in the twinkling of an eye. The shadows of the mountains on either side plunged the road into grateful gloom: this, and the solemn aspect of the great heights touched Marian and Lawrence to something like awed silence. The trees that grew a thousand feet above them seemed to bend their heads in prayer as the breeze silently offering adoration and homage to God.

The ground rose, the mountains receded; they emerged upon a tiny settlement with people wide awake and going about their morning duties. Black were the faces everywhere, but kindly, and the children waved them a friendly welcome, and the women curtseyed and the men touched their foreheads, unwearied in courteous salutation. Over another bridge, from which they glimpsed a perfect picture of bamboos dipping their graceful feather-branches in the water, which now seemed scarcely to move, so deep it was; then again on a road that ran between cultivated fields and pastures, with thick hedges here and there, through which one saw the tiny thatched houses of the peasants and the smoke which had begun to curl in light blue spirals from scores of fires kindled for the morning meal. Higher and higher rose the land, and sometimes they were travelling through a forest of thick trees, with houses nestling among them, and the scarlet and yellow of tropical shrubs glowing admist the mass of variegated green. Now and then Lawrence would name the trees to Marian: orange and starapple, breadfruit and akee, and the shurbs he might mention as coffee and cocoa and the like, until she realised that what she would have taken for a mere tangle of tropical vegetation was often the farm of some peasant-proprietor whose dwelling could not be seen.

"Do you love this country?" asked Marian suddenly.

"I must explain that we Colonials of English descent have two countries," he answered, "England and Jamaica. England is always 'home' to us, even to those of us who may never have seen it. But Jamaica is home also, as many find who leave it, forever as they believe, but pine in colder lands for its bright sunshine and radiant skies. I could have left Jamaica for good five years ago," he continued thoughtfully, "but did not care to do so. Yes, I love this country it is backward but beautiful; sleepy but good-natured. We drift too much perhaps, but we do not hate bitterly. We are dreadfully snobbish, but there is almost always a helping hand for the man who is down and out."

"That would never be you," said Marian; "I can't imagine you 'down and out.'"

"No," he agreed quietly, "I can't imagine myself so. But here one has to fight against climatic influences, you know: in the very warmth and brightness and beauty that we see around us now there lurks a danger. It is so easy for the weak to drift and be content: to give up struggling and see life slip away while resolutions are made that are never intended to be kept. Not many of us yield in these days to the temptation of going down unresisting with the stream; there is some public opinion, some ambition, to keep us from that; but a few do; and there is always the danger. I could leave Jamaica tomorrow if I wished," he added suddenly, "or if you wished." His voice sank upon these last words.

"You are not afraid of the natives, the people here?" she asked, ignoring his last remark.

"What is there to be afraid of?"

"They are so greatly in the majority; they are everywhere; if they chose they might be dangerous."

"They will not choose to be dangerous," he smiled. "Some day you might ask Mr. Phipps what he thinks of that situation; he is a stranger, and may see it differently from me."

Without waiting for another time, as Lawrence's remark suggested, Marian leaned forward and called to Mr. Phipps. He turned at once, the first time he had done so since they started. "Well, what is the idea, my little movie star?"

"Mr. Beaman and I have been talking about the natives here," she began.

"Is that all you have been talking about?" he interrupted. "I admit that the topic is full of interest; still, I don't exactly think that I could spend the whole of a bright morning discussing the sons of Ham, unless there was some politics in it. I think I should find other matters of more absorbing personal concern. Well, and what do you think of them? You think, I suppose, that they are oppressed, like a man from Ireland I met the other day who said to me that coloured people of this country were terribly oppressed and kept down and trodden upon, and robbed and exploited, and I don't know what else besides. He looked like a philanthropist all right; generosity from the word 'go.' But I happened across that same bright leader of light and liberty the next day, and he was having a deuce of a dust-up with a Kingston cabman about sixpence. He seemed to think that the cabman wanted to oppress him, and the cabman had no sort of doubt at all that my philanthropic friend was one almighty thief. My friend wanted to give the cabman in charge, but I cut in and pointed out that native labour must be allowed to cheat the stranger if it is to be restrained from forming trade unions, and, anyhow, the cabman was quite right. I don't say that, as a rule, the cabmen are right; but by sheer perverse accident this one happened to be, and the Irishman had to produce another coin. I guess that when he returns to his own peaceful and harmonious country he will give it out that the white man in the English tropics is terribly oppressed and trodden upon by the black."

"Never mind you friend," cried Marian, "we wanted to know whether you think the people here are dangerous or not."

"I'll bet you anything that friend Lawrence doesn't want to know anything of the sort," said Mr. Phipps. "But if your mind's uneasy, I'll set it at rest at once by saying that they are terribly dangerous to any stray coconut you might leave loose about; while to a bunch of ripe bananas, hanging temptingly and promiscuously within reach, they will become positively hostile. At such times no coconut is in safety and the life of the banana is apt to be short. But that's about all, or nearly all, anyhow. So you don't need to worry."

Mr. Phipps turned his face, away, and settled himself in his seat again as though he had nothing further just then to say.

"Why did you bring him into the conversation?" whispered Lawrence. "It is not often that we have a chance to talk by ourselves."

"He would have thought it very strange if all during this trip we said nothing to him," Marian whispered back. "He would have wondered what we could have to say to one another to his entire exclusion. You must think of appearances, sir!"

"I don't think Phipps is troubled much about appearances," he rejoined; "he usually sees through them."

Marian nodded her head. "Yes," she answered seriously, "he is the sort of man whom one would be afraid of if he were not one's friend. He is always gay and cheerful, but sometimes his eyes and his mouth are hard: I have seen that once or twice. But he is your friend, isn't he? I believe he likes you very much."

"And you too," said Lawrence; "but you are right. He's got an iron strain in him somewhere."

XIV

The Devil's Mountain

The car stopped. The chauffeur slowly and methodically got out and walked towards the fore of his car, opened the bonnet, and began to probe into and tinker diligently at the machinery. Mr. Phipps, after watching him for a moment or so, turned towards Marian and Lawrence with the remark—

"You know, I don't believe there's anything at all wrong with the car?"

"Then what is your man doing with it?" asked Marian.

"Making sure; taking precautions, and all that sort of thing. It is a habit of his, a rather unusual habit in this country, and therefore I do not discourage him, even when I feel he is overdoing it We are at the foot of the Devil's Mountain now, and Arthur is fixing up things against accidents. Accidents may still happen, of course; but he'll have the consciousness, if he is not killed, of knowing that he did everything possible for the sake of safety. And that's about all that any of us can do," added Mr. Phipps, "when once we have started, or been started, on any course. We can take precautions against accidents and surprises: the rest we must leave to—shall I say Providence?"

"You are in a peculiarly moralising mood this morning," remarked Lawrence.

"Must be the effect of Sunday," returned Mr. Phipps smiling; "I am finding sermons in stones and moralities in motor cars."

"This mountain; you call it the Devil's Mountain," Marian observed: "why?"

"The old owners of this country, the Spaniards, called it that long ago. They named it la Moñtana del Diablo, because it was long and steep, with dangerous precipices; and in those days the road was bad. I think there is a Devil's Mountain, and more than one, in the life of everyone of us, little movie star, and if we cross it successfully there are scenes of beauty and delight on the far side, as there are on the other side of this 'Mount Diablo'; and if we do not cross it safely—well! But it has to be attempted, for there is never anyway round, once we have set out on the journey."

"But," said Lawrence, falling in with Mr. Phipps's rather unusual mood, "we need not begin the journey."

"No; sometimes. But that is if we know we are about to begin it and can stop ourselves. Often we do not know until we are well on the way, and then it is too late to do anything except—take the best precautions."

"And those?" enquired Marian.

"Those each of us must find out for himself or herself, my dear. . . when we begin to see where we are going to."

Marian's eyes contracted slightly at these words; she seemed to find a hidden meaning in them. Lawrence, who had never before heard Mr. Phipps speak like this, lifted his eyebrows in astonishment and wondered at his friend's lapse into something like sentimentality. He changed the conversation by saying abruptly to Marian, "You must not imagine that there is anything dangerous about Mount Diablo in these days, no accident ever occurs here now: the road is perfectly safe."

"Yes," agreed Mr. Phipps, "with careful driving it is. With indiscreet driving it would not be, of course: it would be terribly dangerous. There is always danger, Lawrence, on the Devil's Mountain. But I see that Arthur has done fooling with the engine, and we are about to do some pretty climbing. Look to your right, movie star!"

The car had started with a powerful movement, not swiftly but steadily, for the frequent curves and sharp turns of the narrow road would not permit of high speed with safety, as the chauffeur knew full well. Marian, obeying the injunction of Mr. Phipps, turned her eyes in the direction indicated, and uttered one low sound of delight.

To the left and so near that one could almost touch it with outstretched hand, a mountain lifted itself out of range of vision; to the right the ground broke away, sloping to a hidden valley a thousand feet below. Far, far in the distance rose the hills that shut in the valley on the other side, their summits sharp-defined in delicate azure against the bluer sky, their slopes and bases covered with a moving misty mantle of purest white. The mist rolled and drifted incessantly, silver here and there where the sunlight touched it, rising now to blot out as if forever the vivid verdure of some dew-drenched hillside, then disappearing as if dissolved into the air and leaving tree and fern and gleaming frond to emerge into view once more. A garment of green picked out with scarlet and purple was flung over the body of the precipice close by; the overarching sky seemed to sparkle; a glint amongst the trees suggested a waterfall leaping and hurrying to join some placid river down below.

Deep shadows brooded above the mist and beneath the radiant hilltops, shadows dark and still, and save for the throb and purring of the car no sound was heard. A dreamy silence hung above the scene and wrapped it all around; and Marian felt again, as she had felt before in her own beautiful and romantic country, the charm and mystery and wonder of "the sleep that is among the quiet hills."

Higher and higher they climbed, the road twisting and turning like a mighty snake, with precipice succeeding precipice, and mountain range after mountain rage rising in the distance, and the air growing colder and colder. And to their right the precipices yawned always, grim and menacing. But the chauffeur, with his hand upon the steering wheel, looking neither to right nor to left, nor halting nor hurrying, held the car upon its course: there was danger, Marian saw, but only to the careless, or to the incompetent or reckless, and she remembered what her old friend had said about taking all due precautions. Again she began to wonder if there had been a hidden meaning in his words—she had become very susceptible to veiled suggestions and indirect allusions of late. Now and then she thought that Mr. Phipps wished to convey to her something that he could not say directly. . . or was he seeking to find out something from her, and had adopted this means of doing so? Or was it that he meant just nothing at all, and that she was allowing her imagination to play tricks with her, to worry her incessantly, to—

"The top of Mount Diablo, and not a jar to our smooth progress," cried the voice of Mr. Phipps. "We are beginning to go downwards now, out of the silence and cold into the warmth of the sun and the sound of human voices and beasts and birds. It is strange how one's surroundings affect one: I don't think any of us uttered a single word since we began the ascent of Mount Diablo."

And now, as he had said, they moved downwards, and the chasms to their right passed quickly into elevated valleys, and the hills receded farther and farther, and pastures began to appear, pastures with grass of emerald green, and smooth, still, lichen-covered ponds, and copses of tress with thick umbrageous branches. The pastures were fenced with stone, and on these low stone hedges grew green and purple creepers; the scene was fair and park-like, the atmosphere had the quality of sparkling wine and was filled with the scent of pimento leaves, and the sun, the great god and tyrant of the tropics, was here a mild and beneficent deity, calling forth sweetness and giving light.

"We are in the Garden of Jamaica," said Lawrence: "the most beautiful part of a beautiful country: the whole parish of St. Ann is called the Garden of Jamaica."

"Is your old home far from here?" asked Marian.

"Some miles distant; we turn to the north and travel for a while along the seashore before we come to Triton."

They passed through the village of Moneague, a valley among the mountains some two thousand feet above the level of the sea, then again began to descend. They went quickly now, for here there are no precipices; here the land fell, not abruptly, menacingly, but with a gradual steady sweep. The wind sang by them; great ceiba trees, with parasitic plants clinging to their huge branches or sending out tendrils which swung free in the air, reared themselves into sight swiftly and were left behind; flocks of birds rose abruptly from among the grass on either hand, spread themselves out into long air-fleets and disappeared, the tang of the sea came suddenly to them, and then—stretching away to the horizon flashing in the yellow light and painted gloriously with pink and blue and imperial purple, lay the Caribbean Sea.

The amber sand, smooth as the palm of one's hand, was caressed softly by the waves as they rolled towards the shore; here and there grew clumps of sea-grape, and groves of coconuts, tall and slender, tossing and rattling their branches gaily and laden with green and golden nuts. Again and again as they sped along the road by the northern shore they cross rivulets that emptied themselves into the sea, and saw the hosts of tiny red and yellow crabs scurrying to their holes or scuttling into the water. Sometimes there was hardly anything but the road between the sea and the mountain to the left; sometimes the mountains were withdrawn and a wide space of fertile land, dotted with cattle or overed with grass, lay between them and the water. These plots of land were cut off from the road by barbed wire fences; a gate not and then indicated the way inward to houses which could not be glimpsed from the open highway. One of these gates stood ajar; Arthur, Mr. Phipps's chauffeur, swung the head of his car towards it, passed through, and drove with practiced ease along the winding inclined way that led from it to some interior mansion.

"Triton," said Lawrence, though Marian knew already what place it was. Soon she saw, parked on a grass plot to the left, the cars which had preceded them, and a large house with a porch which stood on a slight eminence in front. "Triton!" cried Mr. Phipps, as a matter of form, then sprang out of the car as it stopped, and leaving Lawrence to bring up Marian, hastened to join his other guests.

These had already been received by My. Phipps's major domo, a dignified and venerable old man, perfectly black, whom Mr. Phipps has taken over with the house and had dubbed Pluto, somewhat to the bewilderment of the venerable and dignified retainer. Mr. Phipps had explained that morning at the Myrtle Bank Hotel, to such of the guests as had never visited Triton, that his butler and general factotum would be there to receive them, and would do so quite well as he, Mr. Phipps, himself. And Pluto had certainly welcomed Mr. Phipps's guests with great dignity blended with respectful cordiality, and had offered to show them to rooms where they might refresh themselves pending the arrival of their host. They had all, however, preferred to remain on the porch of the Great House until Mr. Phipps himself should make his appearance. On catching sight of him now they have a little cheer, some of them hurrying forward to greet him.

"Come in, come in," cried Mr. Phipps cordially, "come and get the dust off and a cocktail in—no, not a cocktail, a planter's punch. Pluto mixes planter's punch beautifully; it's one of his many accomplishments."

Saying which, he hustled the crowd into the big dining room, through a corridor that led to it from the verandah. The dining room was to the rear of the Great House. There, on a long mahogany table, were already set out all the ingredients that go to make a planter's punch—old Jamaica rum, limes, sugar, water, and nutmeg—while a huge pail containing broken ice showed that Mr. Phipps had forgotten nothing that would make this famous native beverage delectable.

"We'll have the punch first and the wash afterwards," suggested Mr. Phipps; "there wasn't any dust to speak of on the road this morning, thank goodness. Pluto, will you please see to the punch."

"Yes, sah," agreed Pluto, and summoned a woman somewhat younger than himself to assist in the operation.

"We'll have breakfast in half an hour," Mr. Phipps rattled on, "then we'll begin to enjoy ourselves. Make yourselves perfectly at home, you know; I believe it is all in the old Jamaica tradition that a planter's house belongs to his guests. I am not a planter, but that doesn't matter."

While the punch was being prepared, Marian and Lawrence, who had no followed the others inside, lingered on the porch, from which, because of the elevation on which the building stood, an extended view of the surrounding country on three sides was commanded.

Before them lay the sea, its blue and purple horizon far beyond; on either side was broken land, undulating southwards into foothills and covered with grass and trees; neglected land for the most part, only the space immediately around the building being maintained in something like order. The house itself, mainly of brick with a white and green wooden façade, was of two storeys, with numerous windows, and built on foundation three feet high: a large commodious structure originally erected by owners who could afford to live in such a residence when there was plenty of coffee on the property and the price was high. The stone that paved the porch, as Marian observed, was marble; she noticed that the solid doors were of polished mahogany. She knew little of such things, but guessed that a building such as this must have been worth something once, and perhaps was still valued at a fair amount of money. And this belong to Lawrence, though he evidently made nothing of it. This was the home in which his parents had lived and in which he had been born, the home of gentlefolk, evidently, of people who must have been amongst the first and the best of their time.

"Why did you let Mr. Phipps have this?" she asked him, as he brought her attention points of interest about the house. "Mightn't you have been happy there?"

"There is some land," he answered indifferently, "but land requires money to develop, and I had none when my people died. I had to go and earn some. I would have sold Triton, but didn't quite like to; so I left it in the care of the servant you saw a minute ago, and occasionally I rented it to someone who wanted a residence for a few months of the year. Phipps likes it; but, as you can see, he does not cultivate any part of property. He spends money on it instead of making anything out of it."

Just at that same moment Major Fellspar also was asking himself why a man like Mr. Phipps, who was often in Kingston, who went so frequently to his own country, and who possessed in Jamaica no visible means of support (as the local Vagrancy Law put it) should have such a country resident out of which he so obviously made nothing? Mr. Phipps did not in the least look, to the eye of the Inspector General, like a man with any taste for farming or cattle breeding, and it was certain that he neither farmed land nor bred cattle. Then why this property, and why, in a word, Mr. Phipps? Major Fellspar did not wish just then to ask such questions. He had the unpleasant feeling of being the guest of Mr. Phipps, and even then an excellent planter's punch was being prepared. He remembered his determination of the previous day to refuse all refreshment from Mr. Phipps; had he thought of acute indigestion as a sufficiently plausible excuse. But he had not been able at his rather unsubstantial breakfast early this morning to estimate the effect of a long exhilarating motor ride through wonderful country, to say nothing of the pleasant appearance of the punch which was even now being handed round. His was a tragic position, but he braced himself to refuse the punch, though his lips and palate protested strongly against such unpardonable folly. Everybody seemed to be taking some; reluctant but determined, he hung on the outskirts of the crowd.

"What, Major," cried Mr. Phipps, catching sight of him. "Not having an appetiser? Impossible!" and he found a glass thrust into his hand by his host himself. There was nothing to do, he decided, but drink it; common courtesy commanded that course, although morally he did not want to follow it, whatever his physical inclinations might be. He swallowed the drink with more appreciation than he could have thought possible in the circumstances, and felt exceedingly stimulated. This was alarming: the few crackers he had secretly brought with him in his sporting coat might fail, given his present feeling, to deliver him from the temptation of breakfast. And, truth to tell, Major Fellspar had already begun to take an extraordinary personal interest in the question of breakfast. He did not like this inclination of his mind.

The punch discussed, the guests hurried to rooms prepared for them, Mr. Phipps and Lawrence showing the men the way to their suite, Mrs. Hamilton and another lady, who had been to Triton before, conducting the women. When they had all finished removing the slight evidences of the journey from their faces and hands, they thronged back to the dining room, as had been previously arranged, and there they found the long table set for breakfast, with three or four smaller tables also laid for the same purpose. Mr. Phipps's housekeeper had prepared a Jamaica meal. There was fragrant coffee, the berries of which had been toasted and ground the night before, and the essence distilled by an all-night dripping through a cafetiere. A little of this essence of coffee was put into a cup, followed by a cupful of boiling cow's milk drawn that morning from the cow, made a delicious beverage, and with it you had either toast and Jamaica fresh butter, or crisp buttered cassava wafers which melted in the mouth. Salted codfish cooked with golden-hued ackees was one of the dishes, and this was served with roasted yams and steamed yampees; there were also broiled river mullet and crayfish baked in their own shells. Ham and eggs for those who preferred that dish had of course been provided, and juicy steaks from cattle fed of the rich pastures which abound in St. Ann. Roasted green plantains, and ripe plantains fried in olive oil, baked sweet potato, and little cakes of flour, brown and crisp, split in two and richly buttered—there was everything to tempt the early appetite, and there was hardly an appetite that required much tempting that morning.

Mr. Phipps had carefully arranged for the seating of only two of his guests; the others sat where they pleased, and according to their selection of partners for the table. The two persons whom he saw to their seats were Lady Rosedale and the Inspector General: one to his right, the other to his left: an arrangement which Major Fellspar had wholly failed even remotely to calculate upon. In such a conspicuous position, it occurred to him, how was it possible for a man to avoid eating without giving offence? He remembered with great distinctness the he had assured Lady Rosedale that he would touch nothing under Mr. Phipps's roof, and Lady Rosedale could now observe his every movement. She, he noticed, was affected by no sort of scruples or compunctions whatever. It did not seem to occur to her that part of the proceeds of her jewellery might go to paying for this feast; or perhaps it was because she was of opinion that it might that she was so obviously preparing to make a hearty meal. The odour of the coffee was tempting; it seemed to Major Fellspar that the idea of coffee with boiling milk instead of water was one which he would adopt in the future. Clearly, he would have to taste it to judge adequately of its merits; and if Lady Rosedale found no difficult in accepting the hospitality of a man she suspected of dishonesty, there might be some excuse for an Inspector General placed in the most awkward position imaginable, and all because of his devotion to duty. Unconsciously, while pursuing this train of reflections, Major Fellspar carried his cup of coffee to his lips, and continued sipping it with quiet but excessive enjoyment. He next accepting a helping of baked crayfish without even a moment's hesitation. The crayfish was delicious. So were the cassava wafers. And the steak was tender and juicy to a degree. Major Fellspar was fast becoming convinced that a man like Mr. Phipps, who so thoroughly understood the art of entertainment, could not possibly be guilty of a miserable theft. The very idea now seemed preposterous.

XV

THE PHOTOGRAPHS

B reakfast proceeded amidst great merriment and laughter. There was more rum punch for those who wanted it, and the punch exhilarated still further the spirits of people already primed for enjoyment. The service was brisk, and as everyone wanted to be shortly on the move—for there was to be bathing, boating, fishing and motoring all during the day—in half an hour the meal had been disposed of. Lady Rosedale, at the request of Mr. Phipps, gave the signal for adjournment from the table. "And now," said Mr. Phipps, as everybody rose, "before we go out I shall be glad to show you over this old house of my friend Beaman—it is his, you know, and some day I shall have to hand it back to him."

His guests expressed themselves delighted with his suggestion: led by him, they went from room to room; most of the apartments contained some furniture but were obviously in disuse. "This place," Mr. Phipps explained, "was built in the halcyon days of sugar and coffee; it must be a century and a quarter old, but is sound in every stone and timber. I inhabit three rooms of it when I am here, and the bats come in when I am not and take possession. I sleep in a bedroom, I dine in the dining room—it is so large that I quite see plainly the ghost of the first owner standing in one of the corners: he is supposed to be there, and I see him. The other room I call my library or study, though I do not study there: care to see it?"

He flung open the door of a room on the second storey as he spoke, then drew aside to let the others enter. It had evidently been built as a library; the walls were almost hidden up to two feet of the roof by bookcases. But most of these cases were empty now; only one contained a few old books, and a goodly number of large volumes like albums. These bore paper labels with pen and ink lettering. They were all dated. It was Nora Hamilton who casually drew one of them from its shelf and idly opened its stiff pages.

"What is this?" she asked laughing, glancing at the newspaper cuttings neatly pasted within the book.

"My record of interesting happenings," replied Mr. Phipps. "Curious thefts, murders, revolutions and so on are always occurring, and if I find any account of these in the papers that interests me, I just snip it out and paste it in my newspaper-cutting book. When depressed and bowed down by weight of woe—you know the song, Miss Nora—I adjourn to my study, and by the perusal of the story of sensational crime I revive my drooping spirits. Nothing is so entertaining as a murder admirably executed, the perpetrator of which is never discovered—unless it be a robbery."

"What a morbid taste!" cried Nora, "and what a lot of clippings you have made!"

"My collection of newspaper clippings is surely extensive," Mr. Phipps admitted; "it shows that the old fellow is diligent in the pursuit of instructive information. I brought over today all the newspaper accounts of Lady Rosedale's misfortune, and they will be pasted up along with the others, but specially marked, for I know the victim of this latest crime and it makes it all the more interesting."

"Do you mean, Mr. Phipps, that you have been collecting these records of crime for years?" asked Lady Rosedale, "and for mere pleasure?"

"Not records of crime only," explained Mr. Phipps, "and not merely for pleasure. All the stories in these books are not about crime. You will find—" he drew a volume out of its shelf and looked at the index at the back of it—"you will find that there is a good deal in them about revolutions, for instance, and conspiracies, and jewellery—I have always had a weakness for jewellery and its movements. And I don't keep these records for amusement only; I often read them over to expand and enlighten my mind. It's not because a man is getting old that he should neglect his education, and there's a lot of education to be got out of reading about real happenings. But come! We don't want to waste the precious hours of a lovely day among my musty old clippings."

He moved towards the door and the others trooped after him, nothing loth to be out of doors.

Major Fellspar was puzzled. An idea had flashed into his mind. Could it be possible that this man was a detective, a retired detective? But, if so, he was quite unlike any detective that Major Fellspar had ever of; in spite of his occasionally queer locutions he spoke like a gentleman; in spite of his apparent obtuseness to obvious hints he could act the part of a perfect host. He seemed, too, to be a man of means. Then, surely, no one who was a burglar would speak as he did about his interest in theft, in crime, in jewellery, and would so openly invite the Police to inspect the room where he kept his records of criminal and related events. He seemed actually to be inviting suspicion, and no guilty man would dream of doing that.

Major Fellspar glanced at Lady Rosedale. Lady Rosedale was thoughtful and troubled, as the set of her lips and the little horizontal line in her forehead clearly showed. It was plain that Mr. Phipps had set her thinking; she did not look like a woman at east; there was plainly something on her mind. Major Fellspar wondered if she had discovered, or thought she had discovered, anything new in the last few minutes. Major Fellsppar, it has already been remarked, was really a shrewd sort of man. Those who, because of his perky expression, his humorously upturned nose, his great regard for personal dignity, and his snobbishness, took him for a fool, were often disagreeably surprised. That Mr. Phipps had a very definite object in allowing them all to see his newspaper cutting he realised quite clearly; his business now was to ascertain what that object was. He fixed his attention on this, became silent and preoccupied. An idea, a suspicion, had dawned in his mind.

By this time they had got downstairs again, and the men had donned their hats preparatory to setting off for the open-air picnic. The cars were ready and waiting; Mr. Phipps was on the verge of giving the signal for the general departure when Nora Hamilton called out: "Oh, I say! Do let us take some photographs before we go!"

Major Fellspar felt certain that this suggestion had been hinted to Nora by Inspector Harmsworth, and he noted with appreciation this proof of resourcefulness on Harmsworth's part. The suggestion came much better from an attractive girl like Nora, whom everyone would be willing to oblige, than it would have come from his subordinate.

"Good idea!" exclaimed one or two of the younger girls, and those who said nothing nevertheless looked their readiness to have their pictures taken. The objection came from Mr. Phipps.

"Why waste precious time taking photos now?" he urged; "lets get away to the river."

But Inspector Harmsworth had already unslung his camera, and some of the younger people were preparing to pose. Mr. Phipps say that there would be a friendly contest with him should he persist in pooh-poohing Nora's suggestion; he saw that he could not, without being positively rude, insist that no photographs should be taken. So he shrugged his shoulders slightly, and at the same time glanced in Major Fellspar's direction. Major Fellspar had a self-conscious look. He was uneasily aware at the moment that the only two persons who had brought cameras with them were he and Harmsworth, two members of the Police Department. He wondered whether Mr. Phipps had observed that circumstance. He would not have wondered if he had caught the glance which Mr. Phipps directed at him.

The photographs were taken in groups of four and five, the ladies removing their broad-brimmed jippi-jappa hats for the purpose. Major Fellspar himself was photographed with Lady Rosedale, Mr. Phipps, the moving picture director and the company's principal actress. Stephen posed beside Nora Hamilton, and Lawrence stood by Marian's side. Lastly, Inspector Harmsworth, handing his camera to the moving picture director, was photographed, with Nora and one other girl to make up a group. He promised to show the negatives to everybody within a day or two, and then they streamed, laughing and talking, towards the waiting cars. Major Fellspar was delighted that he had had nothing, directly, to do with this business: he was satisfied that he could not, with any dignity, have acted as amateur photographer to the crowd. He could not have carried off the thing with the lightness and ease of Harmsworth; but Harmsworth had not been ordered by the Governor to do a disagreeable piece of work, and in all probability, Major Fellspar now concluded, was totally unconscious of why his chief had asked him to take these photographs.

They had set on for the picnic ground, a picturesque spot some two miles away, admist the foothills and close to the sea. There was a little house on the ground, and this Mr. Phipps had borrowed from its owner. Here they would lunch, the lunch being packed in a light motor lorry; here, too, they could change for bathing in the river that flowed through the property, or in the sea if they preferred sea-bathing. Arrived at this place, the party separated into groups, each group going its own way, or coalescing with another as it thought fit, during the couple of hours that preceded luncheon. Thus each group followed the bent of its own collective mind, and pursued its own idea of pleasure. When they all reassemble at sometime after one o' clock, it was evident that they had all exceedingly enjoyed themselves.

They were not so much inclined to strenuous exercises after lunch as they had previously been; indeed; the tendency of the younger people particularly was to stroll off in pairs and lose themselves among the surrounding trees. One of the first couples to do so was Nora Hamilton and Stephen Braeme, thanks to Major Fellspar, who called to Inspector Harmsworth just when the latter was about to ask Nora to accompany him for a walk. He would probably have made a party of three, for Stephen had shown clearly that he too was determined to be as much as possible with Nora that day. But Major Fellspar imagined that he had something to say to Harmsworth just then, and Major Fellspar was precisely the one man in the party whom Harmsworth could not put off for another occasion. By the time the Major had finished his remarks—he had merely intended to be nice to Harmsworth, who had executed so neatly the task entrusted to him—Nora and Stephen had disappeared from view, and Harmsworth could not bring himself to hurry purposely after them: that would have been much too marked. Marian and Lawrence too were among those who went off soon after luncheon; so in a little while there were only about half a dozen of the more elderly people remaining in and about the little house.

Lady Rosedale has decided that too much movement just then would be bad for her digestion; she was therefore holding a sort of court just where she was, and was duly being made as much of as though she were a scion of royalty. Major Fellspar, also, saw no sufficient reason why he should perambulate about. Mr. Phipps had lingered behind, his eye on all his guests and ready to anticipate their wants. He had in the meantime kept a particular watch on Inspector Harmsworth, and as soon as he could join them and, after a few commonplaces, casually turned the conversation to the subject of amateur photography.

Mr. Phipps asked to be allowed to look at Harmsworth's camera, and loudly admired it. He spoke of different makes of cameras; in a little while Inspector Harmsworth discovered that Mr. Phipps knew a good deal about photography: far more indeed than Harmsworth knew himself.

"Do you often take pictures?" enquired Mr. Phipps carelessly; "but I suppose you don't get much opportunity for that sort of thing in Kingston?"

"No," admitted the younger man; "when I was stationed in the country I did more photographing in a month than I have done in Kingston during the last year. I am very much of an amateur, I am afraid."

"Then you don't develop your own photographs?"

"I don't know how to," Harmsworth candidly confessed, "and it isn't really necessary, you know. You can get developing work done quite well and cheaply in Kingston."

"Quite true," admitted Mr. Phipps; "but there's some drawback: sometimes you may have to wait long for your pictures. The photographers are so busy that they may keep you any length of time before giving you the negatives. I guess we shan't see those photographs you took today for quite sometime."

"I have already promised to show them to you tomorrow evening," said Harmsworth, "and I'll do it. These are for the old man, you see,"—he indicated Major Fellspar, whose short, sturdy figure could be seen through an open window in the house. "He seems to be keen upon photographs just now: every now and then he has a new hobby. He asked me to take those I got this morning. They'll be a memento of a very pleasant day with you."

"That's kind of you to say so," said Mr. Phipps heartily, but his eyes were narrowed and his look piercing. "You can get those photographs developed in a very short time, then?" he asked, returning to the subject.

"Naturally; if the old man wants them, and he usually wants everything in a hurry. Any photographer in Kingston will finish them in a few hours."

"What does he want them for?" demanded Mr. Phipps sharply, as if to surprise Harmsworth into a truthful answer before he could pause to think.

"Blest if I know," replied the young man; "just wants them, I suppose. He's a man of moods, you know."

"I suppose so," agreed Mr. Phipps. "Shall we go for a stroll? We are certain to meet some of the others."

Inspector Harmsworth consented, saying that he would be able to get some pictures of the scenery for his chief, which remark caused Mr. Phipps to smile.

They went by easy ways, Harmsworth now and then stopping to take some particularly pretty or striking bit of scenery. Mr. Phipps talked, and Harmsworth listened with a preoccupied air, and whenever they saw some couple or group of persons in the distance the younger man's eyes scanned them closely, then left them with a disappointed expression. They must have spent an hour thus, when, their steps having taken them southwards among the rising ground, they came suddenly to the verge of a bluff overlooking a little glade forty or fifty feet below and surrounded by great leafy trees. Paths from the bluff led downwards to this glade. Mr. Phipps's eyes swept over the ground beneath them. He saw, at the same time Inspector Harmsworth saw, Nora Hamilton and Stephen Braeme.

XVI

"I Speak as a Spaniard"

They were seated on a fallen tree trunk, side by side; Nora had taken off her wide-brimmed hat and her bronze hair gleamed in the tempered sunlight. Her face was directed towards the ground; Stephen, in stooping posture, was talking to her eagerly; his attitude, the movement of his lips, showed that. Her left arm hung loosely by her side, and, as they stared Inspector Harmsworth and Mr. Phipps saw Stephen's hand steal slowly towards it.

Harmsworth rapped out an ugly oath, and stiffening himself. "What—what is that damned moving picture man saying to Miss Hamilton?" he exclaimed: "what right has he—"

"We seem to be spying upon a scene that is not intended for our eyes," said Mr. Phipps. "You don't approve of it, Harmsworth?"

"What's going on down there? No! By God, I don't. And I am going to stop it."

"You can easily join them," suggested Mr. Phipps, indicating one of the downward paths; but Inspector Harmsworth had already seen it. Mr. Phipps did not look at him as he dashed off; instead, his gaze fastened itself on a spot on the opposite side of the glade, where a flutter of white had a moment before indicated the advent of someother unwitting intruder. There were two persons there; his keen glance identified them: they too must be spectators of the little love scene—for there could be no doubt it was a love scene—that was being enacted in the glade. Mr. Phipps was deeply interested.

Inspector Harmsworth made no effort to conceal his swift approach as he strode down the path which led from the bluff into the open space below. Stephen heard the noise and loosened his clasp of Nora's hand; she looked up, a little startled; there was a fluttering of her eyelids, a slight quivering of her nostrils, a mantling of her cheeks with pink, as Inspector Harmsworth marched up to them, endeavouring to appear as if he had noticed nothing, but with a brusque constraint of manner that was not lost on Stephen.

"I thought you would find us," exclaimed Nora quickly. "We saw that you were with Major Fellspar, and so did not wait for you."

"How did you find us," asked Stephen haughtily. "Followed us?"

"You promised to go for a motor ride along the seashore this afternoon," said Harmsworth, ignoring Stephen altogether, and addressing Nora. "You haven't forgotten, have you?"

"No," answered Nora, who was already recovering from her surprise of a moment before. "We, the three of us, can go: when do you propose to start?"

"Perhaps Mr. Braeme might not want to go," said Harmsworth directly, and even rudely. "I thought we could go together and take some pictures."

"May I ask why I should not want to go for the ride?" demanded Stephen, and there was an angry note in his voice. "I do not think my going depends upon you. As Miss Hamilton has suggested that I might do so, I am certainly accompanying her."

"Yes," cried Nora, with a nervous little laugh, for the anger in both men's faces was plain for her to see, the antagonism in their tones and attitude patent. "A lot of us can go together: here's Marian and Mr. Beaman now: let's get a big car and go together."

Mr. Phipps, from his point of observation, had watched Marian and Lawrence as they entered the glade, unseen by those already there. Lawrence and Marian, he was quite sure, had been witnesses of what both he and Harmsworth had observed, and probably would have withdrawn unnoticed had not Inspector Harmsworth made his sudden appearance. Maybe something in the attitude of Harmsworth and Stephen had suggested to Lawrence that a quarrel, disagreeable to Nora, would be averted if he and Marian joined the group. Whatever their reason, Mr. Phipps saw them emerge into the open, and decided that he also would go below.

"Quite a pleasant reunion," he called out, as he stepped briskly towards them; "we have all been wandering round and about, and yet we are not much more than a furlong from our headquarters."

He was speaking to everyone, but it was on Marian's face that his gaze was fixed. It was absolutely bloodless, and her eyes held in them a strange and angry look. He remembered what she had said to him about Stephen's lack of earnestness, about his being able to love none but himself. She was looking at Stephen with the bitterest, most scornful expression he had ever seen on her face. Stephen was staring stormily at her, while Harmsworth was eyeing Stephen in a very unpleasant and challenging fashion. But Nora had already recovered her pose and was her bright and cheerful self again. She looked from one wrathful face to the other, then burst into laughter.

"Well, aren't we all serious!" she cried. "What is the matter? I have had a very pleasant time walking and talking with Mr. Braeme, and we are going for a motor ride later on. Won't you all come? You, dear Mr. Phipps, will, I know. You won't refuse me anything, will you?"

"Not even in my life!" returned Mr. Phipps, in the same spirit. "A motor ride is just what I myself was going to suggest. We'll take my car, and do an hour's spin: those who want to follow the good example can do so. But, say, we had better be going back now to look after that car. You must come with me, Miss Nora; you and I are the bosses of this particular show."

"I am coming," said Nora, taking Mr. Phipps's arm gaily.

They moved off in a bunch, but Mr. Phipps was to Nora's left and Inspector Harmsworth to her right. There seemed no place exactly for Stephen, who showed no disposition to join his sister and Lawrence. Constraint was visible in everyone's attitude, for even Nora's buoyancy could not successfully contend against the glumness of the others, and Mr. Phipps appeared to be thinking seriously. Fortunately they had no far to go, and as soon as they came to the house, Mr. Phipps began giving directors to his chauffeur to get ready for a drive along the sea coast.

They started soon after, going westward; they went at a moderate speed, and every now and then stopped for a few minutes if anything striking caught their attention. But the drive, from the viewpoint of genuine enjoyment, was not a success. There were many angry passions at work, and these inhibited any feeling or expression of pleasure. It was with a view to interesting the others in something, and so taking their minds off their several annoyances, that Mr. Phipps ordered Arthur to stop when they came to a little bay in which a few boats, tied with ropes to the shore, swung idly to the motion of the sea. He suggested that they should take a walk about this bay. "It is interesting," he said, "for here are the last of the old masters of this island made his escape; they call the place Runaway Bay."

They looked about them curiously. The little inlet was almost completely surrounded on the landside with trees and shrubs; the few natives about, fishermen and boatmen obviously, were taking their ease in the boats or on shore; there was nothing particular, nothing significant about this spot, save that the last Spanish Governor of the island had embarked from here for Cuba after his final attempt to drive the English conquerors out.

"Runaway Bay," laughed Nora, "prosaic but true."

"Runaway Bay," repeated Stephen, "prosaic and uncomplimentary, señorita." For the first time since he had known her he spoke to her as he would have addressed a lady of Spain or of Peru.

He was now no longer angry or sulky. Stephen was by profession an actor, and he had an instinct for the dramatic. The scene, and especially its historic associations, seemed now to stir that instinct into vivid life; he was standing erect, dark, handsome, with flashing eyes, and surveying land and water with a mingled expression of pride and regret. "And not only uncomplimentary, but untrue," he urged, fixing Nora with his eyes. "Think of it, señorita: an old man—for he was old, as I have heard—comes over the sea from Cuba with but a handful of followers to win back a land won generations before by his own people, and which had been wrested from him, not by superior bravery, but by superior fore and by surprise. He struggles hard, he does his utmost; he is unfortunate, but still he strives; the dice are loaded against him, but he fights with fate itself. Then, foot by foot, fighting always, he is forced backwards, and at last realises that the task of regaining Jamaica is beyond him. He comes to this little spot, with a mere handful of men. Here they make their last stand, but they know that the enemy pursuing them is in overwhelming numbers. So they depart—these few—in an open boat, braving the storms of the sea and the other perils of the deep, preferring death from the elements rather than capture and humiliation at the hands of the English. In Peru we should not have given such a spot as this so poor a name as Runaway Bay. We would have called it something like 'The Last Stand of the Spaniard'—*El ultimo parada del Español!*"

He spoke with fire and eloquence, and as he spoke admiration flashed from Nora's eyes. Unconsciously, Marian also had drawn her form erect, while her cheeks glowed and her delicate head was proudly poised. Mr. Phipps recognised that the Spanish blood was stirring in both of them; Inspector Harmsworth felt that Stephen was appealing to the romantic in Nora's disposition and was posing almost as a hero of Spain just then, as one who in a desperate emergency could also make a last stand and make it bravely.

"Well," said Mr. Phipps, "your poet has asked, 'what's in a name?' So why quarrel about 'Runaway Bay'?"

"My poet, señor?"

"Sure. Bill Shakespeare, you know; he said that and a good many other questionable things, and since your father was English you should have no kick about the English calling this place Runaway Bay. It don't seem to be in the nature of the ordinary Englishman to be over-poetic in the naming anything; and, anyhow, if one half of you was driven out of this country, the other half was the driver. So you can sympathise with both side."

"I confess I am that I am thinking of my Spanish side just now," replied Stephen a trifle coldly. "The side which has so often been unfortunate, but which has covered itself with imperishable glory. You may wonder that a Peruvian should say this, remembering that Peru revolted against Spain and declared her independence under the great Bolivar. But Peru revolted against the Spanish Government, not against the Spaniards and the Spanish blood: that had been impossible. Besides, I come of the blood of the Spaniards in Peru, of the blood of the conquistadores, the men who conquered the New World for Spain, and did so much to make her glorious. I speak as a Spaniard! You understand now what I feel about Don Arnaldo de Sassi and his last stand here. 'Runaway Bay,' indeed!"

He was striking to look at as he spoke; and even Mr. Phipps, not easily impressed by anything, felt that there was true fervour in the tribute this young man was paying to Spain and her wonderful past. Mr. Phipps saw Nora's eyes meet Stephen's, and there was a look of deep sympathy and admiration in them.

"Runaway Bay, indeed!" Mr. Phipps repeated with a little laugh, not offensive, but sufficiently derisive to discount some of the heroics of Stephen: "I don't think, friends, that there is so much 'indeed' about it as you say, or perhaps it is 'indeed' in a very literal sense. I am talking now to the son of an Englishman, and talking merely as a hundred percent American who would have fought on the side of George Washington in the Revolution if he couldn't have avoided doing so, fighting not being much in my line. And, believe me, there wasn't much of a 'last stand' about old man Sassi when he got to this spot in those historical times you've been reciting about. Sassi was running all right enough, and the only question with him was whether he could run faster than the English folk who wanted to get him. He made a beeline for this spot, having been careful to map out his retreat beforehand, in case o accident. When he reached it, he stood not upon the order of his going, but went at once. I guess it was a real runaway and no mistake. And I don't blame him: I should fancy that the fellows behind him were one almighty terror and had precious little use for a Don."

"That's your version," said Stephen, "but if he had been a coward would he have come back to try to reconquer the country, and would he have left it at last in an open boat, as I have read in one of your local publications that he did?"

"No, I allow he wasn't a coward," returned Mr. Phipps, "but his valour was liberally tempered with discretion. As for the open boat, he did escape in one, it is true, but what else could he do? Wait for a caravel? I am afraid he would have waited forever!"

It was Nora who turned the conversation into a different channel, wishing to save Stephen from the polite but unmistakable raillery of Mr. Phipps.

"But think of an open boat living in the sea from here to Cuba," she cried; "I can hardly believe it!"

"It is done even now, Miss Nora," put in Inspector Harmsworth. "These boatmen, in ordinary weather, will go very far out to sea, and Cuba is only about a hundred miles from the nearest point in Jamaica. A boat like that—" he pointed to a fairly large boat in the bay—"could carry a dozen men over to Cuba without tremendous risk, except in the hurricane months."

"A little boat like that?" she asked incredulously.

"They would sail all the way; they only row when going for short distances along this shore."

"Well, one not unlike them carried Mr. Sassi for good out of this island, and I think he was wise to go," said Mr. Phipps turning away and moving towards the car, so as not to give Stephen another chance of breaking out into another rhapsody. He saw that Stephen was about to do this, and that Nora at any rate would listen to him. It was all very romantic, but, in Mr. Phipps's view, decidedly unsafe. After what he had seen in the glade, Mr. Phipps preferred sober prose and prosaic conduct. He was not sure he could depend on Inspector Harmsworth's temper.

XVII

Mr. Phipps Changes

They went back to their camping place, and thence to Triton, in good time for dinner. The picnic had been on the whole a great success, and when Mr. Phipps announced that he had arranged for a light supper at the Myrtle Bank Hotel on their return that night, it was voted that the ending of the day would be perfect. Even Lady Rosedale appeared satisfied, for again and again had the conversation turned on her great loss, and she felt that the seriousness of this subject had not been unduly obscured. Lawrence, who had been most of the time with Marian, looked quietly happy; Nora was bright and brimful of excitement. Stephen, too, for whom the day had begun in disappointment, and who had been angry at his sudden and almost rude interruption in the glade by Inspector Harmsworth, had now apparently recovered his good spirits: he had not failed to notice the impression he had made at the Runaway Bay, in spite of the good-humoured chaffing of Mr. Phipps. But Marian and Inspector Harmsworth were troubled and depressed, though they did their best to stimulate light-hearted enjoyment. It would not have required a particularly observant person to notice that these two were completely out of tune with the rest; and there were one or two who noticed it. Lawrence did, and it was patent to Stephen. Mr. Phipps not only perceived it, but seemed affected by it. Even he was not his usual gay-hearted self.

The short twilight had faded into dusk, the sea had changed from purple to slate, and the stars had begun to peep forth one by one when the party started on their homeward journey.

Mr. Phipps saw Stephen step into Mrs. Hamilton's car, with Nora and Mrs. Hamilton, and made no effort to repeat his manoeuvre of the morning and send him to sit beside the chauffeur. Lawrence, on his part, was much surprised when Mr. Phipps, whom he had fully expected would ride beside Arthur as he had done during the drive to Triton, got into the hinder part of the car with Marian and himself. Mr. Phipps murmured something about its being chilly in front, and spread the rug in the car with great solicitude over the knees of the three of them; but Lawrence, who ordinarily would have done anything for the comfort of his friend, had the feeling that this was an unnecessarily selfish act on his part, since Phipps was a tough and wiry person who would as a fact think much less of the cold than he or Marian. Of course, his sitting with Marian and Lawrence rendered anything but conventional conversation impossible.

Marian was placed between the two men and did not seem inclined to any conversation; Lawrence was not then prepared to indulge in common-places; Mr. Phipps himself, form whom a constant stream of talk might usually be expected, sank into a profound reverie, making no attempt to excuse it.

Lawrence's hand sought and found that of Marian under the wrap; but Marian gently disengaged her hand. Lawrence wondered why a day, which for him had been so full of happiness, seemed about to end so sombrely. He knew Phipps too well not to feel certain that something of more than unusual importance must have occurred to send him into such a brown study, to render him so inconsiderate of what he must have known would be the wishes of younger people who found pleasure in each other's society.

The night was beautiful, with the silver sickle of moon to the west, the looming shadows of hills before them, the vast splendour of the star-besprinkled sky. But Lawrence gave no glance to any of these things; he was trying to puzzle out the explanation of the depression of both his companions. True, there was that scene with Nora and Stephen; but was there so much in it to affect these two so intimately? He also had felt angry, alarmed, at the scene in the glade; he was incensed at the idea of Stephen making love to Nora Hamilton, though, inconsistently enough, he had been doing the same to Stephen's sister.

Stephen's effort by the bay to appeal to Nora's admiration, to show himself romantic and at his best, had not been lost on Lawrence, who had felt that it was not merely a pose. But Lawrence knew that Harmsworth cared for Nora; that had been made quite patent today: he was satisfied that Harmsworth would see the danger of allowing Nora to be subdued by the assaults of the brilliant Peruvian. He could not believe, indeed, that Nora was yet in love with Stephen: he felt certain that she was only flattered and pleased by Stephen's attentions. He could not agree that it was solicitude for Nora that so filled the minds of Mr. Phipps and Marian that a day which had begun happily for both was now ending in silence and gloom.

It was nearly ten o' clock when they got back to the Myrtle Bank Hotel. Here Mr. Phipps roused himself, and springing lightly out of the car, began to marshal his guests for supper. All, however, were not staying to supper. Mrs. Hamilton and Nora were going home, and Stephen, as he did not live in the hotel, announced that he would leave with them. So would Inspector Harmsworth have done but that Major Fellspar suggested that he should remain, and undertook to take him home: which suggestion Harmsworth interpreted as a command. To Lawrence's delight, Marian also said that she did not care for any supper, and asked him to take her down to the hotel's pier for a few minutes. "You had better come in and have something before you go to bed," Mr. Phipps said to both, but Marian was firm. Mr. Phipps lifted his eyebrows a little and went off to his other guests. Lawrence determined to ask Phipps what his change of attitude meant, and why he did not seem to want the two of them to be alone together anymore.

"Phipps is a peculiar fellow," he remarked, as they strolled down to the pier. "This morning he acted so nicely: left us alone, I mean; and tonight he planted himself along with us so that I could not say a word to you."

"He is your friend," said Marian quietly, "and would do nothing against you: we both agreed on that this morning. So he must believe that he is helping you, and he is right."

"What do you mean, Marian?"

"He doesn't want you to be alone with me; he thinks that it is bad for you, harmful; and—and for me also. He is right; but it is not about that that I want to talk to you now. I know you are on friendly terms with Mr. Harmsworth: are you not?"

"Yes; you are referring to Nora and Harmsworth, aren't you?"

"Yes. You saw today what was happening in that wood, and afterwards by the sea you saw—didn't you—how Nora looked when my brother was speaking. Nora likes him, she thinks—she thinks a lot of him: oh, I know; I know how well Stephen can speak, and how he can flatter and make love. Your friend Mr. Harmsworth cares for Nora, doesn't he?"

"That is apparent enough: it was quite plain today," said Lawrence.

On a bench at the head of the pier they seated themselves. There was no one else in sight.

"You want me to speak to Harmsworth about your brother and Nora? I think he has seen as much as we have, and is far less pleased than you and I could feel. I fancy that Harmsworth is in much the same position as myself. He is a man of ordinary salary, and Nora's parents are very well off: that is his difficulty. But now that your brother—well, I think I can say, if I know anything at all about Harmsworth, that he will no longer allow the grass to grow under his feet where Nora is concerned. She used to like him; I have no doubt she likes him still."

"Tell him," said Marian tensely, "that he should show her plainly that he loves her; that he should tell her so and be with her as much as he can, so as to prevent Stephen from being with her; he should prevent Stephen from making love to her, he should tell her father, her mother, that Stephen should not be in her company, should not touch her hand, should not speak to her! Tell him tonight! Will you do it?"

"I will do whatever you want me to, Marian," said Lawrence; "but, remember, you are asking me to derate your brother."

"I would do it myself if I could! I *will* do it! I will speak to Nora about him; but—but would that be of any use? She might think he is being badly used and that might cause her to care for him. What am I to do?"

"Leave the matter in Harmsworth's hands," counselled Lawrence; "I don't think he will require any prompting from anyone after today. And don't worry yourself about other people, dear; surely they can look after themselves. I want you to talk about yourself; I want to talk to you about yourself. You are not happy; I see that; and it is not about Nora that you are unhappy. Won't you tell me what is the matter? I love you, Marian, and I want you to be happy. Dearest, dearest!"

She was crying quietly, her face in her hands. His arm slid around her waist and clasped it firmly; quickly she sat upright and pushed him away, drew herself a little from him, then suddenly she swayed towards him and her head was on his shoulder and his lips on her lips.

"Oh, this is wrong, all wrong," she muttered, "it is the Devil's Mountain, Lawrence, and there is danger."

"There are beautiful fields and the blue sea beyond," he whispered.

"No," she murmured, "for us there is only the precipices, and that is why your friend told us of them today and did not wish us to be alone together tonight."

For answer, he kissed her on the lips again and again, and she made no resistance; but still she continued weeping and murmuring tat it was all wrong. At last she drew herself resolutely away, and when he would again have put his arm around her she rose, and began to wipe her face nervously with her little lace handkerchief. "Let us go back," she pleaded. "I go out to work tomorrow; I must go to bed now."

"And tomorrow night; shall I see you here?"

"Yes—no," she corrected herself; "at least, not alone."

"But why, Marian; for you care for me a little darling, do you not?"

"I love you," she answered simply; "but I ought not to love you; and you too—it is silly for you to care for me dear. I should not have let you kiss me tonight; but I was weak, and I know that I shall be weak again if we meet alone. . ."

She had left the pier, he at her side, and there was no chance now of a last embrace. When they reached the verandah she gave him her hand, saying goodnight. He pressed it, and her fingers tightened on his convulsively, and her eyes looked love into his. . . then she was gone.

Without waiting to see his friend Phipps, or any of the others with whom he had been that day, Lawrence hurried out of the hotel. His heart was beating wildly, his brain was on fire. Marian loved him; that he knew now; she had told him so, and her look was even more eloquent than her words. And, for the first time, tonight she had called him Lawrence. But something kept her from him: her brother no doubt, her brother who was all vanity and self, who sought his won pleasure where it might be found and denied her anything save what he decided was good for her. Well, that brother should learn in no great length of time that there was a limit to selfishness, and that even the Spanish-American doctrine and custom of the subjection of women to their men folk, which so often makes of the Spanish-American woman a mere plaything, had its limits, especially outside of Spanish-America. This gentleman who so proudly boasted of his descent from the conquistadores, who was so evidently prouder of his Spanish than of his English blood, would shortly find that English vigour and determination were something with which he would be compelled to reckon.

Thus with the fixed idea in his head that Marian should only leave the country with him, if she left it, Lawrence went home to think all the long night of his great happiness and of the poor little girl's so evident distress. And all that night Marian lay awake, staring with open eyes into darkness, crying softly now and then, perplexed and wretched. "What am I to do?" she moaned, again and again, "What am I to do?" And could find no answer to her question.

XVIII

Major Fellspar's Belief

M r. Phipps's supper was quickly despatched. Shortly after Marian had retired and Lawrence had left the Mrytle Bank Hotel, the party broke up, and Major Fellspar took Inspector Harmsworth into his car, which he had ordered to meet him that night at the hotel. Inspector Harmsworth was in no mood for conversation with his chief; in fact he felt that Major Fellspar was an infernal nuisance whose main object that day had apparently been to keep him from Nora Hamilton. Therefore, to the Inspector General's remarks, he returned cold if strictly polite rejoinders.

Major Fellspar had promised to take Inspector Harmsworth home; arrived at the Inspectors' quarters, he got out of the car, and drew Harmsworth out of the chauffeur's hearing. "I'll not be in the office in the forenoon tomorrow, Harmsworth," he said, "and you must take this matter in hand. Have those photographs developed by afternoon—the men and women, not the scenery: I don't want that. They must be at King's House before four o'clock. That is understood?"

"Yes, sir."

"Very good. Now about this Mr. Phipps."

"Yes, sir?"

"You noticed what he did today? How he showed us his newspaper records of criminal cases, and talked, as he is so fond of talking, of his interest in crime and jewels and revolutions, and so on?"

"Yes, I noticed it, and it struck me—"

"What?"

"That he had a purpose in doing all this, but still I do not think he is a thief."

"He is none," said the Inspector General briskly; "he is trying to confuse us, and he is the sort of man who will play with fire for the mere love of doing so. He would actually lead us to arrest him, if that suited his purpose. Well, I am glad that your views agree with mine. He knows who the thief is, Harmsworth!"

"You think so?" questioned Inspector Harmsworth.

"I am sure of it. Brown, you remember, suspected Miss Braeme from the first."

"Yes, sir; but surely—"

"Anything is possible. Do you forget Miss Braeme's brother?"

"Good heavens! Then you think?" . . .

"Phipps doesn't care a brass farthing about the brother; but he is interested in this girl. The brother, with all his airs and good looks, is probably a damned thief, and his sister must be in collusion with him. Phipps is a keen sort of man, with evidently a good deal of experience of criminals; he knows we can't touch the brother without bringing the sister into it, so you see—"

"I do see," interrupted Inspector Harmsworth slowly, with his mind riveted upon the fact that Stephen Braeme was trying to make Nora Hamilton love him. "Shall we arrest him, sir?"

"I could wish to with all my heart, Harmsworth, but we must have some evidence. At present we have only a feeling of moral certainty, and that would not go in a court of law: we should be made ridiculous if we charged a stranger with burglary and could not present even a decent case to the jury. Phipps apparently has lots of money and is just the sort of person to bring out from England the most famous criminal lawyer to defend the girl, if he thought the local barristers would not be sharp enough. We must get some good evidence against them before we lay any charge. Tell Brown to be at my office at two o'clock tomorrow afternoon, and be there yourself at the same time. Goodnight."

"Goodnight, sir," replied Inspector Harmsworth, saluting, and went into his quarters.

His mind was a whirl of conflicting emotions. He was conscious of an active feeling of dislike for Stephen Braeme, and now he believed that he had always disliked that young man and been suspicious of him. He found nothing extraordinary in Major Fellspar's suspicion; he did not think of asking himself whether he would have been more charitable towards Stephen if the latter had not happened to be his rival. But when he thought of Marian, for whom he entertained a genuine liking, his heart turned sick within him: surely if her brother were the guilty party she must be in collusion with him: and, if she were, what sort of character could she have, and how could she escape, assuming that the Police could bring the robbery home to both of them? This brought him to another train of reflections: how indeed could the

Police bring the robbery home? They had made no progress whatever in the last three days.

For what were the photographs wanted? Evidently they had some connection with the case: the Governor himself was to have them. He would have liked to ask Major Fellspar for an explanation, but deemed it wisest not to: no doubt the chief would tell him in good time. What was expected of him was simple, and he would see that it was done. Consequently, on the following morning, Inspector Harmsworth took his negatives to a well-known firm of photographers who developed them by noon; at two o'clock that same day the photographs—several sets of them—were lying before the Inspector General on his desk, Inspector Harmsworth was seated near the desk, while Detective-Sergeant Brown stood waiting to hear what the chief might have to say to him.

"I suppose, Brown, that there is little use in our going on with the search our habitual criminals' rooms, is there?" asked Major Fellspar, as a sort of introduction to what he had to say.

"None at all, chief, we have searched nearly all of them," answered Brown, "and that sort of people don't rob big things."

"I am sure you are right," said Major Fellspar, and Brown's eyes brightened at this word of praise.

"I think," continued the Inspector General deliberately, "that Miss Braeme's brother has had a great deal more to do with this robbery than we have thought."

"Yes, chief," replied Brown without hesitation; "he and the young lady, and Mr. Phipps."

Major Fellspar looked keenly at his detective. "Did you suspect Mr. Braeme?" he asked.

"No," answered Detective Brown truthfully, "I didn't, sir: but seeing as he is the young lady's brother, and that she and the old gentleman, her friend, knew about the necklaces, it is to be supposed that Mr. Braeme knew about them too. All these foreign people are not too honest chief."

"That may be so," returned Major Fellspar, "but I do not think that Mr. Phipps has had anything to do with the robbery, or does more than know who is the thief. And he is trying to shield the thief—either Miss Braeme herself, or her brother, because he is her brother. Do you understand?"

"Yes, chief."

"So there hardly seems anything to be gained by watching Mr. Phipps. It is on the other man that we have to keep a sharp and wary eye; we must find out all about his movements on the night of the big dance at the Myrtle Bank Hotel, and since then: as a matter of fact he ought to have been watched from the moment the robbery was discovered. You will therefore watch Mr. Braeme very closely, and you will make all possible but cautious enquiries as to what he did and where he went on the night of Thursday last."

"Yes, sir."

"And Mr. Phipps we'll leave alone."

"Yes, chief. . . but, begging your pardon, chief—"

"Well?"

"I was just wondering why, if he had nothing at all to do with this business, Mr. Phipps so quickly slipped out of the hotel last Friday morning. He was the only one to do it, and his action was very funny."

"He probably wished to divert suspicion to himself," said Major Fellspar. "That is what I am now convinced he has been endeavouring to do all the time. He knew"—Major Fellspar paused at the beginning of his sentence. If Mr. Phipps really *knew* anything on the morning of which they were speaking, his knowledge must have concerned Marian Braeme. There was no getting away from that. So it was probable that she was the thief and her brother merely an accessory! Secretly, Major Fellspar wished that it was he other way about; yet that Marian was implicated he had no doubt at all. As to Lawrence Beaman, there was really nothing against him. His being in Mr. Phipps's room before midnight could not be any possibility account for thefts which, quite obviously, must have taken place two or three hours after. With Phipps and Lawrence eliminated, there were only Marian and Stephen left. He would arrest them both the moment he had one really damaging fact to produce against them!

"Chief!"

"Yes, Brown?"

"Begging your pardon, sir, but I would just like to say a word to you before I leave."

"Go on, Brown."

"Begging your pardon, sir, I would like to say that nothing can get it out of my mind that when Mr. Phipps walked out of the Myrtle Bank Hotel on Friday morning, he went away with the jewellery. I don't know where he managed to hide it; Sampson said he only went to his lawyers, but there are other people in the same building with his lawyers. Mr. Phipps had the jewellery, chief. I feel that I could swear to it."

Detective-Sergeant Brown spoke with the utmost conviction. Ordinarily, had the matter been of trifling importance, Major Fellspar would not have permitted this implicit criticism of his theory to pass without severe rebuke; nor, indeed, in such circumstances, would Detective Brown have ventured to offer it. But this matter was serious, and the detective knew that Major Fellspar had a high opinion of him. "Then where does Mr. Braeme come in, Brown?" asked Major Fellspar quietly.

"That's what I can't tell, Chief; but three of them know about the jewellery, and Mr. Phipps is one."

Major Fellspar thought deeply for a moment. "Very well Brown; I am glad that you have told me just what is in your mind. Carry out my instructions with regard to Mr. Braeme."

"Yes, sir," said Brown respectfull, saluted, and withdrew.

"Brown has a conviction that Mr. Phipps is one of the culprits," said the Inspector General, thoughtfully, "and his insistence on that tends to complicate the issue. And he has more, at this moment, to urge in favour of his belief than I have in favour my conviction that Braeme is the man we want to law our hands on."

"It is the most baffling case I have ever had to do with," said Harmsworth. "I agree with you, sir, that Braeme is in it: but he does not live in the hotel. . . that puts us off somewhat."

"We want to find out where he was between one and three o'clock on Friday morning," said Major Fellspar. "When we have done that, we shall really be on his track. Enquiries must be made, Harmsworth. Someone at the place where he lodges must surely know, at least approximately, the time at which he came home on the night of the dance. We must find that out."

"I will do my best, sir."

"Very well. Report to me tomorrow morning."

Both the Detective Inspector and his subordinate made the most of that afternoon. Inspector Harmsworth went himself to the house at which Stephen lodged, ostensibly to call upon a lodger there, and had a talk with the landlady, an intelligent widow lady of middle age who was fairly well-known in the city. The house was one of the best of its kind, the lodgers were given private keys if they desired them, consequently anyone could let himself in at night without disturbing the rest of the household by ringing or knocking, and no one need know who came in and at what time of the night. Brown, on his part, found opportunity of questioning the two servants who lived on the premises. They knew nothing of the movements of the lodgers after nine o'clock at night. His enquiry was therefore fruitless.

Inspector Harmsworth, thanks to an apparently casual question, learnt the location of Stephen's room; it was on the first floor, with two large sash windows opening to the north. It required no particular knowledge of Jamaica houses of that type to know that any man who wanted to enter the room at night by either of those windows could easily do so, if they did not happen to be fastened, without any fear of being seen from the street. The high brick wall and the darkness would effectually screen him. The report that was handed in to Major Fellspar on the following morning was therefore of a highly discouraging nature; it led absolutely nowhere. "We are in a blind ally," confessed the Inspector General dismally. "We must keep on watching carefully, but—" he shook his head, discouraged.

"Suppose this man Braeme, or anyone else whom we suspect tries to leave the island shortly," said Harmsworth; "what are we to do in that case?"

"I have thought of that and arranged for it," answered Major Fellspar. "No one can leave without a passport, and, in the circumstances, it will not be possible for Braeme to obtain a passport without delay. I understand too that these actors and actresses are engaged for sometime; so it would be a highly suspicious circumstance for any of them to want to quit before their work was finished. If any did manage to go, he or she would be met by detectives on landing in the United States."

"You have it all nicely fixed, sir!" Inspector Harmsworth desired to show his loyalty to his Chief, and to hearten him.

Major Fellspar was sensible of the compliment, but his face expressed nothing. He felt that he was training this young man to his work. He also felt that the Governor did not adequately appreciate his efforts.

"We must keep our eyes open," he said. "Of course, the public and press will say that we have failed utterly. There are suggesting it already."

With what had been written in that morning's papers in his mind, it was impossible for Inspector Harmsworth not to agree with his superior officer. The papers still expressed a belief that the thief or thieves would be discovered, but they did so in a very lukewarm and unconvincing manner. Major Fellspar and Inspector Harmworth knew what would shortly follow. They did not appreciate the prospect.

"We can't prevent the newspapers from saying what they please," said the former, looking very much as though he wished he could prevent them. "If we arrested anybody in mistake, if we failed to secure a conviction, those same papers would be the first to hound us down!"

"They have no principle, sir," agreed Inspector Harmsworth.

"Nor any intelligence. They are not concerned with helping justice, but with selling their miserable rags. They are a curse to this country."

Inspector Harmsworth thought that, very soon, the newspapers were likely to prove a curse to the Police, but he kept this reflexion to himself.

"Yet," continued Major Fellspar, "it might actually be an advantage if, for some little time, it got about that we had entirely failed. That will be rather unpleasant for us, but it may help."

Inspector Harmsworth agreed.

XIX

LAWRENCE AND MR. PHIPPS

By the end of the week the local press and the public had openly come to the conclusion that if Lady Rosedale's jewellery were ever found it would be by the merest of accidents and in no wise due to the ability and activity of the police. Such a view was vastly consoling to newspaper writers and correspondents who, having nothing to lose, professed to be frightened by their insecurity from terrible loss and by the risk they ran of having imaginary valuables subtracted from their places and persons at anytime of night or day. One nervous gentleman even wrote anonymously to one of the papers describing his arrangements for protecting himself and detecting the advent of a thief. Not only had he placed innumerable bells on all his gates and doors, with wire netting over the windows, and bars where bars could scarcely be an advantage, but he had employed a watchman to sleep in a room on his premises, the leg of this watchman being attached to a stout cord which led from his habitation into his employer's bedroom. A tug at this cord was supposed to be an effective awakener of the soundest sleeper, and the man so awakened would spring up ready to fare forth silently and to attack and capture the most daring rogue. On the very night of the day this device was described, the cord was vigorously pulled by the gentleman in question, he being under the impression that he had heard distinctly suspicious sounds in the backyard. Unfortunately the watchman forgot that his cue was perfect silence at such a thrilling conjuncture, and, at the first tug, which threatened to dislocate his leg, he fell violently from his bed, broke loudly into blasphemous execrations, and challenged all the thieves in the neighbourhood to await his coming and then see what horrible punishment he would inflict upon their miserable bodies. The thieves, if any, refused this invitation, and when the story found its way into the press it caused philanthropists to abandon their efforts to instruct other persons as to how they might render their houses burglar-proof.

During the first few days of all this heated correspondence and scathing editorial rebuke, Major Fellspar and his lieutenants suffered greatly in temper, especially as they were permitted no reply. One reporter even had the temerity to approach the Inspector General for an interview on the robbery and on the efforts at discovery put forth by the Police; he subsequently declared that if ever a man looked assault and battery it was the Inspector General. Then, after a week of much ink-spilling and excitement, the press and the public gave up the jewels for lost and offered their sincerest condolences to Lady Rosedale.

She was now, of course, the most talked of person in the country. No social gathering but mentioned her name; at every dinner table everything that was known about her was amply discussed, with details invented for the purpose of making such discussion piquant and interesting.

She received innumerable callers. All the grandees of the official, professional, planter and mercantile world felt that they owed it to themselves to make the acquaintance of so remarkable a woman. By the popular imagination she was endowed with extraordinary qualities. No one troubled to ask himself this simple question: "what has this lady done, and in what way has she benefited art, religion, science, or anything or anyone indeed except herself?" Such a question would have been deemed irrelevant impertinent, if not indeed almost impious; for, after all, anyone might do something for art or religion—that sort of thing depends upon an accident of mind or temperament. But how many persons could afford to lose a splendid diamond necklace? It was generally admitted that Lady Rosedale bore her loss, not only with Christian fortitude, but with patrician calm. "Her manners," remarked one enthusiastic lady admirer, "have all the repose that stamps the case of Vere de Vere." This being said in Mr. Phipps's presence, he observed that he didn't know the de Veres, but supposed that they were quite nice and respectable people: did they often come up to the city? A remark which was regarded as purposely offensive, and so a coolness sprang up between the enthusiastic lady and Mr. Phipps.

To know Lady Rosedale was a very great privilege. It had always been a privilege—she had taken good care to make it so. But not it was a greater privilege than ever, for now her acquaintanceship was more sedulously sought than ever. Her afternoon teas were receptions. She required a small army of the Myrtle Bank Hotel's waiters to attend on her guests alone. On these occasions she sat in the midst of her admirers, saying kindly but condescending things about the police and local matters in general, and introducing Marian and her brother, when these happened to be back from work in time to meet her guests. She still patronised the director of the moving picture company and his leading lady, and these were happy in the knowledge that they were moving in the very best social circles of the colony. But Lawrence Beaman was father off from grace than before, while even Mr. Phipps, though he did sometimes enter the charmed circle of Lady Rosedale's acquaintance, was not regarded by her as belonging to it by right.

Lady Rosedale, if her wish had merely been to have Marian about her for her own convenience, could surely have dispensed with Marian now. That is what Mr. Phipps pointed out one afternoon to Lawrence, when the latter was again reproaching Lady Rosedale with arch-selfishness where Marian was concerned. But Lady Rosedale showed no desire to drop her young friend: "she's genuine where the girl is concerned, sure thing!" said Mr. Phipps; "it's the one redeeming feature in a character and career otherwise reprehensible." And Mr. Phipps did nothing in these days to prevent Lady Rosedale from monopoloising Marian, a circumstance which Lawrence was not slow to perceive.

It was about ten days after the picnic at Triton, and Lawrence by then had realised beyond the shadow of a doubt that Phipps had ranged himself amongst those whose object was to keep Marian away from him. He had hinted at this on one or two previous occasions, and Mr. Phipps had dismissed the subject as trifling; but Lawrence had become imbued with the belief that Marian was avoiding him, not only because she herself thought it best to do so but because Mr. Phipps had in some way, by speech or manner, suggested to her that she ought to do so. Phipps, he decided, was not quite candid with him; there was some reason for this decided change on his part, and he was keeping that reason secret. Phipps actually avoided him now, whenever he could do so without appearing rude; the old spontaneous cordiality that had existed between them—did it any longer exist? Ever since that Sunday night when, on their return from Triton, Marian had said that Phipps was his friend and knew that it would be best for him and her that they should be apart, Lawrence believed that he had seen some constraint in her manner when in the company of the older man. Once or twice what she had told him about her being suspected of stealing the necklaces flashed across his mind, and the question framed itself: did Phipps suspect her of being connected with the robbery? He dismissed the idea as impossible. But what was the true explanation of Phipps's change of manner?

On this afternoon, ten days after the picnic, and while Lady Rosedale was entertaining some friends, with Marian among them and he entirely outside of the circle, Lawrence was at the hotel, whither he had gone determined to have a talk with Phipps about Marina. He had seen neither of them during the previous four days. Marian had been away with some members of the moving picture company who had been taking pictures in a little town to the east of the island, some thirty miles away; Mr. Phipps had left the hotel within one hour of her departure, and had only returned this afternoon, his return synchronising with hers. Lawrence concluded that there was deliberate intention in the coincidence of Phipps's movements with those of Marian. So this afternoon he would have with Phipps what that gentleman himself would call, "a heart to heart talk."

Mr. Phipps was among Lady Rosedale's guests. Lawrence deliberately sent a bellboy to ask him for an interview. When she heard the message Lady Rosedale's eyebrows went up in astonishment at this impertinence; some of her guests, observing her look, glanced in Lawrence's direction, then glanced away as though he were of no importance. Marian kept her eyes steadily from him; but Mr. Phipps rose at once. Lady Rosedale did not particularly desire Mr. Phipps to remain, but she objected to anyone being so unceremoniously summoned from her party. "Can't you send and tell him that you will see him later on?" she suggested to Mr. Phipps.

"I can, Lady Rosedale," he replied; "but I gather from the attitude of that young man that he means to see me just as soon as he can: so I might as well go now. If needs be, he's going to fight on these lines all summer."

"Fight on these lines?" questioned Lady Rosedale, puzzled.

"Merely an amiable remark made by an American general during our civil war when he didn't know what else to do," explained Mr. Phipps to the further mystification of Lady Rosedale. "Our young friend wants to have a conversation with me, and he intends to have that conversation. So, if you'll excuse me, I'll trot over right now and hear what he has to say." And Mr. Phipps left the group and went towards Lawrence.

"I tried to get you earlier today," began Lawrence coldly, "but you could not spare me anytime."

"That's true enough, son; as you know, I have been coming and going from the country to the town these last few days, and have been almighty buse all the time."

"Not busier than usual," said Lawrence bluntly; "but simple too busy to see me. You have been avoiding me, Phipps. You have joined Stephen Braeme and Lady Rosedale against me: why?"

H. G. DE LISSER

"Lawrence," said Mr. Phipps quietly, "do you really believe I would join anyone against you?"

"At any rate, you are acting as they do where Marian is concerned, and that amounts to about the same thing. Why do you do it?"

"You forget," returned Mr. Phipps, "that the last time I asked you questions about yourself and this young lady—taking advantage of my superior years and friendship for both of you—you said that you had nothing definite in mind with regard to her, and that you couldn't think of doing heaven only knows what, and all that sort of thing. Seem to me, in the circumstances, that if I were the young lady's father I would feel that you had no serious intentions and ask you to discontinue your visits. That's a big mouthful to say to you, son, but you recognise the justice of it, don't you?"

"I did say something of what you have just repeated," admitted Lawrence, "but it was nonsense. You know I care for Marian. I have asked her to marry me."

"Of course, you did! Guessed it years ago, and saw on the night of the big dance down here that she had refused you. You had a look that night that recalled a Cuban revolution to my mind. Well, she's refused you more than once, hasn't she? She knows her own mind, and that's all that there is to it."

"She—she cares for me," said Lawrence, reddening; "but something keeps her back: her brother's objection. I do not set much store by that; there are limits to her brother's authority. But he is helped by her fear of him—it cannot be affection for him—and by Lady Rosedale's dislike of me. I have a few friends here; you I have always believed to be my friend, but you do not help me now. You could bring us together if you like, Phipps. She has great faith in you."

"She's a charming girl!" exclaimed Mr. Phipps; "but I don't think she's exactly the girl for you, Lawrence, and—"

"That is what I must judge for myself."

"She seems to think as I do," returned Mr. Phipps a trifle dryly.

"She would not if she did not believe that that was your opinion. You are influencing her in this matter."

Mr. Phipps shot a sharp glance at Lawrence. Mr. Phipps had hoped that Lawrence would not easily discover that his influence had been used to strengthen Marian's resolve to keep away from her love. Mr. Phipps had been very discreet in his actions and his hints and suggestions. But here was Lawrence openly charging him with doing what Lady

Rosedale had done ever since she had perceived that Lawrence was in love with Marian. He fenced.

"'Youthful jealously is a liar,' as one of your poets has so forcibly expressed it," said he; "you are rather hard on the old man, son."

"This is my belief," replied Lawrence; "you can easily prove that I am wrong. I have told you that I intend to marry Marian, who cares for me. She is keeping away from me because of some wild notion of hers that she ought to do so, and she is being encouraged to do so by the woman she is always with, and by her brother. You are a close friend of hers. Talk to her honestly about me, about herself—you know everything about me that is to be known, Phipps. I am not asking you to do anything you could regret."

"I cannot do it, Lawrence!"

Mr. Phipps voice was firm, his look resolute. The iron strain in him, which both Lawrence and Marian observed, was showing plainly now.

"You cannot do it?"

"No."

"Will not, you mean."

"Well, it amounts to the same thing, I suppose."

Lawrence was silent for a little while. When he spoke, his voice had a rather harsh tone.

"Your friend, Mrs. Hamilton is giving a party on Saturday night," he said; "Marian is invited and is going. You are invited, of course."

"The old lady has sent me a ticket yes," Mr. Phipps said lightly, "but that doesn't mean that I am going to claim admission."

"You are very friendly with the Hamiltons: can you get me an invitation? She will invite me if you hint that she might."

Mr. Phipps thought rapidly. Only because Lawrence knew Marian would be at this party, and that, once there, no one could prevent him from being with her—only because of this had Lawrence brought himself to ask that he should be invited to the party. Mr. Phipps realised that it must have cost the young man much to make the suggestion, the request, even to him. And if he refused to have anything to do with this invitation also? Something in his friend's face told him that Lawrence had made up him mind to be at the Hamiltons on Saturday night, even if he had to ask a dozen different persons to get him an invitation. And Nora would do so if she were asked. Mr. Phipps decided. "I'll fix it for you, if you like," he said.

"Thank you," said Lawrence briefly.

"And look here, Lawrence, I want you to understand that I am your friend, and that I am not acting against your interests. The girl herself has told you that she cannot marry you—hasn't she? Why not leave it at that, and go your old way like a man? You are not a weakling; you can stand a pretty hard blow. And you can't force her against her will."

"Is it really *her* will, Phipps?"

"She has said so, hasn't she?"

"That is not what I asked."

"I can say nothing more," replied Mr. Phipps firmly. "She has refused you, and that is enough for me. Remember, Lawrence, I am her friend as well as yours. I am acting as her friend."

"Yes?"

"Yes!"

"And only on that Sunday at Triton," continued Lawrence slowly, "did you discover that we had better remain apart? You said just now that you know that on the night of the dance down here—I asked her—you know what I mean."

"Clear as a crystal! Yes; it was on that Sunday at Triton that I made up my mind that you and she had each better go your own different ways; but I had been thinking something of the sort before. I wasn't quite certain before: that is all."

"And so," said Lawrence with asperity, "you were kind enough to give us the benefit of the doubt up to then. You thought you had the right to interfere in our business in any manner you liked."

"Do not let us quarrel, son: that would be foolish."

"I wish I understood you, Phipps," exclaimed Lawrence bitterly: "you sure do not think, do you, that Marian had anything to do with those infernal necklaces? She told me—but you would not dare to think anything of the sort! You haven't a mean mind. Even Lady Rosedale knows better, and if I thought that you—"

"I am her friend as I am yours," broke in Mr. Phipps, "and I am not in the habit of discussing the character of one friend with any other. One man's business is not another's, and you must not ask me too much."

"So then," began Lawrence suspiciously, but Mr. Phipps had begun to walk back to the party on the lawn.

When Lawrence passed him a little later, and he looked into the young man's face, he was not surprised that Lawrence deliberately avoided his glance. He had expected some action of the sort.

XX

A SLIP OF THE TONGUE

The next day, at about noon, Lawrence received from Mrs. Hamilton an invitation to her party of the following night. He regretted now that he had not withdrawn his request to Mr. Phipps that the latter should secure for him this invitation; he had no desire to be further indebted to his whilom friend. Becoming convinced that Phipps suspected Marian of the robbery, Lawrence had angrily resolved to sever all cordial relations with him; he as in that frame of mind when he was fain to regard as positively inimical those who appeared to be not unequivocally with him.

As for himself, he had made up his mind to induce Marian to marry him, and so to put an end to all her expressed and suggested fears, and to his own uncertainties. If he could not offer her affluence, at least he could provide her with comforts and protect her against annoyances. Of two things he was certain: that she did not like the life she was leading and that she cared for him: he therefore considered that there was sufficient justification for his urging upon her an immediate marriage. He would not be put off by Lady Rosedale's interferences or Mr. Phipps's manoeuvres; as for Stephen's objections, they should be altogether ignored. Having thus made up his mind to act promptly, he repaired that afternoon to the Myrtle Bank Hotel, where, happening to see both Mr. Phipps and Lady Rosedale, he pretended to be unaware of their presence. Stolidly he waited in the lobby until Marian should return from work, and when the car in which she rode drew up at the porch he was on the verandah to meet her. Marian, glancing at his face, perceived at once from its expression that Lawrence was determined to speak to her, and that not merely for a minute or two. Her eyes fluttered in the direction of Mr. Phipps: there was something of a question in them. Mr. Phipps shrugged his shoulders almost imperceptibly; then Marian seemed to make up her mind for herself. She readily assented to Lawrence's suggestion that they should go down to the seawall, his favourite rendezvous for a talk with her. Not until they had reached it, and seated themselves out of the hearing of other people there, did Lawrence speak.

"I told Phipps yesterday," he began abruptly, "that I felt he was endeavouring to influence you against me, and he did not deny it. Will you tell me why he is doing so, Marian?"

"Perhaps I ought," she answered in a low voice. "It would be fairer to you. But—but I am selfish; I am thinking of myself, and that has kept me from being as frank with you as I should be."

"Then it is not you, of your own will, who have tried to avoid me these last few days?" he asked, though he knew it was not she.

"No," she answered, after a moment's hesitation; "No. Your friend is right Lawrence, and I am wrong; but I want to be with you. . . I saw you here yesterday, and wished to come to you; but I could not, as you saw, and I thought I was glad I could not. But I wasn't really glad, dear. . . but Mr. Phipps is right. . ." Her voice trailed off into silence.

"I do not agree that Phipps is right," he replied in quiet, level tones. "I wish and intend to marry you: there's nothing I can think of that would prevent me now. Don't let us talk about what Phipps or any other person may think is best for you or me. Neither of us is a child to be hedged about with protective devices or frightened by solemn warnings from anyone."

"You can speak for yourself, but what about me?" she asked with infinity sadness.

"You too can judge for yourself; it is not what others think, but what you think about yourself think that matters."

His face was set and hard: the peculiar half-suggestions of Phipps, the insistence of Marian herself that Phipps was right, had not failed to have a certain effect upon him. What could it be that made Marian speak so despairingly as she did? The necklaces? But, good God! She could not be a thief. Even if she had—he forced himself to face that issue—even if she had taken the necklaces, she was no thief: there must surely be some reason for her action, something that she could explain. He dared not put his thought into words; dared not tell her that, even though she had taken the necklaces for some extraordinary reason which she could not now explain, he was satisfied that was no guilty thing, that her soul remained unsmirched. He knew that the moment he began, haltingly, painfully, to protest his belief in her uprightness and honesty, a barrier would build itself between them. She herself shrank from mentioning what stood between them. She had spoken to him, nearly two weeks ago, of the suspicion which she was sure was entertained with regard to her, and he had bade her dismiss the very idea from her mind. How could he now dare say that if even the suspicion were still held, even if she had had something to do with the disappearance of the necklaces, that could make no difference to him? And then was he so certain after all that it would make no difference to him? Perhaps she saw farther than he did, knew him better than he knew him. . . no; he wished to hear nothing from her that would make him believe that she had been in anyway connected with a crime. He did not believe it, and would not believe it. There was some miserable mistake somewhere. He had made up his mind.

"If you will marry me, by special license if you like," he said, "we can let the others think what they please about our act. You and I alone are concerned."

She smiled faintly; she had been watching the various expressions as they swiftly followed one another over his face, had guessed something of what he had been thinking. "Let us put marrying out of the question," she said definitely; "and as for not meeting in the future. . ."

"Yes?"

"I think it is useless my trying not to meet you; useless, because you will insist, and because I want to meet you, to be with you."

"Then, Marian? . . ."

"Let us be as we were before we went to Triton. And don't think harshly of your friend; he has meant well. He is wonderful, he is a clever man; but he thinks I am stronger than I am, Lawrence, and that you—"

"It doesn't much matter what he thinks of me."

"And that you," she continued, as if he had not been interrupted, "are less determined than you are.

"I knew you better than he did," she went on, with perhaps just a little thrill of pride in her belief that she understood Lawrence's character more thoroughly, in this particular connection, than even the penetrating Mr. Phipps. "I knew that nothing I could do would keep you away from me."

"I love you, and nothing will keep me away from you," he said, with a ring of determination in his voice. "But there must be no talk, now, you say, about our getting married?"

She noticed that, "now," but she resolved not to argue with him on it. It did not matter much one way or the other.

"No; we must meet and act as friends, not lovers: you will promise?"

"It is hard," said he, "but I promise—to do my best."

"That will make it easier for both of us."

He knew that she would have to go to her room to change for dinner: he asked the old question, which indeed she expected:

"I shall see you down here tonight?"

"Yes," she consented; "and remember that your friend has been right."

But although Marian had spoken of Mr. Phipps as having acted rightly, Lawrence was still conscious of a marked coldness in his heart towards Mr. Phipps. He could not forgive Phipps for feeling or believing that there was something wrong about Marin; Phipps, he argued, should have found such a feeling or belief impossible; should resolutely have crushed it out of his mind. It was awful to think of his friend entertaining any suspicion of Marian: all the more awful because he, Lawrence, was usually prepared to back Phipps's judgement against that of any other man he knew. That very fact irritated him. It might not, had he himself not been haunted with a secret longing for certainty which he would not frankly acknowledge. There was something to be explained, that was patent; and when Marian left him her words came to life again in his memory. Nothing could come between them, and yet this terrible uncertainty, mystery, whatever it was, would continue to haunt and harass him, as—her look and voice proved that—it was harassing her. So some of the rage against inexplicable circumstances that possessed him was directed against his old friend, whom he again avoided as he left the hotel that afternoon. And Mr. Phipps divined the reason of his aloofness, and had a shrewd idea that Marian also was not as kindly disposed towards him as she had been before he had endeavoured to put barriers between herself and Lawrence.

Nor was she. Marian was not vividly conscious that she entertained any sort of resentment against Mr. Phipps; but she knew that he would not approve of her meeting Lawrence frequently, of being much alone with him. Mr. Phipps had suggested to her that it would not be wise: delicately suggested it, vaguely, hinting at reasons without specifying them. She had said nothing, but had resolved to follow his advice, but now she felt that she could never maintain of her own will and motion that resolution to the end, and she concluded that Mr. Phipps would blame her, not openly, but in his mind. That moved her to resentment, a vague, undefined, unacknowledged resentment; it meant that henceforth she took, like Lawrence, would hold herself aloof from Mr. Phipps.

He realised this quite clearly that evening; her hurried greeting and passing of him as she went upstairs to dress for dinner brought it home to his quick mind—a mere gesture was often enough for Mr. Phipps. "It seems to me that I haven't a friend in this blooming caravanserai," he mused half-humorously. Nevertheless he met the two of them later that night and offered to take them up to Mrs. Hamilton's party in his car. Marian thanked him, but said she would go with Lady Rosedale; Lawrence said that he had already made other arrangements for going to the party. So the next night Mr. Phipps went alone.

The Hamiltons lived about four miles from the Myrtle Bank Hotel in one of the handsome villas situated north of the city. Their home stood in several acres of land, the area immediately in front of the building being laid out in walks and flower gardens, and in a spacious lawn for tennis. To the left of the house, a little distance away, were rows and clumps of great trees with here and there a garden bench or chair for any who might choose to wander among them. The house itself had been built with an eye to elegance of appearance as well as comfort; it was two storeys high, the apartments were commodious and lofty, and tastefully furnished.

Over eighty people were assembled in the big drawing room and on the adjoining verandahs upon which the drawing room opened; amongst these were about ten members of the moving picture company. Inspector Harmsworth came early, and Mr. Phipps, observing him closely, noticed that he seemed contented with the number of dances with Nora which he jotted down on both their programmes. From this Mr. Phipps concluded that the young man had been making excellent use of his time during the last few days, though Stephen still seemed a high favourite with Nora. Other admirers, of whom Nora had many, were definitely far behind these two in securing her for a partner.

Lawrence knew most of the persons present, slightly for the most part. But if he, as was his habit and inclination, were disposed to be reserved, a few of them, and those the most highly placed, gave him no chance of being so. They were friendly. Lady Rosedale observed and was somewhat impressed. For that lady, though affecting great independence of judgement, was secretly influenced by what other people said and did, and her hostility to Lawrence had had its origin as much in her belief that he lacked social position as that he was a sort of poor struggling employee. Noticing that he was genuinely welcomed by some of Mrs. Hamilton's friends, she was not, on this occasion, inclined to regard as a positive calamity his temporary close association with Marian. One night would not greatly matter. Still she felt he must be watched, as all ineligible suitors should be, even though, as Major Fellspar had assured her, there could be no possible connecting of him with her recent loss.

Promptly at nine o'clock the hired orchestra struck up a dance tune and the dancing began. Those who did not care to dance, or could not, either watched the others from the vine-sheltered verandah where the white stephanotis filled the air with pleasant odour, or wandered into the grounds now deep in darkness and fragrant with the perfume of flowers.

The moments flew quickly away to the accompaniment of merry music, and the sound of laughing voices and swiftly-moving feet. As midnight approached, the tropical moon, now some days past its full, emerged into the sky. The brilliant sphere of cold, clear light rose in a heaven of pale blue, obliterating almost every star, and everything touched and illuminated by its glow assumed a soft distinctness, fairylike and beautiful, while gentle breezes murmured through the branches of the trees, which cast vague, tremulous shadows on the ground.

About this hour Marian and Lawrence were sitting out one of the dances that she had given to him. On a garden bench set in the midst of a group of high, heavy-foliaged trees they sat, silent for the most part, an access of delightful emotions inhibiting expression. Now and then other couples came near to them or passed by, each intent on its own affairs; in that crepuscule no face could be distinctly seen, and the forms as they moved seemed but dimly familiar. Sitting thus silent, Marian and Lawrence were scarcely visible save to any who might come directly upon them. They heard footsteps, apparently, of people approaching them, but took no notice. Two figures, a man's and a woman's, came into view. Then the man's voice murmured softly but distinctly, "I love you," and Marian sprang to her feet.

Lawrence was startled. He had always regarded Marian as one too timorous by nature for bold and decisive action; in a moment he was undeceived. She had stepped towards the two, the man and the woman, who had come upon them, and in a voice pitched low, but vibrant with anger, she was addressing the man. "You have no right to say that to Nora!" she exclaimed, "you know that you have none! You told me you would leave her alone, though I might have known that nothing you could say would mean anything to you." She ceased, breathing quickly; one could guess, if not see, that her body was trembling violently.

"Marian!" cried Nora Hamilton sharply but quietly, and in her voice anger struggled with shame for the mastery. Nora was ashamed at having been caught in the midst of what seemed to be a proposal, though she felt that she had done nothing to be ashamed of. She was angry, outraged, that Marian should thus dare to intrude upon her. But even at this moment Nora remembered that Marian was her guest.

"This is not the first time you have spied upon me," retorted Stephen, controlling his voice with a mighty effort, "you and this gentleman, who seems to have made himself your constant companion—or more! As you are so much interested in each other's company, I should think it would be only good manners for you not to thrust yourselves where you are not wanted."

The rudeness of this remark moved Lawrence to begin a protest, but Marian was before him. "I overheard purely by accident what you were saying to Nora," she said, "though I should certainly have followed and interrupted you on purpose if I had known beforehand what you were going to do. This man,"—she turned to Nora—"has no right to speak to you as he is doing. He is infinitely beneath you. He is only—only playing with you: it is a habit of his." She faced Stephen again, and her voice quivered with contempt as she cried, "You to make love to any girl—you—you—thie—"

A sudden exclamation from him silence the word which trembled on her lips, but Lawrence guessed instantly what it was, though Nora did not.

"You are inclined to be abusive and shrewish," retorted Stephen hoarsely, but still keeping extraordinary control over his voice. "I am afraid we do not appear to you as a well-bred family, Miss Hamilton. Shall we go inside?"

Nora moved off with him without a word, and Lawrence waited until they disappeared. Then he would have retaken the seat they had vacated, but Marian shook her head. She seemed afraid to speak; she had said more than she had intended, Lawrence felt. In sympathy with her feeling, he wished to pretend that he had not understood her meaning. They went slowly back to the house.

On the verandah they found Stephen waiting for them, with hat and cloak, ready to take his departure. His face was set, dark and grim; there was a menacing glint in his eyes. "I am going down to the hotel Marian," he said quietly, "and I want you to come with me." He spoke in a manner which showed that he intended to insist upon this: the look in his eyes left no doubt as to his determination.

H. G. DE LISSER

"Very well," she replied, and slipped into the house to say goodbye to her hostess and to tell Lady Rosedale that she was going. She returned to the verandah, accompanied by Lady Rosedale. The three of them went down to the hotel together.

Almost immediately after, Lawrence took his departure. He wanted to think over what he had just heard and seen. The key to the mystery of Marian's conduct, her hesitancies and her sadness, the key to Mr. Phipps's hints and warnings, he felt that he had discovered by the mere utterance of a half-formed word. Stephen Braeme was the man who had robbed Lady Rosedale's jewels, and Marian knew it and dared not say a word. She was his sister, the disgrace if not the penalty of the act would be equally hers if the truth were known. But she was making far too much of her connection with Stephen: how could she be in anyway responsible for what he did? Who could blame her for his acts? Who could point to her in reproach? Lawrence went to bed that night with the determination to urge this aspect of the matter upon her when they should meet again.

The next day when he went to the hotel, he was told that she was keeping her room. On the following afternoon he was again at the Myrtle Bank waiting for her return from work; but when she came she greeted him with the most formal of bows, and went direct to her room. He sent her up a note, asking if she could see him then, or later on; the reply was brief: "Not now, nor at any other time. You must respect this wish of mine. M. B." And that evening she never left Lady Rosedale's side, never looked in his direction, and he noticed that her face was pale and drawn, her whole attitude that of one whose mind is made up irrevocably. Lawrence realised that it was hopeless to attempt to approach her. There was no breaking through that armour of reserve.

XXI

The Stranger

N o, my dear," Lady Rosedale had said with an expression of intense disinterestedness, "It is you who must make the presentation to dear Marian: I could not think of doing it. I dislike being in the limelight. Of course, there are certain social duties which one cannot escape, and one's position entails obligations. I have recognised that even here: but I much prefer to remain in the background; my disposition is essentially retiring."

It was to Miss Hellingworth, the star actress of the moving picture company, that Lady Rosedale was thus giving an entirely inaccurate description of her character; and as the star actress was a young woman with some insight into character she was not in the least deceived. Yet she was flattered. Lady Rosedale desired that she should occupy the leading place in a little function to take place on the following afternoon, and to stand socially just next to Lady Rosedale was a distinction not to be despised even by a star of some magnitude in the moving picture firmament.

Some two weeks before, as has already been mentioned, it had occurred to the chief actor of the moving picture company that a broach in lieu of that which Marian had lost in the burglary should be presented to her, and among the members of the company and the guests at the hotel no less than eight hundred dollars had been subscribed for the purpose. The order had straightway been despatched to New York, and now the broach had arrived. This was Wednesday: the presentation would be made on the next afternoon, and arrangements for it were already forward. Tonight invitations would be sent out, and Lady Rosedale had kindly consented that they should be sent in her name.

But there was one thing upon which Lady Rosedale was firm: she would not present the broach to Marian. That must be done by someother lady. She herself suggested Miss Hellingworth who, in her way, was decidedly a personage and could also dispense social benedictions, though not of course with the same amplitude and recognised graciousness as Lady Rosedale. Lady Rosedale, in determining to play second fiddle in the pleasant little ceremony of the coming Thursday, was conscious of that virtuous glow which accompanies an act of self-abnegation. Subconsciously she may have felt that while Marian was to receive a broach, Marian's loss was nothing compared to hers; consequently it was inevitable that during the speeches to be made she herself would be awarded, as it were, a vote of condolence. Indeed, given the character of the star actress, it could confidently be predicted that for every reference in her address to Marian, there would be two at least to "dear Lady Rosedale." So nothing could move Lady Rosedale from her determination that not she, but Miss Hellingworth, must take the leading part in the presentation. "You will do it so well, my dear," she graciously remarked, "and I am naturally retiring."

The manager of the hotel, obliging and indefatigable as usual, insisted upon arranging a proper *mise-en-scène* for the function. The moving picture company was to return on Thursday afternoon a little earlier than usual from work; at half-past four precisely the function would begin. The eastern section of the big ballroom was accordingly decorated most tastefully with flags; a low table, behind which three chairs were set, was placed in this part of the room; on this table would repose the box containing the broach to be presented, in these chairs would sit Lady Rosedale, Miss Hellingworth and Marian.

At about three o'clock Mr. Phipps appeared upon the scene and surveyed it with what appeared to be quiet satisfaction. The manager happened to be showing Lady Rosedale the arrangements he had made; naturally, Mr. Phipps joined them. "I wish," said he to Lady Rosedale, "that there were going to be two presentations this afternoon: the broach to Miss Braeme and two necklaces to you. I guess, though I know you can stand a loss like a British regiment of soldiers can stand a charge, Lady Rosedale, that you would not mind having that diamond necklace back."

"It is natural that I should wish it, is it not?" she asked.

"Natural," agreed Mr. Phipps sympathetically, "but of course you have given up expecting to see even a single pearl or a single diamond returned to you, haven't you?"

"I am coming to the conclusion that I might as well give up any hope," replied Lady Rosedale with intense bitterness. "The police here are quite incapable. Even Major Fellspar, who promised so much, seems to have given up trying. A really capable policeman would have done something by now."

"He may yet do something," said Mr. Phipps soothingly. "He may at any moment determine to arrest some perfectly innocent person: I have been expecting that all this time. At one time I thought he was going to arrest me."

"Do you feel that you should be arrested?" Lady Rosedale asked; "perhaps it may happen." She spoke with some attempt at badinage, but there was a note of seriousness in her voice.

"Well, I don't know," returned Mr. Phipps judicially. "More or less, we all do things for which we might righteously be arrested; and in dealing with a man like Major Fellspar one must expect the unexpected. By the way, you never wore your diamond necklace here, did you?"

"It was a very gorgeous affair," said Lady Rosedale coldly; "and at my age I do not consider that it is proper to deck myself out with jewellery. I was very fond of wearing it ten years ago."

"Dignity unadorned is dignity at its height," cried Mr. Phipps in tones of admiration. "Expect plenty of people here this afternoon?" he continued, quickly changing the subject.

"Quite a number is sure to come," the manager remarked. "I expect that not only this part of the room will be full, but part of the verandah. We shall have a tea dansant afterwards."

"Such is life in the tropics," commented Mr. Phipps, "the life of those who can afford it, I mean. A nice young lady gets a fine diamond broach, there is dancing afterwards, and only Lady Rosedale is reminded of a cruel loss. Yet I doubt if anyone here will feel happier than Lady Rosedale this afternoon."

"Why?" enquired that lady.

"Because," said Mr. Phipps, with a gallant bow, "you always prefer the happiness of others to your own, and that brings me true happiness."

Lady Rosedale, for a moment, concluded that Mr. Phipps was a man of real discernment, he seemed to read her character so well!

"We'll see each other a little later," said Mr. Phipps, and took himself away; but there was already a crowd on the spot when he reappeared and he was separated by many persons from Lady Rosedale.

Lawrence was there. He had heard about this function, and if he could do no more than merely bow to Marian, at least there was some pleasure in seeing her, in being near to her, in waiting with what patience he could command until her strange and sudden reserve disappeared and they should be as they had been before. Major Fellspar came also in response to Lady Rosedale's invitation; the Hamiltons came, and many others who were residents within three or four miles of the hotel. All the guests in the hotel were on the spot. There was quite a crowd assembled when Miss Hellingworth rose to express her great pleasure at having been asked to present to one of the most charming and popular members of the company a slight token of the esteem in which she was held, and to express the regret which everyone felt at the great loss sustained by Lady Rosedale, for whom everyone who knew her entertained the highest affection and most unbounded regard, etc. Thus the lady proceeded for a little while, with Lady Rosedale's name figuring in her speech sufficiently to gratify even that not unexacting personage, who sat with mien composed as some of her wonderful qualities were detailed for the public's edification. There was a press reporter present: he had asked for admission. His pencil flew busily over the pages of his notebook. Lady Rosedale observed him through the corner of one eye. Certainly she was as happy as anyone else present; perhaps more than anyone; which showed that Mr. Phipps's prediction had not been at all extravagant.

Marian sat calm, but pale, with signs of tension visible only to the observant. She appeared to find no pleasure in this function. Lawrence was not far from her, but she never once glanced in his direction. Stephen stood immediately behind her, with other members of the moving picture company, the director being much in evidence, as he always succeeded in being. The chief actor, the man who had made this presentation possible by suggesting that Marian should be given a broach in place of the one she had lost, was called upon to speak after Miss Hellingworth, and this he did as briefly as possible, but made no sort of allusion to the fact that he had had anything to do with the making of this present. He also said nothing about Lady Rosedale. His remarks were not loudly applauded.

Then the little package on the table was opened, the broach extracted and placed in Marian's hand, and a murmur of admiration immediately made itself heard both from those who saw and from those who did not see it. This murmur was, so to speak, ready-made; but the little trinket was really a pretty piece of workmanship and deserved appreciation. Marian at once handed it to Lady Rosedale, who glanced at it and passed it to Major Fellspar. It went from hand to hand amongst those acquainted with Marian, who at the same time was heartily congratulated by those standing nearest to her.

While the broach was still being admired there appeared one of the hotel's bellboys with some letters and parcels that had arrived by the last afternoon mail. He moved leisurely, chanting the names of those for whom he had anything, and delivering these when claimed. "Miss Braeme," he called, and approached Marian, who was now standing, the ceremony in which she had figured being practically over. To her he handed a small parcel, very like that which had contained the broach; she held it in her hand mechanically, making no attempt to open it, until Miss Hellingworth laughingly suggested that it might be another present. Miss Hellingworth said this, animated by curiosity; Marian, smiling slightly, undid the string and the wrapper, opened the little box, gasped, and sat suddenly down in the chair behind her. She was staring at the thing in her hand with undisguised amazement, even with consternation; and as Stephen caught sight of it a sharp exclamation escaped him.

"Well! What is this!" exclaimed Lady Rosedale, in tones of wonder, and Major Fellspar, being forwarded, perceived, nestling in a bed of cotton wool, glinting back the light that fell upon it, a beautiful diamond broach.

"It is Marian's broach, the one that was stolen when my jewellery was robbed!" cried Lady Rosedale; "where had it come from?"

Stephen had snatched up the broach and was turning it over in his fingers. "It is either the same or identical with hers," he admitted: "what does it mean?"

Mr. Phipps, aware that something unusual had happened, now rapidly edged himself backwards towards the verandah's railing. Thursting his heels into the open woodwork of the railing, and resting his hands on the top of it, he managed with a jerk to elevate himself a few inches above the heads of those who were standing about. His quick eyes took in the scene at a glance; he saw that Marian had collapsed, thought already she was endeavouring to regain her self-possession; Stephen was darting sharp enquiring glances around as if to discover the sender of this last broach; Major Fellspar, who had the trinket in his hand, was looking at it minutely. There was a babble of voices, a confused interrogatory addressed to no one in particular.

"Where did this come from?"

"Who sent it?"

"The thief, is it not?"

"But why?"

"If the thief sent it back, what about the necklaces?"

"If we can find out who sent this, we shall know where the necklaces are," cried one of the guests; and Mr. Phipps saw Major Fellspar return the broach to Marian, then stoop and secure the box and the wrapper in which it had been enclosed and put them in his pocket. Mr. Phipps, watching the Inspector General closely, noticed that there was a look of quiet reserve on his face, and when Major Fellspar had secured the box and the wrapper he began glancing about him as if to find someone whom he evidently expected to be present.

Mr. Phipps tried to follow the direction of his glances; suddenly, and entirely by accident, as his eye swept over a group of persons standing by the wide southern door of the section of the room in which the presentation to Marian had been made, Mr. Phipps saw a tall, clean-shaven man, who, quite obviously, was a stranger; evidently one of the new arrivals who had come by the New York boat the day before. There was a number of other new guests present, but Mr. Phipps paid no attention to these. The man on whom his eyes were fixed, he perceived, was intently noting the confusion in the group amongst whom was Marian. A look of recognition flashed over Mr. Phipps's face; at once he sprang from his point of vantage and mingled with the people about. He seemed anxious to escape observation. As unobtrusively, but as rapidly as he could, he began to move towards the northwestern end of the verandah.

Arrived there, Mr. Phipps, threw a quick glance around to see if he were noticed. He was not; everybody's back was turned to him; everybody seemed eager to see the broach that had so strangely been returned. Satisfied that he attracted no attention, he cast, as it were casually, one leg over the railing, followed it with the other leg, and jumped into the garden but two feet below. He hurried round to the hotel's front entrance; then, with calculated leisurely step, entered the lobby and went up the steps leading to the first floor. He passed into his room, closing only the slat-door behind him, then sat on the edge of his bed listening sharply. Three or four minutes afterwards he heard footsteps; measuring the distance with his ear, he concluded that the steps paused just about where Marian's door should be. "The girl is ill, and they have brought her up," he mused; then he heard the footsteps repass.

Silently opening his slat-door, he peeped after the retreating figures: there were two. "Lady Rosedale has remained with her," he thought, and again sat down to wait.

In about ten minutes he heard Lady Rosedale's well-known tread; to make absolutely sure, he peeped out when certain that she was a little distance away from his room door. He recognised Lady Rosedale's unmistakable back, as she pressed on, anxious to get downstairs once more to hear all that was being said about the strange reappearance of Marian's broach and the possible recovery of her own jewellery.

Mr. Phipps had counted upon her doing something of the sort; he had always said that she was true to form.

No sooner had she disappeared than he sat down and scribbled a brief note. "You must make an effort," he wrote, "and get down to dinner. Go down early, say half-past six: there will not be many people about then. I will be at the pier; meet me there. Never mind how ill you feel; you must see me before dinner. It is absolutely necessary. Write your answer on this same sheet of paper and send it back by the bearer, in an envelope." He signed the letter then rang for a bellboy and bade him to take the letter to Miss Braeme's room and wait for an answer. In sealed envelope from him, handed him a shilling, and sent him downstairs for a cocktail. When the boy left the room, he read Marian's reply: two words only, "all right," and her initials. He tore the sheet of paper into tiny fragments and threw them into the basin in his room, turning on the tap as he did so and watching the fragments disappear down the waste pipe. The boy came back with the cocktail and went away again, and Mr. Phipps sent the liquor the way that the pieces of his letter had gone. He went and stood by his window for sometime, scanning the people passing the hotel westward, in motor cars and in cabs.

He was not certain if he saw in one of these the stranger at the sight of whom he had been so startled a little while before; but he thought he did. Others he recognised quite plainly. The guests were leaving the hotel, to spread the news of the remarkable reappearance of a broach reported stolen, and to revive once more the faded interest in the jewel robbery. When it was about twenty minutes to six, and Mr. Phipps judged that all those who had been at the presentation must now either have gone home or have retired to their rooms to change for dinner, he went downstairs and strolled idly towards the pier. As he had anticipated, there were very few folk about, and none of them was the man for whom his eyes searched keenly. After a swift but searching exploration, Mr. Phipps's face assumed a relieved expression.

In another few minutes he saw Marian approaching, and went casually to meet her with a gesture of welcome. "Will you take pity on an old man and talk to him for a while before dinner?" he asked, loudly enough for one or two people to hear; "I have to go out to dine this evening, and am trying to kill the time before then." There was no one on the seawall; he led her there; then at once he began to talk in earnest, low, incisive tones. Marian was desperately nervous. Mr. Phipps himself was grave, graver than she had ever seen him before, and with a strength of purpose showing in his set mouth and narrowed eyes that seemed to contradict entirely the reputation he had gained for light-hearted and even fussy frivolity.

Anyone could see them, but none could overhear, for Mr. Phipps's voice was purposely lowered, and Marian spoke in a voice audible to his ear alone. What he was saying was evidently of the utmost importance to here, for her face went deathly white, her hands were clenched, and perhaps only the influence of his stronger personality and the need there was for self-possession on her part prevented her from again collapsing as she had done that afternoon. She spoke with effort, with eyes that looked straight in front of her, seeing nothing; and for over an hour this queer, earnest talk in an undertone went on. Then he suggested something to her and she shook her head sharply as if the very idea were impossible.

"You cannot avoid it," said Mr. Phipps tensely, "and it would be serious if anyone thought you were deliberately trying to do so. People will want to talk to you about the robbery and the broach: you will have to go through with it. Oh, I know it is awfully hard, but you'll have to go through with it. You have grit; that is why I am talking to you like this, why I have told you everything. I made a great mistake today: I am a big fool," he added half whimsically, "but I could hardly guess that that man would be there. Yet—who is to tell?—Perhaps I have drawn a red herring across his trail. Pull yourself together, my dear, and go through with the game bravely tonight; tomorrow we'll get on the right side of circumstances somehow. You can trust me that far."

And when they went back to the verandah he ordered a half bottle of champagne and insisted on Marian drinking a full glass of it. It brought some colour to her cheeks. His talk, his self-assurance, made a deep impression upon her; when Lady Rosedale came down and joined them she was more her normal self than she had been an hour before. Mr. Phipps surrendered Marian to Lady Rosedale with a few inconsequential words, and with a half-pathetic lament that he was compelled to leave them. Then he ordered his car, having observed that the strange man, for whom he had not ceased to watch, was nowhere to be seen. "But he is on the job all right enough," he muttered, and (as he drove out of the Myrtle Bank Hotel), "I wonder if he recognised me?" Mr. Phipps thought not, but knew that recognition was in any case bound to come within the next twenty-four hours.

"But I have a few hours' start of him anyway," he concluded, not without satisfaction.

XXII

The Stranger Explains

The stranger, as a matter of fact, had left the Myrtle Bank Hotel shortly after Marian had gone upstairs subsequent to the extraordinary reappearance of her diamond broach, and the confusion occasioned thereby. On leaving the hotel he drove straight to the high-walled principal police station of the city in which were situated the offices of the Detective Department. There he was met by Inspector Harmsworth, who informed him that the Inspector General would be calling round later on, and that Detective Sergeant Brown had been ordered to report himself there as soon as possible. Brown had been in Spanish Town that day, but was expected back the last passenger train, which would arrive soon after six o'clock.

At about half-past six Major Fellspar arrived, and almost upon his heels came Brown. It was evident that the stranger was held in high respect by Inspector Harmsworth, while Detective Brown regarded him with something approaching awe. Major Fellspar, as befitted his position, evinced no emotion whatever. He immediately addressed to the stranger a question which showed that he had met and talked with him before. "Is it the same man?" he asked, without any preliminaries.

"Sure," returned the other laconically; "have you many formalities about extradition to go through down here?"

"You will have to see the Attorney General tomorrow, and then you must appear before a judge and swear to your charge. We can expedite you; in a day or so everything should be fixed," explained Major Fellspar.

"And he can't make a getaway?"

"He hasn't had his passport vised, and he couldn't attempt to get it done without our knowing. He can't even hide as a stowaway on board a ship, for all the outgoing ships will be warned and watched. Did he see you?"

"I don't think he did, and I don't believe he would know me if he did; so that doesn't matter."

"Very well; that is all right from your point of view; now what about our own affair? We want to hold him on that too; we want those necklaces back if we can get them."

"I must talk to your men about that, sir," said the American detective. "The return of that broach is a bit puzzling, isn't it?"

"I don't understand it," confessed Major Fellspar; "unless it was sent back to throw us off any scent we might have picked up. But even so. . . no, I can make nothing at all of it. I admit I am all at sea."

The American detective, James B. Baker by name, made no effort to relieve Major Fellspar's perplexity, but, taking out of an inner pocket a packet of papers on the jewel robbery with which he had a earlier in the day been furnished by Major Fellspar, laid it on the table before him and turned to question Detective Brown. Brown looked ill at ease; he had often heard of American detectives and had a keen desire that the Jamaica Detective Department should appear to good advantage before eminent a critic.

"I gather from your chief," said Mr. Baker, "that from the first you suspected this young lady, Miss Braeme, but you didn't think of her brother: is that right?"

"Yes, sir," said Brown nervously.

"Then you have never made any attempt to find out definitely whether Mr. Braeme went upstairs on the night of the robbery?"

"I didn't ask about him specially," Brown admitted; "I asked the night-maid to tell me who she remembered going about the corridor that night, but there was so many people that she didn't know that—"

"I see," interrupted the American; "I guessed as much. And it wouldn't have helped, I am thinking, if you had asked her specially about Braeme, for if she had seen him he would have gone downstairs again."

"You are sure, then," said the Inspector General, "that your man and mine are the same?"

"I have no doubt of it," said Baker with a slight smile; "I was sure of it before I left New York. If you don't mind my speaking plainly, sir, I may say that it ought to have been quite clear that this young woman who calls herself Miss Braeme knew more about the robbery than she tried to make out. This man here—" he indicated Brown—"was on the right track from the start; he even guessed that she had an accomplice who helped her to get away with the necklaces. Who more likely to be that accomplice than her brother?"

"I agree," exclaimed Major Fellspar, "but that did not occur to me until sometime after. Brown did think she had an accomplice, but he suspected someone else, a Mr. Phipps. You see, Braeme does not live at the Myrtle Bank."

"It wasn't necessary for him to do so in the circumstances; his sister was there. When he went into her room that night—"

"So you think he was in her room?"

"Sure. How else could he have got the stuff? She could have passed it out to him through her window, of course, but he would not be sure just when she would hand it over, and he would run a great risk if he was too long on the verandah roof. Sure he was in her room when she retired that night. It was dead easy."

"You mean she had arranged it?"

"Sure."

"But suppose anyone had entered her room with her that night?"

"I went through one or two rooms at the Myrtle Bank today," replied Baker: "I said I would like to see them, if there was no objection, before making up my mind whether I would stay there. Those that I saw had two closets; one curtained and the other with a heavy door. The closet with the door could quite comfortably conceal more than one man; you would only know anyone was in it if you opened the door. See? Now if she had arranged with him that he should hide in her room, she would have left her room door open. He walks up the staircase—"

"He couldn't escape being seen by the clerks in the booking office," interposed Inspector Harmsworth, "You forget that. And they would know him. They would have remembered if he had gone upstairs during that night. There were also certain to have been a few people in the lobby."

The American smiled with the air of one to whom obvious explanations are too obvious to contain the truth. "That's what you might think," he said, "but to notice that a particular man has gone up a short flight of steps, up and down which people are continually passing, means either that you are particularly watching for him, or that something occurred to fix the fact in your mind. The clerks were doing their work as usual, I guess, and weren't looking out to see what people were going upstairs. Nor was anyone else. Had Braeme met anybody on the staircase or in the corridor who knew him and could have sworn to his identity, it would have been different. He would probably have gone but a little way, and then gone downstairs again to wait for another time. Had he met the night-maid or a bellboy or a permanent guest in the corridor, there would have been no robbery that night. But the hotel is built in a sort of semi-circular form—you know that. The night-maid might as easily be at one side of it as the other, and when our man got on to the first floor she must have been at the other side of it. Well, you can easily see for yourselves what happened. The passage is carpeted and he wears dancing shoes. He meets no one, and he knows that it is once chance in a hundred that anyone in the lobby or the booking office noticed that he ran up the steps. They were not watching him, you see, but he was watching them. Besides, could any guest venture to connect him with a big steal on the strength of a sort of belief that they saw him running up the steps, unless the suggestion was squarely put to them? People don't like to make positive accusations that they can't prove. That might get them in trouble."

"Yes, that may be so," said the Inspector General thoughtfully.

"He knows this girl's room," the detective continued, "opens it and slips into it. I should figure that he did this between twelve and one o'clock, when people would be going to bed, one by one, but not as yet in any numbers. She comes up a little past one o'clock and hands him over the pearl necklace. He waits for a little while, then gets into the other lady's room."

"But how?" asked Major Fellspar.

"There are two ways. He could get out of into any room by the windows: there is no difficulty about that to an active man, and he is one. Or he may have had a key to open the old lady's door. From what you have written here, sir,"—(he touched the papers before him)—"I gather that he must have had a false key to fit her trunk."

"But, sir," deferentially suggested Brown, "how could he get one made, unless he made it himself?"

"He could have got a good impression of the key and of the lock through his sister, couldn't he? And he could have sent it over to some pal of his in New York, couldn't he, and have got a key made? There's nothing difficult in that. Or he may have a number of false keys for jobs of this kind: that is very likely. He knew of the diamond necklace and he went straight for it: he knew where to find it—his sister told him. He had now to get away. He doesn't live in the hotel, so he wouldn't dare risk being seen in the corridor or the lobby long after the dance was over. And he couldn't have escaped being noticed if he had tried to leave by the way of the staircase and the lobby after all the other people had gone home. So he just got out of the lady's room by way of the window, and crept along the verandah room until he came to the western end of it, which almost overhands the bar room, as you know. He was dressed in black and the night was dark. There was nobody about at that hour: everyone had gone home or to bed. The only person he might meet was the night watchman, and he kept his eye peeled for him. He didn't see anyone; all he had to do was to let himself quickly down over the edge of the verandah roof: the height is not more than about ten feet, which meant for him a fall of not more than a couple of feet when he let go his hold on the guttering. He landed square and softly on the soles of his shoes; had anyone caught sight of him there would have been a chase, but once out of the hotel he would probably have got away among some of your narrow lanes here. You see, he had it all mapped out beforehand in his mind; he took some risk: that couldn't be avoided. But with a popular sister inside the house the risk wasn't so big after all. That fellow, Quesada, is as sharp as they make 'em."

"Quesada?" questioned Major Fellspar in surprise.

"Quesada?" echoed Inspector Harmsworth.

"That's his real name; Braeme is the name he acts under, though I may say that it is legally his now. He changed it from Quesada to Braeme about two years ago in New York; and as lots of people have been changing their names during and since the war—especially the foreign ones—that alone wouldn't mean anything. But he's a dago all right, is Esteban de Quesada; the name used to belong to a swell Spanish family somewhere down in Peru, and I believe in Boston he claimed that his great, great grandfather or something was a sort of Washington in those parts, and I don't say but what he may be right. He hasn't improved upon the family history, though, by adding burglary to their other accomplishments. But he is cute. I am bound to hand that to him."

"You know a great deal about him," remarked Major Fellspar; "but you have had no dinner; will you go home with me and have some?" Major Fellspar was anxious to be hospitable, but, it must be confessed was thinking of his own physical requirements even more than of those of the detective whom the Police Department of New York had so kindly sent over to help solve the problem that had baffled the Jamaica police.

"I don't mind if I do," said the American.

"Very good. Harmsworth, you must come with us. Brown, report yourself at my office tomorrow at nine sharp; we may need you."

"Yes, sir," said Detective Brown; and then the Inspector General, Inspector Harmsworth and the American detective left the Police Station and were rapidly driven to the Inspector General's residence, which was not quite a mile away.

With the aid of some cold meats a respectable supper was soon provided by Major Fellspar's capable housekeeper; while discussing the meal Mr. Baker talked.

"When your Governor wrote up to New York," said he, "and sent the photographs of the moving picture crowd to see if we knew anything about them, everybody in our Department was anxious to help him. We went over the pictures; there was a man in our force from Boston who was certain that he had seen Quesada's face before; as for me, I spotted Phipps at first sight."

"Phipps!" exclaimed Major Fellspar, "then he too—"

"Wait a bit," interrupted the detective, "I don't say that he has had anything to do with this steal; I don't know that he has. I have run across him more than once before: in Cuba and in Guatemala. Usually he was interfering with what didn't seem to concern him; the Guatemala Government was going to deport him once, but he got out in time. I think he believed that it wasn't deportation they meant, but simple assassination if it could be done without awkward enquiries being provoked. I was down there after a fellow that had absconded from the States, but I didn't connect Phipps with him. Phipps used to avoid me; evidently thought I might spoil his little game, whatever it was. There's nothing against him that we know of, but I regard him as a very suspicious sort of a customer; one that you have got to get up pretty early in the morning to watch. His photo didn't interest me any, however, after our man had recognised Quesada. We knew something about Quesada. The Boston police believe he had lifted some valuable jewellery in the town a little more than three years ago; they know now that he did."

"You have proved that?" asked the Inspector General.

"In this way. After one of our boys recognised Quesada, in one of the photos you sent us, as the man who had been suspected of robbery in a Boston hotel, I was despatched that same day to Boston to see what I could find out about him. You must have noticed, sir, that you can almost divide up the crooks into classes. Those who forge will keep on forging; the yeggmen will remain yeggman all their lives; the jewel lifters are always jewel lifters: each one sticks to his own line. Isn't that so out here?"

"I know that there seems to be any number of damned petty thieves here," replied Major Fellspar savagely; "but I think you are quite right: the same man does the same thing again and again."

"Exactly so. Well, there was a big jewellery robbery in Boston some years ago, and a man called Quesada, who was a movie actor, was suspected. And here we had a photograph of Quesada, a movie actor, and the story of a big jewellery robbery in Jamaica. It looked as if Providence was taking a hand in Quesada's career.

"The police in Boston remembered him quite well. He had been staying at a hotel there—one of the best—when a rich woman from one of the Western States was robbed. The police thought that the crook must have got into her room at night by a false key, or been secreted in it, and they were sure he had a pal in the hotel itself. Quesada had the room next to the woman who was robbed. Early in the morning, before the theft was discovered, he left he hotel, returning a couple of hours later. He was arrested and questioned: he denied having anything to do with the robbery; he said he had only gone out for an early morning walk, as was his custom. He could prove that he had gone out every morning early while staying at the hotel; and nothing was found on him. He was watched all the time he remained in Boston, which he did for three or four weeks longer. He only left when he got an engagement in a moving picture company in New York, who wanted a foreign-looking actor to do some athletic feats. The Boston Police couldn't get a thing against him, though they found that some big steals had been brought off in someother towns where Quesada happened to be at the time. And they couldn't get anything against the fellow who they believed was working with Quesada, one of the night men in the hotel. This man was discharged for carelessness; a year ago they caught him red-handed in a robbery in another hotel, where he was helping an outsider. He went to jail for five years."

"Yes?" queried Major Fellspar, as the detective paused.

"A few days ago we put a lot of photographs before him, with Quesada's in the bunch, and promised that his sentence would be greatly reduced if he could point out from among those photographs the man who had robbed Mrs. Hiram B. Stone's diamonds three years ago. We told him that we had got the dope on that man all right, but that he could help. He had been a year in prison already and he didn't want to stay any longer than he could help. Talked about wishin' to lead an honest life and all that kind of bunkum, and went through the photographs. The moment he came to the group with Quesada in it, he put his finger on Quesada: 'that's the man,' he says, and then he told us the whole story. The police had guessed quite right how the thing had been worked, but they had not been able to dig up a sufficient evidence to bring before a court. But you have only to wait long enough," concluded the detective sententiously, "and you will catch the cleverest of thief at last. They don't vary their methods, you se,, and some day they are bound to make a big mistake."

"But why if Quesada is a professional jewellery thief has he become a moving picture actor?" asked Major Fellspar.

"I don't know that he was a thief before he became an actor," the detective answered; "I rather figure that he was an actor before he became a thief. That is," he corrected himself, "I guess he was always a thief by disposition, but didn't take up stealing regularly until he saw the opportunities that traveling about and having a profession gave him. An actor don't need to be always working; it won't look suspicious if he is on his own for a little while. Then in these movie companies you can go from one part of the world to another where they won't have heard of you, unless you are very high up in the acting profession, and then you don't need to steal. A man like Quesada wouldn't try to rob another hotel in Boston, but he would risk it in San Francisco or in Vancouver, or in Cuba or Jamaica; and as (I suspect) he has always gone for big hauls—nothing less than a few thousand dollars at a time—it has paid him to work that way. He figured that he would always be able to get away with it. That's where he made his mistake. All of 'em do."

"I have suspected him for some little time," said Major Fellspar, "and now we must decide what we are going to do with regard to him. There are still grave difficulties in the way. We have no direct evidence against him. And you say that Mrs.—Mrs. What's-her-name's diamonds were never found?"

"Not one. That's where he had Boston beat."

"I shouldn't care if he escaped so long as I could get back Lady Rosedale's jewels!" cried the Inspector General: "those are what we want. I can have his room search, but I know quite well I should never find them there."

"You are right, sir," the detective agreed, "you won't find them that way. Quesada does not work alone. I am sure he sent Mrs. Stone's jewellery out of Boston when he went for that early walk of his after lifting them. He has done the same thing with Lady Rosedale's necklaces."

"This man, Phipps, may have helped him?"

"I don't know; but I'll tell you what I think. If you want to get rid quick of any article likely to land you in jail you will try and get it out of your hands by a simple and yet pretty safe method. You have a fellow that works with you, say over in New York. You put your necklaces in the middle of a bundle of newspapers, or in some such innocent-looking parcel, and it is taken by the mail over to him and delivered. The chance of that bundle going astray isn't one in a hundred. You can afford to take a risk like that, and with plain-clothes men watching you for weeks and ready to arrest and search you anytime, you want the goods to be far from you. Quesada knows quite well that he might be searched on landing in New York even three months hence, so he wouldn't have kept them with him. He would have to get someone to dispose of them for him, anyhow; someone in touch with jewellers and that lot. If he has a good arrangement, he would supply the goods by mail, so unless you catch him within a few hours after he has stolen 'em, it's goodbye to the booty."

The situation looked appalling to the Inspector General. To discover the thief and not the things stolen would afford but little satisfaction either to Lady Rosedale or the imperative Governor, through whose communication to New York this American detective had been sent down. However illogically, the Jamaica Police Force would be blamed. He simply dared not give up the hope that the necklaces would be discovered and restored. There was Marian Braeme's diamond broach. . .

"The return of Miss Braeme's broach," he suggested, "shows that the rest of the things taken may still be in this country."

"Miss Braeme and her brother would hardly steal from themselves," mused the detective; "or, if they did, it was on purpose. I can't think just now what that purpose was, and I don't know that it matters much. You may find out when you take some steps against the pair. What are you going to do, if I may ask?"

"I am damned if I know!" said Major Fellspar flatly.

"I should like to carry my man away with me as soon as I can," the detective went on; "but my instructions are to place myself at your service. We have got him nailed anyhow; he'll be put away safe and sure for a few years up North. But naturally you would like to nail him on the spot. Couldn't you arrest him and summon the girl as a witness against him? You might be able to find someone who will, if the question is put direct after Quesada is arrested, remember seeing him going upstairs that night, and as he doesn't live in the hotel he would have to do a lot of explaining away his presence where he had no right to be. But it's the girl who should be of the greatest use to you.

She's likely to break down and give the whole show away, especially if she knows that unless she tells the true story she herself will be put in the dock. You might convey that to her, in a delicate but explicit sort of way."

"I see what you mean," said the Inspector General, "but I shall have to take the opinion of the Attorney General tomorrow on that plan."

"H'm," said the detective.

"It will be the wisest course to adopt," urged Major Fellspar, "and nothing can be lost by it. Let me see; today is Thursday. I shall be able to have a talk with the Attorney General in the afternoon, about two o'clock: he'll be engaged otherwise in the forenoon. If he approves of the plan you suggest, we can arrest Quesada either tomorrow afternoon or on Saturday. In the meantime you will be able to attend to that extradition business of yours. I think, too, Mr. Baker, that you had better go with me tomorrow afternoon to see the Governor; it is due to his suggestion that we are able to avail ourselves of your valuable services."

"I am at your disposal, sir," replied the American with a friendly bow.

"And you are sure that nobody knew your recognised you at the hotel this afternoon?"

"I didn't advertise myself any; and I am sure Quesada doesn't know me. I can't think how he could."

"But Phipps was at the function this afternoon."

"I didn't see him."

"No, but he might have seen you."

"Quite possible, sir; now what is troubling you about that?"

"He's very friendly with this girl, and he has acted peculiarly ever since the robbery. He knows something about it."

"I see; but you say that Quesada cannot make a getaway."

"Not possible," affirmed Major Fellspar positively.

"Then it seems to me that this Phipps can't do much harm, even if he's inclined to play monkey tricks with us. I would advise that you have a man to watch Quesada, though."

"He has been watched ever since the day I suspected him," said Major Fellspar grimly, "though we have had to be careful that he doesn't know it."

"Right!" said the detective. He thought a moment, then added: "And perhaps you'd better have the girl watched too."

He rose to go, and so did Inspector Harmsworth.

"I'll send you both home in my car," said Major Fellspar. "I hope, Mr. Baker, that you find your room at the Inspectors' quarters comfortable."

"Quite," said Mr. Baker; "goodnight, Major. By Saturday something should be doing with those two birds."

"Something will be done," promised Major Fellspar; "but whether that will get us back the necklaces—"

He left the sentence unfinished.

XXIII

Mr. Phipps Explains

Lawrence was surprised when, on going himself to answer a rap at his front door, he found Mr. Phipps on the doorsteps waiting for admission. Mr. Phipps was about the last person he expected to see that night; he was keenly aware that Phipps must have perceived, and probably had resented, his recent attitude of aloofness, his undisguised efforts at avoidance of personal intercourse. Yet his immediate emotional reaction to the presence of Mr. Phipps was one of pleasure and satisfaction; he vividly realised that he had missed his cheerful friend far more than he had believed; he was conscious of a feeling of elation at this obviously friendly overture on Phipps's part.

There was another and equally potent reason for Lawrence's feeling. The scene at the little presentation ceremony of that afternoon was still vivid in his mind; he had been puzzled by it; ever since Marian had retired upstairs at the hotel and he had left the building for his own house he had been pondering its possible meanings. That something new had developed with regard to the robbery was certain; that Marian was in some way involved in it appeared probable. And perhaps the only person who could throw light on all this complicated business, or at least could make a good guess at what it might mean, was Phipps. And now, here was the man himself. "Come in!" he cried warmly, taking Mr. Phipps by the hand, and pulling him inside. "I am awfully glad you came round."

Lawrence lived in a little bungalow by himself on one of the main roads to the north of the city; his wants were attended to by an elderly native woman, who, with a boy that looked after the garden, constituted the domestic establishment. "If you haven't had dinner yet, you are in time to join me," he said; "Matilda can always dish up something. We'll only have a few minutes to wait."

"I came to have dinner with you," replied Mr. Phipps with equal warmth: both men had automatically slipped back to the old relationship of mutual confidence and friendliness. "I wanted to have a talk with you, and I thought I'd invite myself to dinner. Anything will do for me."

In the light of Lawrence's sitting room, a bachelor's apartment sparsely furnished with a few wicker lounge chairs, two or three small tables, a couple of bookcases filled with books, and a large crex carpet, the two men glanced enquiringly at each other, and each pair of eyes saw worry and anxiety in the face into which they looked. Mr. Phipps was not surprised at Lawrence's troubled expression, but Lawrence knew that it required something of more than ordinary moment to disturb so markedly the habitual jaunty cheerfulness of the man before him.

"You want to talk to me?" he asked, making no attempt to pretend that he did not know of whom Phipps wished to talk. "About Marian and the curious thing that happened this afternoon?"

"Bull's eye again, son," said the other, with something of his old manner although the effort was visible; "you have a gift for deduction which must be singularly unnecessary in the shipping business." He stretched himself in a lounge chair, and Lawrence sat facing him. "You saw what happened this afternoon, of course?" he asked.

"Of course," said Lawrence; "it puzzled me as it puzzled everybody else. The sending back of the stolen broach at that particular time, when the occurrence could not fail to attract great attention, the breakdown of Marian, her brother's evident apprehension—what in the name of God does it all mean! Who could have sent that broach?"

"I," said Mr. Phipps. "Didn't you guess as much?"

"You?" cried Lawrence; "You? But how could I guess, man, and how did you get it? Why did you choose such a moment for its arrival?" He was sitting straight up in his lounge chair, his whole figure tense with astonishment. "You sent back the broach, but the necklaces—Phipps, I don't understand!"

"You won't until I have explained. I have had the broach, Lawrence, from the night on which it was lost."

"Lost? Stolen you mean."

"'Lost,' I said. It was never stolen."

"But the necklaces: they too were taken. And don't you see, Phipps, that the man who has been keeping them—"

"Is a thief? That may be, son; but I said nothing about the necklaces; I was speaking about the broach, which is quite a different matter."

The tinkling of a bell in the adjoining room intimated that dinner was served, but neither man took any notice of the call. Mr. Phipps resumed.

"You will remember that on the night of that big ball at the hotel, Marian wore her broach. She used it to pin some flowers to her waist. I noticed that the catch was loose and called her attention to it. She seemed careless and indifferent: I thought I guess the reason of her indifference. She had just come back from a long talk with you: you call that to mind?"

Lawrence reddened slightly, but said nothing.

"I rallied her about her carelessness; later on that night she was sitting next to me on the lawn; after a while she left with the man to whom she was engaged for the next dance. While she was siting down, or on rising to go off with her partner, she dropped her broach."

"I see."

"I was in a low rocking chair, my fingers easily touching the ground: my hand came in contact with the broach before she got far away. I picked it up and was going to take it to her, when I thought I would teach her to be more careful in the future by letting her discover her loss. I slipped the thing into my pocket, not mentioning it even to you. You wouldn't have been much interested anyhow. You were thinking your own thoughts then, and it didn't require a mind reader to know that they weren't very happy ones.

"I intended to produce the broach the next day, when Marian would have given it up for lost, and after Lady Rosedale would have suspected everybody of having stolen it. I wrapped it up neatly when I went upstairs that night; the following morning I put the parcel in my pocket after I had dressed; and then there came the alarm about the robbery."

"And you said nothing?" Lawrence observed.

"Not having any desire to be instantly arrested, I did not. But that wasn't my main reason for keeping silence. If I had confessed to having the broach I should have had to explain how it had come into my possession. But Marian had already distinctly said in the hearing of many people that her broach had been stolen along with Lady Rosedale's pearl necklace. Marian stated quite positively that she had taken off the broach in her room that night. It wasn't the truth and she knew it."

"Phipps! Do you mean—"

"You'll get my meaning in good time, Lawrence, and you will need all your calmness and wits during the next twenty-four hours so don't get excited now. Marian must have realised after she got up to her room that night that she had lost her broach. But if she had told that quite truthful story, and yet asserted that the pearl necklace had been stolen, who could possibly have believed her? Her tale would have sounded like a silly attempt to deceive. There was nothing for her but to say that all the jewellery she had worn that night had been robbed.

H. G. DE LISSER

"The moment I heard her say that, I had to make up my mind. For me to have produced the broach then and there, after her positive assertion, might have had an ugly result for her. If the police chose to believe me, she must have been arrested on suspicion. If they preferred to believe her, and came to the conclusion that I was the thief and was merely trying to throw suspicion on her they would have arrested me. I guess I could have cleared my character all right, but her own story would have been terribly against her. There was only one thing to do.

"I had to get away with the broach as quickly as possible; it was burning a hole in my waistcoat pocket at that moment, I can assure you. I left the investigation suddenly and went round to my lawyers, Jones and Bedlaw, and asked them to let my deposit the little parcel along with someother things I keep in their safety vault. I put the broach away with my own hands, talked to them a little while about business, and then I went back to the hotel in time to find the detectives preparing to search my room."

Again the dinner bell tinkled, but neither man seemed to hear it. "You saved Marina that morning from arrest," said Lawrence gratefully; "tell me, did you believe that she had anything to do with the robbery?"

"Yes."

"She had not, Phipps: it was Stephen Braeme who was the thief."

"I know that, son; but she knew how the things had been stolen; and don't you see that that connects her with the wretched business? She pretended not to know; she was therefore, technically, an accessory to the act. She might with one word have indicated the culprit. She did not. What would a judge and jury say about that in a court of law?"

Lawrence answered nothing, but waited, with fear peering out of his narrowed eyes, to hear what more his friend might have to say.

"The moment Marian said that her own broach as well as Lady Rosedale's necklace had been stolen from her room, I realised that she knew who had taken the necklace and was trying to screen him, perhaps acting under instructions from him, for friend Stephen knew that no one would readily accuse Marian of being a thief. Her face, too, told its own tale for those with eyes to see. She was desperately frightened, though she had nerved herself to go through a terrible ordeal. Happily for her, the positive statement of Lady Rosedale about the handling of the jewel box made it impossible for anyone to connect Marian directly with the diamond necklace. The case would have been a simpler one without the diamond necklace; but no one could imagine Marian stealing into Lady Rosedale's room through a window to extract it, and if any did think she may have had an accomplice it was not of Stephen that they thought. It was of me. I was the red herring across his trail.

"Fortunately, the police here are more circumspect in dealing with people of our position than they would be in the States or in England. A white man here is a person of importance. Marian was suspected, you also for a little time, and I—that black man, Brown, would have had me arrested first thing if he had had his way. But his chefs were more circumspect; they have been waiting for evidence; and now I am beginning to fear that they may get some—enough, at any rate, to make serious trouble."

"Do you mean," asked Lawrence in a voice that trembled slightly, "do you mean that Marian is in serious danger?"

"I am afraid she may be," Mr. Phipps answered gravely, "and that is why I think it is best that you should know exactly how matters stand."

"I am listening," said Lawrence. "I want you to keep nothing from me."

"I didn't think the police would find out enough to make much trouble for anyone, for the scent was clean away from Stephen, and Marian kept up wonderfully. But that Sunday, at our picnic in Triton, young Harmsworth began taking photographs, and I knew at once that he was acting for someone else. He admitted it to me that same day. I got worried then.

"Everything depended on whether Stephen had left any bad record behind him in New York or the other States; if he had, his picture might be recognised—and then! It was a cute idea that, sending up all our pictures to the New York police; for I know now that is what they were taken for; indeed, I suspected it at the time. Well, the plan has succeeded."

"They have discovered something?"

"I believe so; and they have sent a man down here who will discover something more if I am not mistaken. I have met that man in other countries, Lawrence; his name is Baker, a rather slow but a dreadfully shrew and persistent fellow. Take it from me, he is on Stephen's track—and Marian stands in that same track!"

"Marian? But Phipps, you know she did not steal the jewels. Good God man! You know that she did not help him to steal them. All that might be charged against her is that she knew he was the thief, and who would expect a sister to send her own brother to the prison?"

"Marian has told me the whole story. I guessed most of it before, but she has filled in the details. I am afraid that she is in more danger than you seem to think, Lawrence, and I want her to get out of it and not wait to face it. She must leave this country within the next twenty-four hours."

"Alone, or with her brother?"

"Alone. I believe that Stephen is being watched. That man, Baker, if he has a line on Stephen, will not let it go until he pulls him in with it. Stephen cannot escape; there is no possible way of escape for him. But with Marian it is different. I am sure Baker knows nothing against her, thought he may advise that she should be arrested along with Stephen. But he will hardly believe that she will try to get away within the next day or so independently: anyhow I hope he won't. Now if we could get her away. . . you will help, I know."

"I will do anything for her, Phipps; *anything*; though I see no reason why she should attempt to fly and thus perhaps stain her name. Do you really believe that she runs a serious risk? I do not believe it. The idea is monstrous!"

"You have ships running to Costa Rica, haven't you?" asked Mr. Phipps, ignoring Lawrence's indignant protests.

"One goes tomorrow night, at about two o'clock."

"I gathered that from your advertisement in this morning's paper. You know, of course, that Costa Rica is a country which has no extradition treaty with either England or America. Once Marian is in Costa Rica, she could not be brought back here.

"I know the Costa Rican Consul quite well. He'll make out a proper passport for Marian tomorrow; so there won't be any difficulty about her landing on the other side. The difficulty will be to get her aboard your ship without anyone seeing her who oughtn't to; but I think that can be managed. You'll call to take her out for a ride; you will take her to the ship; it will all be done so openly that no one will suspect anything. Even if they do they can't stop her unless they have orders to do so; they can only ask her to show her passport, and she will have one all properly made out."

"And when she is in Costa Rica, what?"

"Time will have to answer that question. She'll have enough money to live on there for sometime anyhow."

"I am not thinking of that, Phipps. She'll be there alone. . . that's what I'm thinking. . . but no; she will not be." The last words suggested some thought that was passing through Lawrence's mind.

Mr. Phipps fixed a penetrating glance on his face and read there a dogged determination upon which mere argument could have no effect.

He saw that Lawrence did not approve of Marian's endeavouring to escape from Jamaica; and he had felt all along that if Marian went to Costa Rice, where she would be but two days' journey from Jamaica, Lawrence would go with or follow her—unless. "Unless," he repeated to himself, and weighed the question in his mind.

Lawrence broke in upon his reflections. "You haven't made somethings clear," he said. "You haven't explained why you sent back the broach in so extraordinary a fashion, or how Stephen managed to steal the necklaces out of Marian and Lady Rosedale's rooms."

"Marian long had a shrewd suspicion that I knew a great deal about the theft," Mr. Phipps replied, "but it was only a suspicion based upon little hints I had thought it wise to let drop. I used to say things that made her thoughtful, sort of pulled her up, you know; and they puzzled her."

"You distressed her, Phipps; and God knows she had enough to distress her without your adding to it," said Lawrence with some bitterness. "You once said to her something about the Devil's Mountain, and she wondered what you meant. From that to this she has been a changed woman: why did you do it?"

"She guessed I was acting for the best, even if that did not altogether prevent her continuing to trip up the Devil's Mountain," retorted Mr. Phipps grimly. "My hints warned her, but hints would have been of no avail with friend Stephen. I should have had to tell him plainly that I knew he was a thief, and that was not what I wanted to do in cold blood. I would have done it, though, if I hadn't had that broach, for it was necessary that he should clear out of this country. He had nothing to fear by going openly; they would have found nothing on him; he's too smart for that. It was Nora Hamilton that was keeping him here, or he'd have said goodbye already. I didn't think it was good for Nora that he should remain, and it wasn't good for you that Marian should remain."

"Of that, Phipps—"

"You are not the best judge, son," said Mr. Phipps decisively; then, noting the angry light that leapt into Lawrence's eyes, he held up a deprecatory hand, and hurried on. "Marian agreed with me, though we never talked the matter over in so many words. She knew that I knew quite enough about her and Stephen to come to a sound conclusion. But I had to frighten Stephen into making up his mind to leave. A broach was to be presented to her this afternoon. I got her old one, posted it to her, knowing when it would arrive, and I trusted to luck to its being opened at just the right time to give Señor Stephen a turn. It did. It hit him like a blow. He must always have been puzzled by the alarm raised over the diamond necklace which he never took; and with the reappearance of the lost broach he must have had a shock."

"Then who stole the diamond necklace?" demanded Lawrence astonished.

Mr. Phipps, despite his gravity, smiled mockingly.

"No one stole it," he said; "there was none to steal."

"None to steal?" repeated Lawrence incredulously.

"Not a single diamond. Has it never struck you, son, that no one in the hotel had ever seen this necklace, but had only heard about it from Lady Rosedale? Not even to Marian had she shown it. She announces its loss with a little scream one morning, but she was not really perturbed until she learnt that her pearl necklace was gone. Then indeed she showed consternation and distress. She has talked a lot about her pearls since then, but not very much about her diamonds: it was I who did that. And she could be very positive that Marian had not stolen her diamonds because she knew that there was none to steal. Besides, I don't think she would ever have believed Marian capable of such dishonesty."

"But her motive for saying they had been stolen? What on earth caused her to raise that hue and cry?"

"A silly hunger for notoriety. The woman simply loves to be noticed and made a fuss about; she'd do anything to get her name in the papers, to be the centre of attention, to be always talked of. For years she must have lived mainly for this sort of thing, and now she cannot do without it; behind all her self-possession is an enormous vanity. The same craving for notoriety makes men anarchists sometimes; they want to be conspicuous in the world's eyes. She had the diamonds once, but four years ago, when the price of everything was high in America, she sold them at a handsome price. There were some paragraphs about the sale of her beautiful stones in the society pages of some of the New York papers, and her photograph appeared. She didn't imagine anyone down here could have heard of that: she wanted a fuss made about her, and so she put up that stupid story about her trunk being opened and her necklace taken. All she had to do was to open the trunk, say she had been robbed, and pretend to be distressed and indignant and outraged. That would secure for her all the notice and publicity she could possibly desire.

"And now we come to the really curious part of this whole affair, the sort of thing which may not happen once in a thousand times, but which does occur on occasion and upsets all one's previous calculations. It was probably because she had lent her pearls to Marian, and believed that they were perfectly safe in her room, that the idea occurred to Lady Rosedale to give out on the morning after the dance that she had been robbed. It was then or never; there might be no other such opportunity; for of course she could never venture at anytime to say that her diamonds had been stolen and a fine pearl necklace left. That sort of tale might go down where only a few small trinkets were concerned, but it would not otherwise be credible. The idea must have come to her in a flash; it could hardly have been premeditated; she is always, consciously and unconsciously, seeking opportunities of being in the limelight, and that sort of folly will give rise to all sorts of extraordinary resolutions and projects. The one thing that did not enter her mind was the possibility of a real theft having taken place; it would scarcely have occurred to anyone to suppose that on that Thursday night, seeing the pearls within his reach, a professional rogue would plan to steal them. But with Stephen too it was a case of them or never; that Marian should be wearing Lady Rosedale's pearls must have seemed to him the most wonderful piece of luck. And if Lady Rosedale was thunderstruck to find that an authentic robbery had taken place, Stephen was no less astonished to learn that her diamonds had been stolen at the same time.

"I fancy that Lady Rosedale would not have said much about her reputed loss, after the publicity she craved had been secured, had she not actually lost her pearls. She could not have wanted to injure anyone by throwing unjust suspicion on him; she did not pause to consider whether anyone might be injured; she probably believe that an investigation by the police would end in nothing. But with the disappearance of the pearl necklace the matter became serious; she desired very much to recover her pearls. Recently, however, she had not said much about them. I figure that she has been wondering whether anybody would find out that she had been pulling the leg of this whole community over those diamonds. She knows I keep track of good jewel stories, for I told her so, and she has seen my scrap books at Triton. She isn't any too comfortable in mind, for she doesn't know what I might say or do. I am sure she'd prefer now to hear no more about the pearls than hear too much about the diamonds.

"Now Stephen, don't you see, has felt that someone else besides himself has been at work on Lady Rosedale's property, and that, up to a certain point, was in his favour. There would be somebody else to suspect.

H. G. DE LISSER

But with the broach returned, he would be likely to think that the man who had had it all the time knew something about the diamonds also, and might know who took the pearls. He couldn't be certain that he was not suspected; to a guilty mind everything is suspicious, even normal happenings assume a significance which is really created by fear. Still, I ought to have given Stephen a direct warning before, and not have waited to make a fool demonstration like the one today. I have done the same thing before and regretted it, yet I don't seem to learn any lessons from that—disposition, I suppose. I am a bit too fond of creating dramatic situations; that's why I delayed until Mr. Detective Baker turns up and queers the whole bally pitch. You can't know how badly I feel about it."

"You would have allowed Braeme to take the pearls with him, Phipps?"

"Take them? Do you believe he is fool enough to have them with him? If he hasn't got rid of them long ago, I am a Chinaman! Stephen has some brain son; and this is not the first time that he has got away with the goods."

"Well, then," insisted Lawrence, "they will be able to prove nothing against him if he is arrested, and Marian will have nothing to fear. There will be the scandal of her brother's arrest. I know—"

"And of her own: would you like her to be arrested?"

"Ah!"

"Besides, there may be some definite charge that the Government of the State of New York can lay against Stephen. That would insure his arrest even here. Remember, he probably has something against him. In fact, I know he has."

"But Marian has none."

"No, she hasn't; but—"

"If she runs away, Phipps, her character will be smirched. People will believe the worst about her. I have agreed to your plan, and am prepared to carry it out if there is nothing else to do, but I do not like it. Perhaps she will accept no advice just now from me, but she knows you are her friend. Tell her that it is best that she should confess the whole truth about her brother if her silence cannot save him."

"She would not do that, Lawrence, and you would think the less of her if she did. You will agree with me later on."

Lawrence shook his head obstinately; he could see no reason why Marian should make any sacrifice for Stephen.

"And besides," continued Mr. Phipps, seeing the look, "when all the truth was known, her evidence would not even be admitted."

"Why?"

Mr. Phipps rose abruptly out of his chair, and Lawrence, attracted by his movement, rose with him. "You have grit," said Phipps kindly, placing his hand on Lawrence's shoulder, "and you have got to hear the truth sooner or later, though I did not want to tell it to you tonight. You are dealing with a bitterly vain and jealous man in Stephen Quesada, and he knows that you love Marian. He will be arrested, and, if he believes he cannot hope to escape, he may drag Marian to destruction with him if she is within reach of his anger and his bitter jealously. It is not only from out of the reach of the law officers of this country that I want her to go; it is beyond that of Stephen. He will strike at her, I tell you, and strike at you, and might even find some satisfaction in his own downfall in knowing that he had injured you both. She told him—I had it from his own lips this evening—she told him before you a few nights ago that he was a thief, and he hates her for having said it, and you for having heard it. He hates her because she loves you, and you because you love her and despise him. He is Spanish, remember, and revenge is part of the Spaniard's nature and tradition: he will destroy if he can because of wounded vanity or of a real or imagined injury. Even now I fear that he may strike at Marian before we can get her out of his way. Until she has gone I shall not cease to fear him."

"But why all this jealously about his sister," cried Lawrence with anger and scorn. "Is the man insane as well as a villain?"

"You have to know, Lawrence, and it will not make you less ready to help the poor little girl if you do. She is no sister of his—"

"Good God!"

"She is his wife."

XXIV

Stephen

E steban de Quesada, scion of one of the best Peruvian families, a descendant of one of those reckless Spanish adventurers who had conquered and dominated the land of the Incas, was but twelve years of age when his father sent him to the United States of America. He was an only child; before his birth his family had fallen in prestige and estate owing to their unconquerable propensity for political plotting and their peculiar genius for favouring as a rule the losing faction in those bitter party struggles which so largely make up the sum of Latin-American politics. His people were conservative, passionate and proud; in former days they had sat in the seats of the mighty. But Esteban's father had concluded, when the boy was still young, that there would be no future for him in his own country were he to remain in it. At that time the life of the father himself was held on a precarious tenure, and there was no saying but that Esteban too might be included in any vengeance planned and prosecuted against the elder Quesada.

So Juan de Quesada had collected what little money remained to him and had arranged with friends in America that Esteban should be put to school there, with medicine as his future profession in view. The boy went to New Orleans; his father continued on his career of political plotting, which was as the breath of life to him, and which was also now a necessity of material existence. In this career he persisted for six years more, then at last passed within the walls of a squat adobe calaboose, whence, a month or so afterwards, it was given out that he had been shot while attempting to escape. Esteban was now eighteen years of age. He found himself thrown entirely upon his own resources. He had to face life in a foreign country with but his own wits to aid him, for he knew that a return to Peru, where his father's enemies were still in power, could but mean his own destruction.

Fortunately, he possessed a good command of English, which he spoke as well as any American. He was tall, too, and strong, with the dark handsomeness of his ancestors and a look of distinction which he had inherited from a family that had always counted for something in Peru. With his knowledge of English and Spanish, he found no difficulty in securing a clerkship in a store in New Orleans, but the life and work were not congenial to him. After a couple of years in this city, in which he changed positions more than once, Esteban drifted to New York, where he managed to secure a footing in one of the large moving picture studios.

He learnt his work, and learnt it well; it was something that appealed to his excitable, romantic nature. But he did not excel in it. He was theatrical but not a great actor; he loved the dramatic but did not shine conspicuously in impersonation. Was this but another illustration of his family's inability during the last three or four generations to achieve any striking or ultimate success? Whatever it was, it is certain that Esteban was but an ordinary actor with an ordinary salary; meanwhile he had developed extravagant tastes and a gambler's disregard of consequences. He was restless, too, going from one company to another. Then, in a Western city, an opportunity came to him of possessing himself of a large sum of money through theft. It was an actress whose jewels he succeeded in purloining, probably with some help, and the crime was never traced to him. He soon came to know others who followed a dishonest career, crooks of a superior intelligence like his; and though the risks were sometimes great the rewards were accounted greater. Nor was constant effort required to bring about rich gains. In one year, by a single venture, Esteban and some of his companions made a haul of jewels in Canada worth about ten thousand pounds.

He was about twenty-two years of age when he embarked on the rouge's profession, and, though the police of different cities had long had their doubts about him, only once had direct suspicion fastened on him. That was in Boston, and for the first time in his life as a crook he had been gravely frightened. Although nothing had been found, or traced to him, he was nevertheless seized with a desire to leave America for a time: while in that country he could not easily conquer a certain nervousness which his narrow escape had engendered. He suddenly became possessed with a wish to visit the land of his birth, to pass sometime once more among the scenes of his early days. He had quite enough money to last him for a while; work was by no means an immediate necessity. He obeyed the impulse; he decided to return to Peru. It was safe for him to do so now; his father was almost forgotten; the party in power might be more friendly than otherwise; besides, he had entirely escaped the infection of violent political sympathies and partisan hates, which were the commonplaces of his own country. He went back to Peru at thirty years of age as a stranger almost. He knew no one as intimate friend. But his name, and the circumstance that he was one of the first families, made his social path comparatively easy for him. Then too he suggested that he was a man of means, and his command of ready money and his manner of assurance seemed to vouch for him. He cut some figure in Lima. He had not been there many months before, at the house of an English lady resident, he was introduced to Marian Braeme.

Like Esteban, Marian had been educated in the United States; there for give years she had remained, returning to her own country at the age of twenty. She was twenty-one when her English father died, a good, kindly, ineffectual man who had but little to leave his daughter save an enduring and beloved memory. Marian wanted to return to America then, but she shrank from plunging alone into the whirlpool of a great American city to fight unaided for her bread. Her father had known some of the English and American residents in Peru; one of these at Lima, an English lady whose husband was connected with the railway system of that country, offered to Marian on her father's death the position of governess to her two little boys. Marian accepted the position. She had been living as one of the family for something over a year when Esteban came upon the scene.

He was brought to the house by the head of it, delighted to meet a companionable man fresh from the United States and full of enthusiasm for modern life and institutions. This gentleman knew what the name of Quesada had meant in the history of Peru. And with a frank sociability, very different from Spanish-American formality and exclusiveness, he had not thought twice about making Esteban one of his circle of friends.

For himself, Esteban took what came to him for granted and as part of his due. Had anyone alluded to him as a thief, he would have smitten down that man: the notion that he was but a thief never once occurred to him. Ever since he was a lad he had entertained the belief that the world had treated him and his in a dastardly fashion. It had impoverished his people (of whom he was genuinely proud), had murdered his father, had left him penniless and forced him to take to tasks beneath his dignity; therefore it owed him not merely a living but reparation. He had been a victim of circumstances; why should he not revenge himself upon others who had been favoured by circumstances? What they had they owed to no merit or virtue of their own; what he took from them would but go to redressing the balance of undeserved ill-fortune. Thus he reasoned in his vanity and overwhelming egoism, being in this quite true to the character of the men from whom he was descended.

Petty stealing Esteban would have regarded with loathing and contempt; he had never stolen anything insignificant. He was no picker up of unconsidered trifles. He was, he doubtless considered himself, a sort of gentleman adventurer risking liberty and life in the pursuit of excitement and gain; so had done that ancestor of his who had helped Pizarro to conquer the Incas against overwhelming odds, so had done many of his subsequent ancestors who had made revolutions or fought revolutionists for place and power and wealth in Peru. To the victor belong the spoils, and his war was with the rich. To most of those whom he victimised he considered himself superior: by birth a gentleman of purest Spanish blood whose family name must live in the history of Latin-America. So it was with no sort of qualms of conscience or sense of social unfitness that he entered the circle of Marian's employer and friend and it was with perhaps the firm belief that he was madly in love with her that he, with characteristic impetuousness and ardour, offered her his hand and heart.

He was not exactly the sort of man that, under happier circumstances, Marian would have listened to with any degree of seriousness. His brilliant theatricality, while it appealed to her imagination, lit no fire in her heart. He was handsome, and that appealed to her sense of physical fitness, yet he lacked that firm strength of character and calm steadfastness of purpose in which her gentler, clinging disposition would have found its complement. That it was this, among other things, that he lacked, she herself did not of course realise; she could not have formulated in words her hidden cravings and desires, was not aware of their specific existence. Nevertheless she felt that Stephen, though she admired him, though she liked hi, was—how should she express it?—not the man she had imagined she could ever marry. Yet there was something in common between them. He was different from the younger men of her own country, the country of her mother. He was fond perhaps of display, but not a fop; his outlook on life was that of a citizen of a great country: his years in America had not been without marked effect upon his mind. All that was English in her blood and American in her training appreciated the differences in him from what was purely Peruvian, differences with which his upbringing and sojourn in the United States had endowed him. To her, when he spoke English (as he invariably did her society or in the society of American and English people), and discussed matters with which she had been more or less familiar in the States, he was, not a Peruvian, but an American. And the American, to Marian's understanding, was first cousin to English, and her father, and all her father's people, had been English. Then she wanted to leave Peru; the nostalgia of the North was in her blood and in her brain. The thought of life as a Peruvian lady, with all the conventions and stifling social restrictions of that life, amazed and sickened her; she could not calmly contemplate it. Her friend, too, in whose house she lived, saw Esteban's infatuation and smiled a benediction on it. It was Marian's golden chance, she said, a marriage with a man like Esteban de Quesada, whose future lay in America. So in three months all Marian's hesitations had been swept away. They were married, and almost immediately after they left for the United States.

For some little while life went smoothly for them; it ran on pneumatic tyres and was clad in silks. But only for a little while. In the intimacy of married life traits of character unsuspected at first peep out, and then stand fully revealed. Marian was conscious that Esteban had not told her the truth, or, at any rate, had caused her to believe what was not true. He spent money freely, but admitted that he had no reserves and began to talk about the need of finding something to do; he hinted that she too would have to work with him. It was not the prospect of having to work that troubled Marian, it was that Esteban had posed as a man of means in Peru; also, she did not quite like the sort of life that he suggested. He was going back to the moving pictures and wished her to go with him; they would act, he said, under an assumed name, her maiden name, and she would pass as his sister. For the mere purposes of acting in a company, she had no objection to her maiden name being used by them both, but she saw no reason why they should not be known to their acquaintances generally as man and wife, and she said so. She argued the point, and then she perceived that she had to do with an imperious man, one bent upon having his way without reference to any other person's feelings. She yielded; soon she began to believe that Esteban's insistence that she should be known as his sister and not as his wife, was motivated by his desire to appear to be a bachelor still, especially among the women of the company for which he worked.

They occupied separate apartments now; sometimes, when moving about, they did not even live in the same building; and again and again she saw Stephen devoting himself to some attractive young woman without much regard to any objection she might have. Withal, he was jealous of any attention which men, believing she was a single girl, might pay to her. His jealously, originating in a desire for exclusive possession, in pure personal vanity, in the feeling that his wife was his property, and that, whatever he might do, her course of conduct was to regard all men as strangers and be as ice to them, expressed itself in bitter rebuke at times, and this unjust. She resented it; the belief in the necessary subjection of women, which she may have inherited from her Peruvian mother, was sapped and mined by the memory of what her English father had thought of women, and of how he had treated and regarded her; it was sapped and mined too by those years that she had passed in the city of New York, in a country where the personal freedom of women is part of the social religion. Moreover, she knew that there was no reason for his arrogant jealousy, that it did not arise from love of her, that he had no right to complain of her innocent actions when he himself flirted outrageously with other women, and did not, she had a shrewd suspicion, stop at mere flirtation only. By the end of a year they were estranged in feeling, completely. They remained as brother and sister, both working for a moving picture company in which she played minor parts, her face and figure ensuring her employment. Marian now began to wonder how long this would last; she would have thought of divorce, but her mother had brought her up a Catholic, and she still clung to that faith. Yet she wondered how long this existence of hers could possibly last.

Esteban not only adopted her name, but presently he legally changed his for Braeme, and so became Stephen Braeme. Years before he had taken out his first papers as an American citizen, knowing that he would never return to Peru to live. He now took out his final papers; henceforth he was Stephen Braeme, and under that name he engaged himself for a term of three months to a picture company which planned some photo-dramas with a tropical setting and interest. His pay was fairly good, and he stipulated that Marian should also be engaged. There was no difficulty about this. And thus they came to Jamaica.

"Most of this Marian told me this afternoon," said Mr. Phipps, "some of it I had guessed, or perhaps not merely guessed, for my deductions have some facts behind them. You may wonder, Lawrence, how I can be certain that, at an early age, Stephen Braeme became a crook. Well, I have records of some big jewels thefts which have occurred during the last fifteen or twenty years, and those that I have mentioned as being his took place when he was in the city, and even the neighbourhood, where they occurred. In one way or other, his name is brought into the reports. He knew the people robbed; he was interviewed; he was questioned; but there never was anything against him save only once, when he was arrested, and even then it was only on suspicion. Clever as he was he could not always entirely throw off suspicion. But what occurs in Vancouver will very shortly be forgotten in Philadelphia, even if it is heard of there."

Lawrence nodded. Since the revelation made by Mr. Phipps he had remained silent, listening. His face was drawn, his eyes fixed on his companion in a stony star. Mr. Phipps resumed his narrative.

Her meeting with Lawrence changed inwardly, if not on the surface, the course of Marian's life. He appealed to her, and this appeal, coupled with her increasing alienation from Stephen, swept her off her feet. She felt herself to be drifting perilously; she struggled against the current that was taking her out to dangerous depths; but she was not helped by the harsh remonstrances of her husband, whose own conduct was so patent an insult and affront to her. On the night of the big hotel dance, when she had left the ballroom for a walk with Lawrence, Stephen had followed her, called her back for a while, and angrily ordered her to have nothing to do with Lawrence. She refused to obey him, and had kept her engagements with Lawrence. She saw nothing more of Stephen that night until she was in her room.

The room was empty, to all appearance, when she entered it. She had not been inside for more than a minute when the door of her clothes closet opened and he stood before her; her first impulse to cry out died away as she recognised who it was. She realised that he must have come up sometime before and had been waiting for her. That he should conceal himself was not very strange, since someother woman might have come into the room with her, and he, in his masquerade as her brother, would not wish to be seen.

She thought he had come to quarrel with her about Lawrence, but he said very little on that score. She took off her jewels and placed them under some clothing in the top drawer of her dressing table; then for the first time she missed her broach, and feared that she had lost it, as Mr. Phipps had warned her that she might. She mentioned the loss to Stephen, who seemed annoyed at it. She then locked the drawer and sat down in a rocking chair to wait until he should say what he might have to say, and go.

He talked commonplaces, touched on how he was running short of money, was moody and evidently ill at ease. They conversed in whispers so as to prevent their being overheard; she grew weary of this at last, and asked him what he wanted with her, and did he not intend to leave the room? She protested that it could only do her harm if he were seen leaving her room at that hour, and bitterly blamed him for being there. "Even if I were seen," he replied coldly, "all could be properly explained by my merely proving that you are my wife. The only person who might be shocked is your friend, Mr. Lawrence Beaman." She did not wish to talk about Lawrence after what had occurred between them earlier that night, so she answered nothing. Both remained silent after this; then, overcome by weariness, she dozed. She awoke with a start. The room was in darkness, and Stephen was quietly leaving by one of the windows which opened directly upon the roof of the verandah below.

At that moment she was too surprised to guess at what had happened; indeed her immediate feeling was relief at his going, though his method of doing so was strange, and appeared even dangerous. He heard her start up, whispered to her to be silent, quietly pulled the window down behind him and disappeared. She stepped hastily towards it and peered through the glass, but she saw nothing, heard no sound, and for another quarter of an hour she waited before turning on again the electric light which he had extinguished while she was asleep. She noticed nothing unusual; she undressed and went to bed In the morning, after throwing on her dressing gown, she went to her drawer with the intention of taking out Lady Rosedale's necklace to return it. Then she knew.

She understood in a flash her horrible position. She could accuse him of entering her room and stealing the jewels, but it would be divulged that he was her husband. . . she shrank from that revelation. And how could she, the man's wife, accuse him of theft? It might be believed that she was a party to it, and had only confessed because her nerve had given way and she was afraid of discovery and punishment.

In an agony of fear and hesitation she was still revolving in her mind what she should do, when she heard Lady Rosedale exclaim from the adjoining room that she had been robbed. At once Marian leaped to the conclusion that, on leaving her room, Stephen had gone to that of Lady Rosedale and had stolen the diamond necklace; and in this also she saw herself involuntarily implicated. Her decision was automatic: she must profess absolute ignorance of the theft and the thief. Stephen did not live in the hotel, he had got away, no one would suspect him if he had not been seen; then too he had taken some of her own things—she was grateful for that—and the broach had gone: she screwed her courage up to the sticking point and fought for concealment and safety desperately. Her nerves paid; but she knew that if she failed the disgrace would be terrible, and so, in a torment of apprehension, she waited to hear if any inkling of the truth was in the mind of any of those concerned with the discovery of the culprit.

She soon perceived that she was suspected; she became passive, waiting to see what would be done. One thing encouraged and heartened her. Lady Rosedale thought she had been a trifle careless, nothing more. She felt that Lady Rosedale, let the worst come to the worst, would be her friend to the last.

"And that's one of the few good things that the recording angel will put down to her ladyship's credit," commented Mr. Phipps. "She cares for Marian in her own way, Lawrence, and I don't know that any of us can do anymore than that."

By the next morning Marian had begun to feel that no one was even remotely connecting Stephen with the jewels. But her own feeling towards him, angry and resentful and bitter before, was now one of absolute loathing and dread. He was a thief; he had not hesitated to place her in a precarious and dangerous position, counting upon her fears and her dread of scandal and disgrace to keep her silent, and perhaps even intending, if he were accused by her, to throw the crime upon her and leave her to sink or swim as best she could.

She felt that she was bound to such a man by legal but no other tie: she hated him. And a question sprang up in her mind: was he merely flirting with Nora, the girl who was so nice and kind to her, or would he not attempt to injure Nora if he could? Nora's friendship for her, Nora's genuine delight in giving her pleasure, Nora's frank comradeship and charm of manner had touched her heard, and it stung her to anger to see Stephen playing the lover to the girl with such assiduous attention. She had no faith in him, no trust; she saw him all black; besides, what right had a man like that to dare make love to a girl like Nora Hamilton? As for herself, she knew it was little less than madness for her to love Lawrence, who could be nothing to her, nothing but a friend, and that for a short time only. But a resolution formed itself in her mind; she would not allow Stephen to dictate to her in the future her course of action, to say what she should do and not do. She did no harm, she assured herself, meant and intended none; and he should not be her mentor, should not assume over her the authority of a tyrant. Thus she justified to herself, as much as she could, though with secret fears and doubts and misgivings, her increasing craving to be with Lawrence often, and she decided to go to Mr. Phipps's picnic without caring whether Stephen approved of it or not, or went himself. He would not now dare advertise that he was her husband. And no one else would know, and in a little while she would leave this country, and, once out of it, would separate from him forever. So she believed, until, on their drive to Triton, an apparently chance remark from Mr. Phipps had opened her eyes to the possibility of others knowing her secret besides Stephen and herself. Mr. Phipps had spoken about a Devil's Mountain in everyone's life, and the need of precautions when one had once begun to cross it: "when we begin to see where we are going to," he had added, with a curious inflection of voice, and Marian had seen more in the words than Lawrence.

Later on that same day, on the return journey from Triton, Mr. Phipps's evident desire to keep her away from Lawrence satisfied her that he had guessed her secret. Her hypersensitiveness, induced by her recent experiences and the tension of her nerves, caused what might have seemed to others to be mere trifles to become symbols and warnings of grave significance to her.

She was right in this reading of Mr. Phipps's words, this interpretation of his tones and looks.

Mr. Phipps had for sometime been genuinely puzzled as to why Stephen should show such aversion to and jealously of Lawrence. Although he knew, as he had told Lawrence, that in Latin-America a girl enjoyed far less freedom than she did in England or America, yet it had occurred to him that Stephen went beyond all ordinary limits; as a brother his attitude was hardly reasonable. Mr. Phipps, always watching closely, began to weave a curious conjecture. There came that scene in the glade at Triton and he caught a glimpse of Marian's face. It was not that of a sister. Marian's remarks to him about Stephen and Nora rushed back into his mind; a man of rapid perceptions and almost instinctive reasoning, Mr. Phipps then definitely and finally accepted the conclusion that had been forming in his mind.

No longer now had he any doubts. What resemblance was there between Marian and Stephen that indicated a blood relationship? None. There was no gesture that either of them had in common, no tone of voice, no trait of character. And the jewels which had been stolen out of Marian's room must have been stolen by someone who knew that he could enter the room. . . he made up his mind immediately. A brother, even if a rogue, might not matter greatly; but a husband! That was an obstacle which Lawrence with all his quiet determination could not overcome. It would be better for both Marian and Lawrence that they should meet as little as possible, best for them both that they should be separated by hundreds of miles of ocean.

Mr. Phipps was genuinely distressed; he was a romanticist at heart; he loved to play the beneficent god out of the machine, but now he must act the part of an unwelcome intruder into other people's affairs. He tried to interfere without showing his hand too openly, but Lawrence perceived and resented this new attitude of his. And Marian, though feeling that Mr. Phipps was right, had not sufficient strength, or rather, experienced no real desire to hold herself aloof from Lawrence. Even while saying that she should and would do so, she was drifting nearer and nearer to him; or, as Mr. Phipps had grimly put it, she continued to Devil's Mountain in spite of the threatening danger.

But a slip of her tongue, on the night of the Hamilton's party, brought matters to a climax. Stephen insisted on taking her back to the hotel, and at parting from her that night he had spoken a few sinisterly significant words. He told her that unless she broke with Lawrence he would make it known that she was his wife; he informed her curtly that he had nothing to fear from anything she might dare to say about the jewels, since not one pearl would be found in his possession, but that, if she uttered one word to direct suspicion against him, he would know the cause and reason of it and would not hesitate to shoot Lawrence like a dog. She knew the temperament that dictated this threat; she believed him capable of carrying it out, if brought to bay.

"And now you know," concluded Mr. Phipps, "why she has not spoken to you since that night. She was thinking of you fare more than of herself, my boy, and now we have both got to think of her."

XXV

LADY ROSEDALE INTERVENES

A m leaving on Cecilia for Costa Rice tonight. Jefferson left in charge. Writing."

Lawrence himself coded this message to his head office in London, signed it, and put it in his pocket to be despatched later on. It was not the first time that he had suddenly left Kingston for some South or Central American country; sometimes he had done this on instructions from his London chiefs, sometimes on his own initiative and judgement, in the interest of the business with whose local management he was entrusted. There would be no questioning his decision to go; the real reason of his present determination, if and when it came to the knowledge of head office, might create some surprise, perhaps astonishment, but he had calmly discounted all that. There was plenty of leave due to him, the man next to him was quite competent to carry on in his absence for a few weeks; they would know in London that only something of vital urgency, imperative in its call, could have induced him to make up his mind to leave so precipitately and without first asking permission as a matter of form; but whatever they might think or do his course to him appeared straight and clear: there was no other.

He could not allow Marian, in her present terrible predicament, to go, a girl without friends and apparently without a future, to a strange country where she might be the prey of awful anxiety, of loneliness, of depression, and even of despair. He had on one or two unforgotten occasions seen something of her distress without realising its reason, he knew how deeply she could feel, how pathetic was her helplessness. The discovery that she was Stephen's wife had come upon him with the force of a blow, half stunning him. He had listened the night before in unbroken silence to his friend's narration of Stephen's life, of Marian's brief unhappy experience as a married woman; and when Mr. Phipps said that both of them must help her now he had come to a resolution which he had not thought it necessary to mention, feeling that his friend would offer opposition, and not being of a mind to argue or discuss the point. Phipps could not decide for him. Phipps was the truest, the staunchest of friends, but it was he and not Phipps who loved Marian, it was he whom Marian loved. He saw it all clearly now: her fight against yielding to his pleasing, her reluctances, struggles, bitter regrets; she was linked to another man, and the secret chain checked her every movement and clanked its warning to every impulse of her heart. But now the whole aspect of her life had swiftly and suddenly changed. She loved him: alone and in a strange country she would be the more unhappy because of her love for him. Surely he could not leave her to face the unknown future alone.

He would not, for her future was ineluctable bound up with his, and he did not wish it otherwise. What was she to this man she had married? He had deceived her, treated her wretchedly, stooped to rob her: was a marriage vow made in ignorance, regarded with contempt by her husband, with poignant regret by herself, to stand between her and happiness? Perhaps she would decided that it should: he would not dwell on that just now. At the least she must have a chance to think it all out calmly, must be free to choose; she must not leave Jamaica as a fugitive, alone, perhaps to drift from one country to another if she found it safe to move about at all, with not one human being on whom she could absolutely rely, with no one who would make the uttermost sacrifice for her sake.

And there was himself. He was no mere youth now, but a man who knew his own mind, one who, for better or for worse, had made up his mind in so far as Marian was concerned. Stephen Braeme would be sent to prison; Marian would be done with him forever. Without her he, Lawrence, could doubtless continue to toil, perhaps to succeed, but his whole being was in high revolt against the hideouts tedium and sordidness and aimlessness of that. He could not be again what he had been; his life had taken a new direction, had been touched to deep and passionate issues; his most vital interest now was centred in someone other than himself. His course was planned; he would go with her tonight, would see that she was suitably placed in Costa Rica, would shortly return to Jamaica to straighten out any matter that might need his personal attention, and then go back to her if she would let him. He would go back to her forever. That was what he desired: the final decision must be left to her. There might be some talk about it in the land of his birth, some gossip, then indifference and forgetfulness. It did not matter. Nothing mattered to him now but Marian: the future would be sharply separated from the past.

"May I come in?"

"Please do," replied Lawrence, recognising his friend's voice on the other side of the door. Mr. Phipps had not troubled the porter to announce him.

"You have seen her this morning?" asked Lawrence, as Mr. Phipps seated himself opposite to him.

"Yes, son, as I arranged to do last night. She is in a bad state, almost broken down at last, I fancy. She could not go out today, but her director said that did not matter. I guess they have nearly finished with her."

"And she will go?"

"She doesn't know what to do; it is terribly difficult for her to make up her mind; but she will go. She knows many people here, and—quite naturally, poor girl—she doesn't want to face a scandal amongst them all. I told her plainly that I had talked over this matter with you, and that you agreed that the best thing she could do would be to leave quickly and quietly, though that isn't exactly what you agree with. I knew she would want to know what you thought; she would be guided by your wishes, Lawrence, far more than by mine, in any great crisis of her life.

"But there is no telling exactly how any woman will act. Last night, after I left her, she saw her husband and warned him that there was a detective from America here. She told him that I feared the worst, and that I knew and had known all along who took Lady Rosedale's pearls."

Lawrence started. "But didn't you warn her against saying anything to him?" he asked quietly.

"I did; but she'll have her own ideas, you know, as to what is right and what not. I suppose she remembered he's her husband, and felt that she ought to give him a warning. He's gone out of town with the company today; gone to work as usual. It seems that he has some pluck or he could never have done that. He's going to show fight, Lawrence. I am afraid we may have to reckon with him."

"But he does not know she is leaving tonight, does he?"

"No. Fortunately she refrained from saying anything about that to him, but she told me quite plainly today that she must tell Lady Rosedale. She said that she must let Lady Rosedale know everything that has occurred— everything. She doesn't want the old dame to think that she had a hand in the stealing of the necklace; she doesn't want to appear ungrateful. I argued against this decision, but she was firm, and now I can only hope the old lady will keep her mouth shut for twenty-four hours. I have got the passport all right. Marian and I went out together and fixed that, but there was a man watching her. It's that fellow Sampson, of the Detective Department."

"And he saw you go into the Costa Rican consul's office!" exclaimed Lawrence; "won't he guess what for, Phipps?"

"He may and he may not," returned Mr. Phipps calmly; "but, remember, the consul has only once office in a big building; there's a dressmaker's parlour in the same building; there is a curio shop, and someother business offices. In spite of all his cleverness, Mr. Sampson could not efface himself before I saw him, and I bought plenty of curios, with Marian's help, this morning. See? The detective didn't enter the building; he watched from outside. By the time that he has reported my movements, and they have thought out the meaning of 'em, Marian should be quite safe."

"Once she is on board, the ship will sail with her," said Lawrence quietly, "whatever they may choose to do. They will not find her, Phipps, or bring her back."

"I guess they won't, son, if you have a hand in this business; the trouble is going to be to get her out of the hotel."

"She can leave by boat from the hotel's seawall; people go rowing from there at night."

"I have thought of that too; she could go for a row with you. But we must leave nothing to chance. She may be more closely watched tonight than she has been today. Then there is her husband: he may be with her. If he is, you cannot be on the spot, Lawrence, and there will be only one thing to do. I'll offer to take Marian out for a ride, and if I am followed I will break every speed limit in this old country and show the natives, white and black, what a real road maniac is. I'll throw 'em off the track, never fear, and get Marian on board, whatever happens. When she is there, the ship must sail at once. Can you do it?"

"The captain already knows that he may receive orders to sail at anytime from midnight. Will that do?"

"You've got it fixed fine," said Mr. Phipps heartily; "I don't see how we can fail."

A knock sounded at the door, and the porter, putting his head into the room, announced that a lady was asking to see Mr. Beaman: "a Lady Rose," he said.

"Ah," said Mr. Phipps and puckered up his lips. "This is likely to be an unpleasant interview, son. You must keep your temper for the little girl's sake."

"Show the lady in," said Lawrence to the porter, and set his lips sternly.

Lady Rosedale entered with her usual self-possession, but it needed no second glance at her face to discover that she was agitated. She look searchingly at Lawrence, noted the drawn lines about his eyes, the set, hard mouth, the rigid attitude of his figure, then she glanced at Mr. Phipps. That gentleman, his face without a smile, was eyeing her curiously. Lady Rosedale perceived that she had a hostile audience.

"Marian has told me everything," she began at once, not taking the trouble to shake hands. "She told me about half an hour ago. I have come here to talk to you about it."

Lady Rosedale addressed her words to Lawrence. Plainly she considered him the principal character in this situation, with Mr. Phipps of little or no importance.

"Well?"

Lawrence's monosyllabic question, and the manner of it, suggested conflict. Lady Rosedale stiffened herself and eyes him squarely.

"You will understand, Mr. Beaman," she said, "that I am speaking as Miss Braeme's friend, her disinterested friend. She had sufficient confidence in me to tell me just what has happened and what she proposes to do. I have suffered a heavy loss through her, but I know it was not her fault, and I never thought it was.

"The poor girl's life must have been a hell all this time," Lady Rosedale went on hurriedly, and the two men observed a visible softening in her tones and look, a slight trembling of her hands. "I can fancy what she must have suffered today when confessing everything to me. She has no mother, no sister: I am the only woman anywhere to whom she can speak. You don't understand that that means, Mr. Beaman! Men don't understand these things."

This was a revelation of an aspect of Lady Rosedale's character which neither man had seen before. The searching, curious look in Mr. Phipps's eyes changed subtly but Lawrence still sat rigid, antagonistic and cold.

"It is very kind of you to arrange to send the poor girl away," she continued; "but tell me, Mr. Beaman, do you intend to go with her?"

The question came suddenly and caught Lawrence unprepared. Mr. Phipps started perceptibly. Lady Rosedale had gone straight to the heart of Lawrence's secret, with an insight for which Mr. Phipps had never given her credit. Both of them noticed the contraction of Lawrence's eyes and the sterner setting of his lips. Lady Rosedale did not wait for an answer.

"I can see that you do," she added, "and I understand. Oh, I know that you care for Marian, Mr. Beaman; I think I was the first to see it. I know how you feel: you are thinking that the world would be well lost for her sake, and that, now especially, you cannot leave her alone. But you mustn't go with her. You must not. That would be fatal to you both, don't you see? And far more fatal to her. Can't you see it?"

"I do not," said Lawrence. "I do not!" he repeated, with the first expression of passion he had displayed since Lady Rosedale entered the room.

"Well, I do, and I am a woman of the world," said Lady Rosedale, with a slight resumption of her old autocratic manner. "She doesn't know that you contemplate going with her, and it is better that she shouldn't, for that would only make her dreadful uncertainty worse. Poor child!" Once more there was a softening of the lines about Lady Rosedale's mouth, just a suspicion of a mist over her eyes. She now turned to the older man.

"The girl lost her mother, years ago; her father, as you know, was an Englishman. Of good family too; she has told me a good deal about him. To me she is an English girl, Mr. Phipps; her father's people and mine are of the same country, and she loved him, and she loves England too, although she never saw it. I have no daughter, no child, and I took to this poor girl from the moment I saw her. She did not need to tell me that she had nothing to do with the loss of my pearls; I should as soon have believe a daughter of mine capable of taking them. I love Marian too," Lady Rosedale went on, speaking with unwonted simplicity, and looking again at Lawrence, "and my affection is more unselfish than yours, Mr. Beaman. You are thinking of her, I know, but you are thinking also of yourself: you cannot help it: you are thinking of your own happiness as well as of hers. The love of a man is far more selfish than the love of a mother, and it is as a mother that I feel towards Marian. You must stay here. If you go with her, her name will be smirched and the things said about her may follow her far: remember, she is a married woman. She will have no place anywhere if you are with her. You can never know what is to happen in the future; meanwhile she is too young to have her life more spoilt than it has been. You must remain behind. It will be hard; I sympathise with you; but you must remain. You see what I mean, don't you, Mr. Phipps?"

"I do, Lady Rosedale," said Mr. Phipps gravely; "and I agree with you. But it is for our friend and for Marian to decide."

"No," said Lady Rosedale decisively, "it is for an older woman than Marian to decide, and one who can see father than Mr. Beaman can just now. Don't think"—(she addressed Lawrence)—"don't think I am actuated by any feeling of opposition to you now. Why, I wish a thousand times that she had met you before she met that miserable man who has brought her so much unhappiness! I am sorry for you both Mr. Beaman; but sorry most for Marian, for she is a woman, and her life has been spoilt almost from the beginning. You must not help spoil it further."

"Spoil her life!" cried Lawrence fiercely, "and what has she before her? Exile, loneliness, unhappiness? I would give up everything for her sake, and you call that spoiling her life? I am going with her to devote my whole life to her, and you call that spoiling her life?"

"Yes, I do. At least, let her leave this country with no one able to say a word against her. If you go, suddenly, on the same ship, to the same country, with her, there will be the gravest suspicions, the worst beliefs. Away from you she may be lonely at heart, but not friendless, Mr. Beaman; you may depend on me for that."

"Ah!" cried Mr. Phipps. "God bless you, Lady Rosedale!"

It was a sudden exclamation, springing from the heart of the man; it escaped him as it were, and the quick working of his face showed already that he was ashamed of this momentary display of emotion. But Lady Rosedale threw a grateful glance at him, and again a mist passed over her masterful eyes. "I am going with Marian to Costa Rica," she continued, "it should be easy to arrange."

"That will solve all our difficulties," murmured Mr. Phipps.

"I can see that," said the Englishwoman, taking charge of the situation at once, as she had taken charge of many a situation in her time. "Marian believes she is being watched; it makes her dreadfully nervous. But no one, I suppose, would think of watching me. She will leave the hotel with me tonight; we can go for a drive somewhere, perhaps to Constant Spring, and then to your ship. I will speak to the manager this evening and tell them that I am going away for a short time but don't want it known. I will retain my room at the hotel and send to the ship only such things as I may actually need; some of Marian's things can go with mine. It is *my* jewellery that was stolen, and even an American detective would hardly believe that I would aid the escape of anyone who had taken them: so they won't follow me tonight. Do you agree?"

She looked from one to the other of the men. Mr. Phipps's face was radiant. He had been more troubled about the difficulties Marian might have to overcome in getting away from the hotel than he had thought it wise to confess to Lawrence.

Lawrence was thinking deeply. He had always known Lady Rosedale as an enemy of his. But now there could be no doubting her sincerity, her genuine affection for Marian. She was a woman, conventional undoubtedly, and the fear that Marian's reputation might suffer if he went away with her touched her to the quick. She was fighting for Marian: he saw that, and fighting because of her love for her. He saw too that she would go with the girl, or, if would not give her a passage, would follow after as quickly as she could; the resolute expression on her face could leave him in no doubt of her intention. And Marian? She had clung to the older woman, instinctively divining, perhaps, that Lady Rosedale loved her; and in her present distress she would still cling to Lady Rosedale as to a mother. He might decide to go, might refuse Lady Rosedale a passage, but she had said that he was selfish in this love of his, in this very resolution to set everything at defiance and go with Marin, and in the depths of his heart he knew there was much truth in this assertion.

And she had used the same argument he had urged on Phipps when protesting against Marian fleeing from the country: her name might be stained.

He could no longer contend to himself that Marian was about to face the future friendless. No one would suspect that Lady Rosedale had left Jamaica hurriedly because she personally desired to escape the attention of the police. She would say that she would shortly be returning, and had taken Miss Braeme as a companion: the act might be regarded as eccentric, but hardly as anything more.

"And I think you could square it with the moving picture director," broke in Mr. Phipps who had been watching Lawrence keenly, but who spoke now to Lady Rosedale. "You might write him a note tonight, to be delivered tomorrow, saying that you suddenly decided to take Miss Braeme for a short tour with you, as you noticed that she was run down and needed a rest. I guess he can do without her. And she may come back with you a little later on: nothing may be said about her, either by Baker, or her husband, once she is out of the way. Anyhow, we must take the chance of that."

"Are they likely to go on with my case in the courts if I am out of the island?" Lady Rosedale asked Mr. Phipps.

"Hardly, unless they have some good evidence on which to arrest somebody, and that could only mean a preliminary investigation. The whole affair may blow over if you are not on the spot."

"Then I'll write to the Inspector General tonight and tell him that I won't be here for a little while, and thank him for what he has done to help me. I will write as if the case no longer interests me."

"You might drop a note to the Governor too."

"I will; I will leave them to be posted tomorrow. I am taking Marian up to Constant Spring after dinner. We'll remain there until—what o'clock shall we come on board, Mr. Beaman?"

"At midnight, or as near after that as you can."

"Very well; I shall see you then?" she said, putting out her hand kindly.

"Yes; and I want to thank you, Lady Rosedale, from the bottom of my heart for your kindness to Marian. I will remain in Jamaica until I hear from her. Perhaps you are right that it is best for her that I should."

"I am sure of it, Mr. Beaman, and so is your friend here. I am going now to see about my passport."

She walked towards the door, Mr. Phipps hastening towards it, to open it for her. She turned for a moment towards Lawrence.

In her eyes he read more sympathy than he would have once thought her capable of feeling. Then she passed outside.

"I take off my hat to that dame," said Mr. Phipps gravely, going back to his seat. "She doesn't like spending too much money; but she's going to keep her room at the hotel so as to make it appear that she may return at any moment, and that's for Marian's sake. She's going to a country which she never before thought of visiting, and that's because she doesn't want the little girl to be alone. I don't care a damn how disagreeable and foolish and pretentious she is; she's pure white where Marian is concerned. I always believed she loved Marian.

"And you, son, are doing a finer thing to remain here than if you went with the little movie star. It is the harder thing of the two to do. But don't think that only you and Lady Rosedale would go with Marian if she could not go alone. The old man has also a warm place in his heart for that little girl."

XXVI

The Only Way

Hardly any of the people moving about the lawns and gardens of the Myrtle Bank Hotel took any particular notice of two dark men, natives of the country obviously, who hovered in the vicinity of the American bar, from which position they commanded a clear view of the four gates—two to the East, the others to the West—which opened on the street. Now and then one of these men would stroll unobtrusively about, going down to the seawall, wandering by the annex, paying marked attention to the boats that came along the waterfront plying for hire. These men were taken by those who saw them to be persons connected with the hotel. But Lady Rosedale knew why they were there, and so did Marian; Mr. Phipps also, and Stephen Braeme.

Stephen was at the hotel this afternoon. It was about six o'clock; half an hour before he had returned from his work with someother members of his company, and he had been keenly conscious that day that one of these men had been watching him. The man had always kept at some distance away; but now he was within the grounds of the hotel itself, and Stephen remembered having often seen him before. He had paid no particular attention to him on those previous occasions; only today, when he knew for certain that he was under the surveillance of the police, did the presence of the man become apparent to him with a sinister significance. He was certain that if he had stopped at the house where he lodged, the detective would have stopped in the neighbourhood also. He was under remitting scrutiny. His every movement was watched.

And the other man was probably watching Marian. And at any moment the order for the arrest of one or both of them might be pronounced.

He had seen Marian the night before: she had warned him, bitterly, despairingly, and he had realised that, with the advent of the American detective there would be put forth a grim effort to trace the man who had stolen Lady Rosedale's necklace. He knew now that it was Mr. Phipps who had returned Marian's broach, and also that Mr. Phipps, for Marian's sake, would give no hint of what he knew.

Stephen was quick-witted. He was terribly startled when Marian broken the news to him of Detective Baker's arrival, of Mr. Phipps's fears that he had something of a record in America, but he did not allow his fright to get the mastery of him; he realised he must have time to think, and that, above all, he must give no indication that he believed himself suspected. Escape by any ordinary means was out of the question. Mr. Phipps had told Marian that it was certain that Stephen would be stopped if he were seen entering a wharf; and no consul of any country in the island would now visé his passport; they had probably all been warned. He was surrounded, as it were, by a cloud of visible and invisible witnesses; along the waterfront were sentinels placed to prevent him from leaving the island; if he left the hotel for an instant, there would be a man in a car in full pursuit. So much he fully realised, and yet, with in instinct of self-preservation, with the instinct of an actor also, he kept a grip upon himself, and strove to appear not unduly concerned.

He had gone to his work that day chiefly to dispel any suspicion that he realised he was in danger. Yet, inwardly, he was fearfully apprehensive. True, he had been in tight places before and had made good his escape. They had discovered nothing against him in the States; merely to have been arrested was quite a different thing from having a conviction recorded against one; yet he knew in his heart of hearts that his former arrest on suspicion, in connection with a jewel robbery, would count against him now with the local police should they know of it, and he was possessed of the conviction that at last they knew.

He had sent away the pearls long since; they had arrived safely in New York; they could not be brought in evidence against him. No one had seen him entering or leaving Marian's room on the night he took the necklace; no one—and yet Marian said Mr. Phipps knew all about the theft. But Phipps would be silent for Marian's sake Phipps would be silent: what then had he to fear? Let him keep calm, let him go about his work as usual, and, no matter what they might wish to suspect, they could not touch him: there was no evidence against him.

Again and again he went over the ground, reaching this conclusion, but not deriving from it that feeling of certainty without which the most hopeful of conclusions is vain. The dread and terror which, three years before, had driven him out of America and to Peru, assailed him now; he was plagued by doubts. Had anything been discovered about the robbery of Mrs. Stone's jewels? Had anything been brought to light in connection with some of his former acts? That question would obtrude itself into his mind. And—would Marian remain silent? She had assured him that she would say nothing, would give no hint, but suppose her nerves gave way? The American detective might question her, press her hardly, might return again and again to the charge: what would she do? She had no reason to wish to deal gently with him, she might think she had a very good reason to do otherwise. She might want to be rid of him: he believed that she did. Fear and jealously and wounded vanity lit a flame of wrath in his heart. What if she should say a word now that should send him to prison and leave her alone with Lawrence Beaman?

He did not believe in the loyalty of women. And then, did not Marian and Lawrence Beaman love one another?

He slipped his hands mechanically into the back pocket of his trousers; he would not go to prison, and Lawrence Beaman should not have her. She should die first: the next shot would be for himself. Beamean would have the awful satisfaction of being a mourner at her funeral. His wife, the wife of a Quesada of Peru, should be no Englishman's leman.

That was one reason why he was at the hotel this afternoon. He booked a room there on coming back to the city. He would remain there for as long as he could. Tomorrow he would insist upon Marian going out to work with him: and if she could not go, he also would find some excuse for not going out with the company: he would keep her under his eyes always, until the end came. If arrested while away from her, he would ask leave to speak with her for a few minutes; he knew the Jamaica police would never refuse such a request, or think of putting handcuffs on him, or of treating him in anyway harshly. If arrested, with this American detective in the island, there would be a small chance of escape. He would act then, swiftly, decisively, but not before. He would not abandon hope until the police took a definite step; not until the last moment would he utterly despair. He drew his hand away from his pocket, and, with the feeling that someone was eyeing him intently, he turned his head in the direction from which this subtle, intangible indication came. He discovered Mr. Phipps looking curiously at him.

And something in Mr. Phipps's face told Stephen that Phipps had guessed his intention from that involuntary movement of his towards his pistol pocket. Mr. Phipps had had no time to disguise the startled expression that had swept over his face: looking full at one another, both men discerned clearly the dominant thought in the mind of each.

Mr. Phipps's countenance assumed a hard expression: the light of a fighter shone in his eyes, his jaw thrust forward as his gaze riveted itself on the face of the other man. Stephen smiled mockingly, and stared defiance at Mr. Phipps. Then, as though moved by a sudden impulse, he walked over to where Mr. Phipps was standing.

The latter met him calmly. "To carry a gun without a license is a punishable offence in this country, friend," said Mr. Phipps softly.

"Indeed," said Stephen; "but how would it be known?"

"Ah, that is the question. This part of the British Empire goes in a lot for all the formalities of law; they make sure of their ground before they lay a charge against anyone. That is why I too think I am safe in carrying a gun." And Mr. Phipps lightly touched his own pistol pocket with a meaning smile.

Stephen understood. He was to be under the surveillance of Mr. Phipps. He shrugged his shoulders carelessly and threw back his head. He was prepared for risks and struggles; he would not be frightened by a threat.

"Let us walk," suggested Mr. Phipps. "One of those men over there is watching us rather keenly. If we walk up and down he can scarcely follow us. I want to talk to you."

Deliberately turning their backs on the detective Mr. Phipps and Stephen strolled eastward until they were out of the man's sight; then they turned and retraced their steps. They noticed that the detective had already begun to follow them, but that he stopped casually when he saw that they were coming back. Again they turned to repeat their walk.

"What are you going to do?" asked Mr. Phipps quietly. "Your wife told you what I said to her, I know."

"I think you already know what I am going to do," said Stephen. "I am a Quesada, and she bears my name. I will not leave her to Lawrence Beaman."

"You are not generous, certainly," retorted Mr. Phipps. "You have treated her shamefully, but you think only of yourself to the very last. If you wish to put an end to your life, do so: I for one would not prevent you. It might be the best thing, all things considered, that you could do: for a man like you there is no future worth having if you are once convicted and sent to prison. But why pursue the poor little girl with your unreasoning hate and jealousy? Be decent to her for once, Quesada!"

"And leave her for your friend, señor?" laughed Stephen bitterly. "That is not how a gentleman of Peru acts; but you, of course,—you

H. G. DE LISSER

would not understand! And let me tell you this: you must not again speak to me as you did just now. If you do—"

"I carry a gun as well as you, friend," broke in Mr. Phipps warningly, "and you are not likely to take me unawares. Please remember, too, that any insane act on your part will only lead to your immediate arrest. You need not anticipate that by some hours."

To and fro, west and east, in front of the main building of the hotel they walked, and the detective, noting that they were talking and promenading without giving him a glance, made no effort to keep them always in sight. But he kept the four gates of the hotel continually under his eyes, and he took the precaution to send his colleague to the southern part of the grounds which ended at the seawall. He knew that Stephen could slip round the eastern end of the building and get down to the seafront if he wished, and there a boat could easily be hailed.

"We came here together, and if I cannot escape she will go the way I go," said Stephen in a bitter voice. "I don't know that I would care to escape without her even if I had the chance of doing so—which I have not."

"Yet—pardon me for saying so Señor Quesada," said Mr. Phipps with elaborate politeness—"yet it is scarcely love that dictates your decision."

"It is pride," answered Stephen, drawing himself up with a flash of the eye. Mr. Phipps say the motion, noted the impetuous, arrogant look, and a memory of a scene by the shore of St. Ann, a scene in which were mingled the sea and some rocking boats, and a far-off horizon, and a little group of people, flashed into his mind.

"Let us stop here for a few minutes," he commanded briskly: they were again out of the detective's sigh. "Listen to me. Beaman knows that Marian is your wife; Lady Rosedale knows it too; Lady Rosedale is very fond of her and will take care of her. I don't think you need to have any fear about your 'honour'—it is that you are thinking of, isn't it?"

"You know, señor."

"So that if you could get away and leave the poor girl in peace— don't try and bluff me, friend," exclaimed Mr. Phipps testily, seeing that Stephen was about to resent his plain speaking: "it can't be done, and you are not the man to do it, anyhow—if, I say, you could get away, she would be all right. She is among friends, and you ought to know, in spite of all your foolish jealousy, that she is not a light character, but a good woman at heart."

"I would not have married her if I had thought she was not what she ought to be," returned Stephen coldly.

"Then there is less excuse for the way you have treated her," said Mr. Phipps firmly. "Now if you could get away—let us walk back: we have been standing here quite long enough."

They retraced their steps again, and the detective, vigilantly waiting, and already beginning to wonder if they had gone round to the opposite side of the building, relaxed his tension.

Mr. Phipps was thinking rapidly. He could inform the detectives that Stephen was armed, and that might lead them to take some immediate action. But that might also lead to Stephen saying or doing something that might render Marian's departure impossible. Such a risk could not be faced.

"You were saying, if I could get away," said Stephen. "But I cannot. I am like a rat trapped: I am hunted, and the hunters are always in sight. I have been thinking, thinking, thinking, and I can see no way. There is only one way," he added gloomily, "but I am not afraid of that. My people have never been afraid of it when it was a choice between disgrace and that only way."

"There was only one way left to Don Arnaldo de Sassi," murmured Mr. Phipps reminiscently. They had again left the detective out of sight, and their pace was slow. "There are boats along the northern shore that even now sail to Cuba with labourers who cannot get a passport here, or with folk who for reasons of their own do not want to apply for one. I wonder."

Stephen stopped dead. "Señor?" he cried.

"My car, which can go fifty miles an hour at full speed, is just over there," and Mr. Phipps pointing east to an open space where waiting cars were parked. "To my chauffeur I have given the evening off; I thought I might want to drive myself. Now if I were leaving this place and did not wish to be seen by anyone on the grounds, I would not make the mistake of going west, for that would take me past the hotel and I should probably be seen. I should go direct east for a block or so, turn north, and then go west—or whichever way I wanted to go. I guess some folk would spend sometime looking and asking for me before they would think of my having driven my car in a direction that hardly anyone ever takes on leaving the hotel. Let us walk back."

"For the last time," said Stephen.

"I suppose you carry plenty of money with you?" asked Mr. Phipps casually.

"I have enough now on my person for any purpose."

"Some food purchased at a wayside shop, a handsome sum to a few boatmen, and I should soon be landed somewhere along the coast of Cuba safely," continued Mr. Phipps, as though he were pursuing a train of personal reflections. "I speak Spanish fluently, you know, and so long as I do not trouble the Cuban officials, and am generous to those of them I come in contact with, I should hardly be molested in Cuba until I could slip out of it. Perhaps I might easily pass for a Cuban—will you excuse me if I leave you here?"

Without waiting for an answer Mr. Phipps walked rapidly away towards the hotel's annex, and did not glance once behind him. Stephen stood still for a moment or two. Already it was darkling; the shadows of evening were dimming the sky; a little while and night would descend upon the earth, night and obscurity. He seemed to make up his mind to a final decision. Hurrying to the park wherein a few cars were waiting, he entered the one which he knew belonged to Mr. Phipps, started it and turned its head eastward. A block or two away from the hotel and he turned the car north; presently he was running dead west towards the only road he knew by which he could reach that little bay on the northern shore from which the last of the conquering Spaniards had, for the last time, embarked from Jamaica. Swiftly he sped towards this road; he remembered it well. In a very little while he must cross the mountain to which it led, the mountain which lay between him and safety. He was leaving Marian. But the imperative need of the moment was to think of himself. To Nora, to be with whom he had lingered longer in this country than prudence dictated, he gave no a thought. His mind was obsessed by what lay before him, by what lay behind—all the selfishness of the man was uppermost and dominant now: with an opportunity of escape had vanished all thought of protecting his "honour" even at the cost of a woman's life.

Once over the mountain that lay ahead, and he had no doubt that he could land safely in Cuba, where he could easily pass for a Cuban, and thence steal away to someother Latin American country where he would need fear no agent of the English or the American police. That was his plan. So, swiftly and ever more swiftly, as the boundaries of the city were left behind, the car rushed forward towards la Montagña del Diablo, as the old Spaniards had named it—towards the Devil's Mountain, as it still is called.

XXVII

Mr. Hammond's Story

A polite request from Major Fellspar, about an hour after Stephen's hurried departure from the Myrtle Bank Hotel, brought Mr. Phipps down from his room (in the seclusion of which he had determined to remain as long as it was possible to do so). He found Major Fellspar in the manager's private office, with Inspector Harmsworth and Detective Sampson: Sampson looking just then the picture of dejection and dismay. And with them was the American detective, Baker, whom Mr. Phipps immediately greeted with well-simulated surprise and cordiality.

"I believe you were the last person seen with Stephen Braeme this evening, Mr. Phipps," said Major Fellspar immediately, after somewhat coldly returning Mr. Phipps's bow: "did you notice where he went when he left you?"

"I can't say I did, Major," replied Mr. Phipps. "As a matter of fact, he didn't leave me; I left him. I had something to do in my room before dinner, so I asked him to excuse me—we had been walking together. What's up, if I may ask?"

"It is very important that we should know where he has gone to," returned the Inspector General gravely; "we believe that he did not come back into this building. He may have slipped behind the annex, of course, and gone out into the lane; it seems that that way of escape was not watched this afternoon"—Major Fellspar glanced angrily at Inspector Harmsworth, who reddened—"but you say, Mr. Phipps, that you did not notice the direction that he took?"

"I did not, Major; and for all you know he may still be somewhere in the hotel. But won't you tell me what you are so anxious to find him you? You have awakened my curiosity. I take it, myself, that Stephen has gone out somewhere in the legitimate exercise of his right to life, liberty and the pursuit of happiness, as is guaranteed to all men by our American Constitution. But you sort of suggest that you want him badly and that he has slipped out of your hands. I'd like to be wise on that."

Mr. Phipps was aware that Baker was eyeing him keenly, but he took no notice of a scrutiny that was too searching to be polite. Baker distrusted him; that he felt certain of. But Baker could not know how much he knew about Stephen, and there he had Mr. Baker at a disadvantage.

"Braeme cannot possibly escape from Jamaica," said Major Fellspar decisively; "so much at least is certain." (Mr. Phipps took these words to mean: "No friends of Braeme's need try to aid him, for they cannot succeed.") "Yes, I will take you into our confidence, Mr. Phipps. Stephen Braeme, or Quesada, as his real name is, is wanted by the American Government for robbery. All the necessary formalities for his arrest and extradition will be completed tomorrow forenoon; in the meantime we have thought it advisable to keep an eye on him. You were seen with him an hour ago. When he had not appeared for a few minutes—that is the time Detective Sampson mentions, but it must have been longer—a search was made for him, and he was nowhere to be found. Sampson then telephoned to Detective Headquarters, and I thought I would come down myself to see what should be done. I tell you all this, because you will suspect that there is something serious about our enquiries after Braeme, and because I should not like you to aid and abet—in ignorance no doubt—a criminal who is wanted for a number of serious offences. That would be a most unfortunate position for you."

Mr. Phipps whistled loud and long. "So this explains Mr. Baker's presence here!" he exclaimed. "Stephen a crook! Say, Major, that will be hard on his little sister when she comes to know of it. I haven't much use for the young man, but I tell you right now that I have a tender spot for his sister. Guess she doesn't know anything about this, does she, Baker?"

"Could you show us where you left Braeme?" drawled Mr. Baker, without troubling to answer Mr. Phipps. The American detective was plainly, thought not rudely, hostile.

"Sure!" said Mr. Phipps getting briskly up from his chair; "come right along." He led them, talking the while, to where he had parted from Stephen not long before. They looked about them: the spot told them nothing. Mr. Phipps still talked.

"Stephen was depressed," he admitted; "talked pessimistically like a man crossed in love; suicide and that sort of thing you know; a desire to be away and at rest. But it isn't easy for anyone to get away from this country, is it, Major? I should find considerable difficulty myself."

"He can escape from no port of this island, not the smallest," said the Inspector General. "There is not a ship, not a vessel leaving, that is not being watched by some officer of the Government. So, if he happens to have become suspicious and is trying to get away, he will fail. I suppose that when he is caught he will blab about any confederates he may have had. I wouldn't trust a rogue to keep his mouth shut out of gratitude or any fine feeling."

"I hope he will blab if he has anything to say," agreed Mr. Phipps. "So Stephen's a crook, eh? Well, I am beginning to feel scared. He didn't pick my pocket this afternoon: that I know, for my watch is still in my possession. But who is to tell if he wouldn't have done me in the eye if he had had half a chance?"

They returned to the building and Mr. Phipps invited the two officials and Mr. Baker to dine with him. They declined, Mr. Baker explaining that he had already arranged for dinner, and that Major Fellspar and Inspector Harmsworth would be dining with him. Would Mr. Phipps join them?

"Delighted," said Phipps, and wished that the three men were miles and miles away; "and after dinner we might go for a spin somewhere in my car, when we can talk at ease over this extraordinary news you have just been giving me. I told my chauffeur that I didn't think I'd want him tonight, but I know where to find him."

Without paying attention to the protests of the other men that they would not care to go driving after dinner, Mr. Phipps called one of the bellboys and precisely instructed him to send a message to his chauffeur, bidding him to present himself for duty at the hotel at nine o'clock sharp. He gave the chauffeur's address, then went in to dinner. As they passed up the dining room they had a glimpse of Lady Rosedale, regally attired, and of Marian, also dressed superbly. Lady Rosedale bowed to them—her face was towards them—Marian did not look round. But of her profile Mr. Phipps had a swift view, and there was a little twinkle in his eye as he saw it. "Rouged," he thought. "Rouged by Lady Rosedale. That old dame can put up a good bluff: no pallor and tears for her. Nothing to give the show away. She's got grit and bounce anyhow."

It was obvious to Mr. Phipps that the Inspector General was just now acting under the advice of Mr. Baker, and that Mr. Baker, for reasons of his own, was determined to stick to the hotel for sometime tonight, and perhaps for the whole night. Phipps felt in his bones that Baker linked him up in some way with Stephen's disappearance and perhaps even thought that he had managed to smuggle Stephen into his room preparatory to smuggling him out of the country. Mr. Phipps remembered vividly an incident of the sort in which he had figured in

Guatemala, and Baker had been in Guatemala at the time. Had Baker heard of it? The latter was now keenly on the alert. He wanted to know more about that last conversation between Stephen and Mr. Phipps; Mr. Phipps knew it, and persisted in talking about all sorts of subjects, Stephen included, without going back to the chief incident of the afternoon. He might have to talk about it later, and he wanted time to make sure of his ground. If Stephen escaped, there would not be much difficulty. If by any chance he failed—well, an explanation would have to be forthcoming, and it would have to be extremely plausible. He must not say too much this evening.

Close upon nine o'clock they finished dining; on going into the lobby they were joined for a moment by Lady Rosedale and Marian, who, after dinner, had gone into the Ladies' Room for their wraps. The American detective swept Marian's face with a searching glance, but bowed politely as he was introduced to her by the Inspector General. Major Fellspar said nothing about Baker's profession to either Marian or Lady Rosedale, and neither of these gave any sign that they knew who Baker was. Indeed, Lady Rosedale rose to the occasion with magnificent aplomb. Seeing Major Fellspar and Inspector Harmsworth with the American detective, and Mr. Phipps in their company, she surmised that they were at the hotel for some reason connected with the robbery, and possibly closely connected with Marian. She addressed herself to Major Fellspar, assuming her grandest manner, which always made the Major feel that Lady Rosedale regarded him as a not very efficient policeman to whom she consciously showed exceeding kindness. "I am sorry I won't have the pleasure of your company this evening," she said to him, "but I am leaving the usual dance here to go and see the dance at Constant Spring, and I am taking Miss Braeme with me. By the way, I have a big surprise in store for you, Major Fellspar."

"What is it?" asked the Major gallantly, "something delightful, I am sure."

"I should be much mortified if I heard that you really thought it delightful!" remarked Lady Rosedale dryly. "I rather hope, in my vanity, that you will feel sorry."

"Ah, now you pique my curiosity," said the Major.

"A woman's curse, Major. Let me keep my little secret to myself, until I choose to reveal it to you. Some future day we shall probably laugh over it. The car is at the door?"—this to a bellboy. "Very good. Goodnight." She bowed to the four men pleasantly, and Marian did likewise, but

Major Fellspar hastened after her to hand them both into the car, and Mr. Phipps and the others followed more leisurely. "You'll get my little surprise before long," cried Lady Rosedale, as the car started, and Major Fellspar bowed his best.

"What's this surprise?" enquired Mr. Phipps, thought he knew quite well that Lady Rosedale had been referring to her intended sudden departure with Marian from Jamaica.

"Some sill fad or other I suppose," said Major Fellspar, who secretly detested Lady Rosedale.

"Curious woman," commented Mr. Phipps; "always saying or doing something strange or eccentric. Now what about this little spin of ours, Major?"

"I don't think I can go," said Mr. Baker decidedly. "I'll just stay here and watch the dancing and things."

"Well, then," said Mr. Phipps, "I think I'll stay too. Here's my boy, Arthur. Say, Arthur, I don't think I'll want you after all. You can put the car up in the garage and go home."

Arthur stood in the driveway under the porch, evidently perplexed.

"The car, sir?" he asked. "I came to ask you about it."

"Yes? Well, what about it?"

"I went over to the park there, sir," said Arthur, pointing with his hand, "and it wasn't there."

"Wasn't there?" repeated Mr. Phipps, "but didn't you leave it there?"

"Yes, sir, this afternoon; but it isn't there now."

"Indeed!" exclaimed Mr. Phipps; "well, let us go and see. There's surely some mistake."

He followed the chauffeur, and Major Fellspar and the other men walked out with him. Arthur led them to the spot where he had parked the car some hours before; there were other cars there, some with their chauffeurs, others unattended. Mr. Phipps's car, of course, was not to be seen.

"Let us enquire of these men here," said Mr. Phipps; "perhaps they can give us some information."

But all the chauffeurs just then in the enclosure had arrived after seven o'clock; they knew nothing about Mr. Phipps's car, had not seen it. It was a cabman who volunteered to help them; he knew Mr. Phipps and his car very well. He had been there a couple of hours before, he said, waiting to be called for passengers, when he had seen a tall, foreign-looking gentleman enter Mr. Phipps's car and drive towards the eastern end of the street. He had thought nothing of the incident, for the man was a white man and a gentleman from the hotel, and he had supposed it was all right. He had seen the gentleman often.

"Stephen undoubtedly!" exclaimed Mr. Phipps. "He's off with my car!"

"I imagined so," said Baker quietly, "the moment I heard that the machine was not to be found."

Baker developed sudden energy. "He would not have taken the car if he was not going for some distance. Where would he be likely to go to get out of the city—most likely, Major Fellspar?"

"There are three main roads leading out of the city," said the Inspector General, "but after any car has got some miles away it can turn from the main highway into someother. If he went east as this cabman say—"

"If he went east it was to throw us off track," interrupted the American brusquely. "Can you get some quick cars and send them all three ways in pursuit? You are bound to hear something about him if you go quick and make enquiries. I want that man, sir, and I am not so sure as you are that he can't get away from this place. We've got to follow him. I'll stand the expense of the cars."

"That won't be necessary," said Major Fellspar quickly. "Harmsworth, go to the Sutton Street Station at once and get some of our men ready. The cars will meet you there. I'll make out warrants for Quesada's arrest on my own authority. I'll take the responsibility. Come with me, Baker!"

Major Fellspar hurried back into the hotel and immediately telephoned an order to a garage, then he rejoined Mr. Phipps and Mr. Baker.

"Harmsworth will go with a detective in one of the cars," he said. "It is not customary, but I myself will go to get this man. My chauffeur is a policeman. You?" he looked enquiringly at Baker.

"I'll go in the third car," said the latter, "thought I feel that it wouldn't be a bad thing if somebody remained here." He looked with unveiled suspicion and anger at Mr. Phipps. "Funny that it is your car that Quesada took," he remarked.

"Not at all," replied Mr. Phipps calmly. "I remember saying to him this afternoon that I didn't think I should be requiring it tonight. If I were trying to get away, and time was an object, I should take a car that was not wanted in a hurry. Wouldn't you?"

Baker answered nothing, but got into Major Fellspar's roadster, which rapidly drove off towards the Police Headquarters. Mr. Phipps watched the car disappear, then sat down, thoughtful, to wait until midnight should be past. He had not deliberately planned getting rid of the two officers and the detective; his sending for his chauffeur, his enquiry for his car, had been deemed by him a prudent precautionary act in view of the enquiries that would be made in the certain event of his car being discovered at Runaway Bay or in the vicinity. It would easily be identified; therefore it was best that its disappearance should be proclaimed as early as was consistent with giving Stephen a fair chance to escaper. Mr. Phipps did not for a moment believe that in a country where many cars travelled night and day over the roads, anyone would take particular notice of his; the darkness of the night would surely aid and shield the fugitive. Besides, Stephen would have had nearly three hours' start by the time the pursuit commenced; already he must be at Runaway Bay; already, indeed, if they had provisions enough for the boat—and there were shops of Stephen's route and the boatmen would have some native provisions—then men must be putting out to sea. Stephen would pay liberally, and these boatmen would take a desperate risk for gold; not until morning would the police discover the car. Stephen should be safe—for the present. What might happen to him after he was out of the country would not matter, for if he was taken in Cuba it would be to the United States, and not to Jamaica, that he would be extradited, and it was only in Jamaica that any harm through him could come to Marian. So far, everything had gone well; in another three hours at the latest the Cecilia would have said, with Lady Rosedale and the girl, and he, Phipps, would be free to consider that he had accomplished in his life another bit of useful work.

He was pleased to think this; his vanity was touched and gratified. It seemed to him extraordinary how often in the course of his existence he had been mixed up with matters which, on the surface, seemed no affair at all of his. Other people had sometimes said that it was he who interfered with things that did not in the least concern him, that he had often, quite unasked, thrust himself into the very midst of other folks' business and made it his own; but that was never his own reading of any situation in which he found himself involved.

It had always appeared to him inevitable that he should find himself just where he happened to be: there was a job to be done, a job that needed doing, and somehow he found himself taking a hand in the doing of it. Curious? Inquisitive? Irresponsible? Well, they did say he was all these things, but if he had let such criticism trouble him, what a useless life (he reflected) would have been his. He was well off; he never had had to do a stroke of work in all his life for his living, thanks to a father who had made money in manufacturing shoes for the multitude, and who had been able to send his son to Harvard and then had allowed him to travel round the world in search of his proper vocation. That vocation had been wonderfully interesting; he was always finding it.

He played a part in Spanish American revolutions, had been an amateur detective, had been a political agent in one of the Western States of American for the mere fun of the thing, had figured in many other roles and situations, and now was in Jamaica helping an unfortunate girl for whom he had a deep fatherly affection. He wondered how she would have fared without him; he concluded that she would have fared but badly.

Then—"I am getting a little too vain," he thought, feeling a trifle ashamed of the elation he experience whenever he surveyed his own achievements. "I am too fond of showing off; I must keep that tendency down. I am not sure I am much different from Lady Rosedale after all. I wonder if vanity is the trye source of all our important actions?"

"A telephone message for you, sir. Please speak at the telephone," said a bellboy.

"Very good, my lad." Mr. Phipps rose briskly, "That's Lawrence, no doubt," he thought "but what could he want to talk to me about? Has anything gone wrong?"

He hurried to the telephone room, carefully closed the door behind him, and put the receive to his ear. Of a sudden he was conscious of being troubled, anxious; he realised then that he had been far more apprehensive about the success of Marian's departure than he had been willing to confess himself. And this anxiety at least had not its origin in any feeling of vanity.

"Yes; this is Mr. Phipps, speaking from the Myrtle Bank. Who is that?"

A strange voice answered. "The Inspector General, sir, ask if you could kindly come up here, to the Sutton Street Police Station, at once. It is very important."

Mr. Phipps's heart gave a tremendous leap. But he mastered his emotions and answered briefly: "Very well; say I am coming at once."

What did this summons mean? Some new development? Some discovery? Stephen captured? Marian's plans found out? Everything gone to ruin on the very verge of success, and perhaps he himself to blame? He would very shortly know! In the meantime he must keep his wits about him; he could not allow people like Major Fellspar and Baker to get the better of him; he must beat them yet if that were at all possible. "I am getting old," he reflected grimly, "for I feel more disturbed and panicky tonight than when I have been in far worse situations. Poor little Marian: I hope she will be safe!"

The cab that he took, driven swiftly arrived at the Police Station within ten minutes. The big gates were shut; Mr. Phipps went through a wicket in one of them, and the wicket banged behind him. "That way, sir," said a policeman, pointing to a flight of wooden steps leading upward, and on the landing above Mr. Phipps found another policeman who immediately took him into a room wherein were the Inspector General, the American detective, Inspector Harmsworth, and a man whom Mr. Phipps knew he had seen more than once before. This man was terribly agitated; his clothes were crushed and stained with earth; his face pale, his eyes eloquent of fear and distress. And the faces of the other men in the room gave evidence that something of a very serious nature had occurred.

"This is Mr. Hammond, Mr. Phipps," said the Inspector General. "We were just about to start out on our business—you know what I refer—when Mr. Hammond came in and told us of a terrible experience he had just passed through. I sent for you, for your car, I fancy, is the one he alludes to, and perhaps you would like to go with Inspector Harmsworth to identify it. Mr. Hammond, will you tell Mr. Phipps what happened?"

The man steadied his voice with an obvious effort.

"I was coming over to Kingston from Trelawny," he began, "in my car, and by eight o'clock I was more than halfway over Mount Diablo. I was driving very carefully; my chauffeur was with me, but I drove myself; I am a very careful driver." He emphasised these words. Major Fellspar nodded sympathetically.

"The night is a dark one, and I sounded my horning whenever I came to a turning. For sometime not a car passed me on the hill. I was glad of that; you know how very narrow in some parts is the road over Mount Diablo."

He paused and shuddered violently, the muscles of his face working and twisting. He was awfully shaken and upset.

"I came up to a sharp curve and sounded my horn as I made the turn. I heard no other sound save my own; perhaps the car coming in the opposite direction may have sounded at the same moment. If it did, I could not hear it, you know; you can't hear another man's horn if it sounds at the same time as yours. But I don't think the other man blew;

at any rate, as I rounded the curve, I saw a car rushing full speed towards me, *and it was on the wrong side of the road*."

He stopped again for a moment; Mr. Phipps's eyes opened wide in horror-struck anticipation of what was to follow.

"I was on the left-hand side of the road, the other car was on the right-hand side, where it should not have been; and both of us, you will understand, were travelling near to the edge of the precipice. But that would not have mattered if the other car had not been going at such a terrific speed. There was no time for me to stop—you know the curves, Major Fellspar—but I did what I could. I was on my proper hand, but I swerved inwards—the only thing to do. That save me a moment too late and I should have been hurled over the precipice. The other car never lessened speed for a second; I think the man driving it must have lost his head. I think he must have swerved a little to the right—the worst thing he could possibly have done. All I know is that his car crashed downwards, and I thought I heard a scream. My God, I never want to go through such an experience again!"

"The rule for cars and other vehicles in America and Canada is to keep to the right," broke in Major Fellspar. "Here we keep always to the left. Mr. Hammon was on his proper hand."

"I was," agreed Hammond eagerly. "I stopped my car, and my boy and I got out and hurried to where the other car had gone over the precipice. It hadn't fallen very far; the trees prevented that. We climbed down to where it was—I always carry an electric torch with me, and it helped me to see my way. The man had fallen out of his car and lay a little distance away. He must have pitched headlong out of it and his head was twisted round. . ."

"Injured or—?"

"Dead, quite dead," whispered Hammond, replying to Mr. Phipps. "The poor fellow! But it wasn't at all my fault."

"Mr. Hammond says he had seen the dead man before; recognised the corpse," said Major Fellspar quietly.

"Yes," assented Mr. Hammond; "it is a man that I have seen at Myrtle Bank; one of the actors that are out here, you know; a tall, dark, good-looking man; but I don't know his name.

"We—my boy and I—tried to get him up to the toad, but we couldn't manage it. So I pushed on to Ewarton, which was not far, and I gave the alarm ther. I hired four men with a car to go and pick up the body, and I sent my boy, David, back with them, to show them the spot and to help them. I told them to bring up the body—I hope I haven't done wrong—and I drove right on to this station to tell the police and give myself up. But I can pledge you my solemn word, Major Fellspar, that it wasn't at all my fault. I suppose I'll be able to get bail tonight?"

"I don't think there will be any difficult about that, Mr. Hammond," said Major Fellspar kindly. "As a matter of fact, this business is within the province of the police in whose parish the accident occurred. But I can arrange that you won't have more trouble than is absolutely necessary. I think you understand what has happened, Mr. Phipps?"

Mr. Phipps nodded.

A picture of that awful accident rose clear and distinct in his mind. He saw Stephen rushing at full speed along the level road, towards the Devil's Mountain, all restrain and prudence through to the winds in that wild, desperate effort to win to freedom and security. Every sound, every ray of light projected from behind him, he must have believed to have come from some car containing his pursuers, every moment he must have imahined that the hunters were relentlessly speeding on his track. Every second was precious; his blood was on fire; his nerves tingling with terror; however fast he went it must have seemed to him he was far too slow, however swift his passage it must have been borne in upon his fear-stricken mind that there might be behind him others who were swifter. And unconsciously, following the practice of another country, he had kept his car to the right-hand instead of to the left-hand side of the road. He knew but superficially the way he was traversing; not to familiar knowledge but to the light from the lamps of the car must he trust when he began the ascent of the terrible Devil's Mountain. And even when the ascent began he hardly slackened speed; there too he hung, as a matter of habit, on the right-hand side of the narrow path, but the edge of the precipice, on the very verge of death.

So, swiftly, up, up, up, he rushed, until the summit of the mountain was nearly reached.

Then had appeared, suddenly, springing as it were out of the bowels of darkness, a car right opposite to him, and flying straight towards him. He may have seen the swerve made by it to escape collision, a swerve made to the wrong side of the road, the side that he himself was entitled to take. Instinctively, he turned his steering wheel, perhaps ever so slightly, in the other direction; turned it ever so slightly, but there was no room for safety, and the impetus of the car could not be checked. There came the made leap of the machine into space, a scream of terrorised realisation, the hurtling of the body through air as the car plunged downwards, then swift and merciful death. Yes, Mr. Phipps understood it all: saw it all with awful distinctness with the eye of his mind. The Devil's Mountain had claimed one more Spaniard. It had justified again the name by which it had been called by its Spanish masters of former days.

"It is Quesada and no other," said Detective Baker; "we are going, Mr. Harmsworth and I, to identify the body. The Inspector General didn't know but what you might want to go along with us and see about you car, Mr. Phipps. Do you care to go?"

"I will follow you immediately," said Mr. Phipps, "please don't wait for me."

Baker and Inspector Harmsworth left the room; Harmsworth taking Mr. Hammond with him; then Mr. Phipps addressed Major Fellspar. "That ends all criminal proceedings, doesn't it?" he asked, and Major Fellspar nodded.

"It seems so," he said; "he would have been taken back to the States, you know. Now, poor chap, he'll never go."

"No, poor fellow!" said Phipps, "poor fellow!" For the fate that had overtaken Esteban de Quesada had touched both men to pity.

Mr. Phipps knew that he had something to do that must be attended to at once. Thanking Major Fellspar for sending for him, and intimating that he would shortly set out to look after his car, he left the Police Station and took a cab down to Lawrence's office, where he found Lawrence patiently waiting until Lady Rosedale and Marian should arrive. "What is it?" asked the younger man at the sight of his friend, for Mr. Phipps's manner indicated news of grave importance. In a very few moments the whole story had been told.

"I'll go up to Constant Spring myself and tell Lady Rosedale what has happened," said Lawrence; "I'll be back in time to see to the sailing of the Cecilia. I wonder how Marian will take it!"

"She had better know nothing about it until she is in her own room at the hotel," counselled Mr. Phipps. "Lady Rosedale will break the news to her. It's the best way out of the whole difficulty, but, you know, I am sorry for that chap. He took the wrong side in getting over the mountain. He seems always to have taken the wrong path in life."

XXVIII

Goodbye

Stephen Braeme had been buried for two weeks now in the cemetery of the Roman Catholics, and among the mourners had been Marian, Lady Rosedale and Mr. Phipps. It was Lady Rosedale who had insisted upon this attendance: it would look strange, she said, if they remained away from the funeral; for Marian's sake they must try to shield the reputation of the unhappy young man.

Nora was at the gravesite, too, regretful and sad, and still wondering why Stephen had gone on that wild night ride which had had so tragic a conclusion for him. The members of the moving picture company, the acquaintances he had made in Jamaica, spoke in tones subdued of his fine qualities, of his generosity, his bonhomie, his striking appearance, as they turned and left him in his grave, and Lady Rosedale supported Marian through it all with the demeanour of one who had suffered the loss of a valued friend. That same day she had a long walk with Major Fellspar, who was accompanied by Mr. Baker. The Inspector General took her completely into his confidence; when he had finished his statement she made him understand that she in no way held the local police responsible for the non-recovery of her jewels. "We don't need to say anything more about the robbery," she said: "I don't want it known that Miss Braeme's *brother*"—she stressed the word—"was a rogue. I shall write and thank your Governor for all you have done for me in this matter, Major Fellspar." The Major felt that this last offer on her part was only, after all, what was due to him; nevertheless he appreciated it, for he knew that one does not always obtain one's due in this ungrateful world: his own career, he was satisfied, was proof of that. He was greatly relieved too that she accepted with calmness and equanimity his announcement that her loss was final.

Three days afterwards, Mr. Baker went back to the United States. Before going he had a long and friendly talk with Mr. Phipps. "I should like," he said, "to know just how much you knew about that chap Quesada's plans when he tried to make a getaway from Jamaica. Where was he going—for he sure was going somewhere when he made for that Mount Diablo on a dark night at full speed. Where did you come in on that business, Mr. Phipps?"

"You should ask me where my car came in, not I," laughed Mr. Phipps. "I shall have to get a new car now."

"Well," drawled the other man, "you were willing enough to risk the loss of that one. I'll tell you what: I'm sure that but for you I'd a had Quesada safe and sure by now. But what beats me is that no one here seems to be able to guess why he was going the way he went; they say that no ship was leaving that night from any of the Northside ports, and he must have known that if he couldn't escape that night we would get him the following day."

"Quesada must have known," agreed Mr. Phipps; "Quesada also knew some history."

Baker looked puzzled but did not pursue the conversation further. But when he repeated it later in the day to Inspector Harmsworth the latter knitted his brows and began to think, as if trying to remember something. But what it was, if he did remember, he refrained from mentioning to the American detective.

And now two weeks had elapsed since Stephen's burial, and the accident had been almost forgotten save by those who had been closely connected with him. It was Sunday night. Tomorrow Lady Rosedale was leaving the island for England, and Marian was leaving with her.

Lady Rosedale was giving a little farewell dinner. On this occasion she had not invited the moving picture director of Miss Hellingworth to dine with her; it has in all honesty to be confessed that she had rather drawn away from those two persons of late, a fact which they had not been slow to observe, and which had caused them to speak of her in terms the reverse of complimentary or even respectful. She herself would have been astonished to learn that she was no longer regarded by them as a woman of remarkable personality, and still more shocked to know that Miss Hellingworth had even suggested in Mr. Phipps's hearing that she was not a lady. Such base ingratitude would have moved Lady Rosedale to indignation, but Mr. Phipps gave her no hint of it. He was on remarkably good terms with Lady Rosedale now.

It was a small dinner part she was giving this evening: Major Fellspar and Mr. Phipps, Mrs. Hamilton and Nora were the only guests. Marian, Lady Rosedale had decided, should not take part in what might be considered a social function so soon after her "brother's" death: Lawrence had been asked, but Lady Rosedale had readily appreciated the reason of his excuse. Marian had dined early, by herself, and even now was somewhere by the waterfront; Lawrence had come into the hotel half an hour before, and had disappeared in the direction of the waterfront. Lady Rosedale knew it all; she looked upon it in Providential manner and saw that it was good. "Marian, naturally, is not yet recovered from the shock of her brother's sad death," she explained to her guests, "but she is very young, and Mr. Beaman is very attentive to her and knows her moods exactly. I think he will make his way in the world."

"Because he knows Marian's moods, Lady Rosedale?" enquired Mr. Phipps innocently.

"Certainly not; how could you ask so extraordinary a question? Because he had many sterling qualities. It is not secret, of course, that he is in love with Marian; I have known it all along. I think I mentioned something of the sort to you, didn't I, Major Fellspar?"

Major Fellspar admitted that she had done so, but took care not to remind her that, at the same time, she had entertain grave doubts about the young man's honesty.

"They have very wisely fallen in with my advice," Lady Rosedale continued. "I am taking Marian with me to England, this country has many painful memories for her: she needs to forget. In a little while Mr. Beaman will follow, and they will be married in England. I am advising Mr. Beaman to try and get transferred to England after he is married; I am sure he'll do very well over there. I spend more of the year in England."

"Have you given friend Lawrence a hint of that?" asked Mr. Phipps.

"Of what?"

"Living in England. I am sure, Lady Rosedale—perfectly sure—that if you mentioned that you would be there it would have great effect." (This with imperturbable gravity).

"He has not yet made up his mind," said Lady Rosedale. "I am speaking to him about it this afternoon when he was here, but he seems to favour returning to this country. I shall persevere, however."

"I am sure you will," said Mr. Phipps, and left Lady Rosedale a little uncertain of his meaning. "Well, I am sorry I shall not be at the wedding."

"You will be invited," Lady Rosedale promised him. "Marian shall be married from my house, and you will know in good time. All of you will be invited," she added. "And I expect, if what a little bird has whispered to me is true, that we shall be hearing of another wedding before long."

She smiled at Nora as she spoke, and her glance at portly, good-natured Mrs. Hamilton indicated that lady was the little bird to which she referred. Mrs. Hamilton might more correctly have been likened to a motherly old hen.

"You will be in England this summer, won't you, Major?" asked Lady Rosedale.

"Yes, I must go home for about three months this year," said Major Fellspar; "I need the change."

"You do, Major," agreed Mr. Phipps. "you'll breakdown if you don't stop working and get away. I always wonder how you stand your job. You are going over too?" he questioned, looking at Mrs. Hamilton and Nora. The latter blushed slightly; the older lady placidly answered yes.

"Wedding trousseau and wedding bells," muttered Mr. Phipps. "I wish everybody the best of luck. And we are all sure to meet again, if not this year, next, and if not next year, then later. I am going away tomorrow, too, Lady Rosedale."

"You also?" cried Lady Rosedale; "you must have made up your mind very suddenly?"

"I did; I made it up yesterday. I am going to the States, and from the States I think I am going to Brazil: I won't be back in Jamaica this year anyhow. I can't keep Lawrence out of his house when he has a wife in prospect, can I?"

"Do you mean that you won't come over to their wedding?" asked Lady Rosedale.

"Can't. Besides I don't cut a good figure at weddings. I am too sentimental; I feel like wanting to cry, you know: I inherited that tendency. No, Lady Rosedale. Tonight I tell my friends here goodbye and I am off. As one of your great poets said, 'Fare thee well, and if forever, then forever fare thee well.'"

"Isn't Shakespeare beautiful," sighed Mrs. Hamilton.

"Supremely," assented Mr. Phipps, without moving a muscle. "Let me wish you every happiness. Miss Nora." He raised his glass, and Nora bowed to him prettily and thanked him.

They left the table, and he asked them to excuse him for a few minutes; then he too disappeared in the direction of the waterfront.

He found Lawrence and Marian sitting side by side upon a bench on the seawall. They rose to welcome him. He waved them back. "Sit still," he ordered in a playful tone of voice; "I know that two is company tonight, and three none, and you have a lot to say to one another."

"You know?" asked Marian softly.

"Trust Lady Rosedale for making the newspapers unnecessary," he replied. "Yes; the old dame duly published it forth that you are to be married in the summer, which I could have told her, for the matter of that; and she seems to harbour some design about living with you a part of the year at least. Take an old man's advice, little movie star, and cut the old lady's sojourn with you down to one month a year: longer than that would destroy the happiness of any home. She wouldn't mean to do that, but she would get upon the nerves anyhow; she's built that way. She isn't a bad sort when you know her, and she loves you all right enough; but I don't exactly see her as a permenant angel in the house. I have come to say goodbye."

"Goodbye?" echoed Lawrence, surprised; "but surely you will be at the pier tomorrow, and—"

"No, son, the ship for the States leaves earlier than the ship for England. I have written to you about Triton; you'll get my letter tomorrow. It's goodbye to you both and to Jamaica, for the present anyhow."

"And when do you return?" asked Marian.

"There's no saying. But some day I'll call in to see you, quite unexpected. It's a way I have. Goodbye." He put out both hands, grasped theirs, turned quickly, and was gone.

They remained quite silent until the sound of his departing footsteps had completely died away, then—

"The best friend I ever had," said Lawrence, with deep feeling, "the strongest and truest."

"He is a dear, strange man," said Marian, wiping her eyes, "queer, but dear and good. I love him. But for him—"

Her hand stole into that of her lover.

The End

A Note About the Author

H. G. de Lisser (1878–1944) was a Jamaican journalist and novelist. Born in Falmouth, Jamaica, de Lisser was raised in a family of Afro-Jewish descent. At seventeen, he began working as a proofreader at the *Jamaica Daily Gleaner*, where his father was editor. By 1903, he earned the position of assistant editor and began writing several daily articles while working on the essays that would fill his first collection, *In Cuba and Jamaica* (1909). His debut novel *Jane's Career: A Story of Jamaica* (1913) has been recognized as the first West Indian novel to have a black character as its protagonist. In addition to his writing—he published several essay collections, novels, and plays throughout his career—de Lisser was an advocate for the Jamaican sugar Industry and a Companion of the Order of St. Michael and St. George.

A Note from the Publisher

Spanning many genres, from non-fiction essays to literature classics to children's books and lyric poetry, Mint Edition books showcase the master works of our time in a modern new package. The text is freshly typeset, is clean and easy to read, and features a new note about the author in each volume. Many books also include exclusive new introductory material. Every book boasts a striking new cover, which makes it as appropriate for collecting as it is for gift giving. Mint Edition books are only printed when a reader orders them, so natural resources are not wasted. We're proud that our books are never manufactured in excess and exist only in the exact quantity they need to be read and enjoyed.

Discover more of your favorite classics with Bookfinity™.

- Track your reading with custom book lists.
- Get great book recommendations for your personalized Reader Type.
- Add reviews for your favorite books.
- AND MUCH MORE!

Visit **bookfinity.com** and take the fun Reader Type quiz to get started.

Enjoy our classic and modern companion pairings!

Printed in the USA
CPSIA information can be obtained
at www.ICGtesting.com
JSHW021625280823
47399JS00001B/37

9 798888 970096